**Acclaim for the authors of**
***Unlaced by Candlelight*****:**

'A wild adventure with rich narrative, authentic dialogue and memorable characters.'
—*RT Book Reviews* on
NOT JUST A GOVERNESS
by **Carole Mortimer**

'Scott pens a deliciously wicked romance.'
—*RT Book Reviews* on
LONDON'S MOST WANTED RAKE
by **Bronwyn Scott**

'Plenty of tension and dangerous excitement blended with poignancy and passion.'
—*RT Book Reviews* on
FALLING FOR THE HIGHLAND ROGUE
by **Ann Lethbridge**

'McCabe's story charms readers.'
—*RT Book Reviews* on
RUNNING FROM SCANDAL
by **Amanda McCabe**

'Kaye offers up another sexy romp.'
—*RT Book Reviews* on
UNWED AND UNREPENTANT
by **Marguerite Kaye**

**Carole Mortimer** was born in England, the youngest of three children. She began writing in 1978, and has now written over one hundred and fifty books for Harlequin Mills & Boon®. Carole has six sons and is happily married to Peter. They are best friends as well as lovers, which is probably the best recipe for a successful relationship.

**Bronwyn Scott** is a communications instructor at Pierce College in the United States, and is the proud mother of three wonderful children (one boy and two girls). When she's not teaching or writing she enjoys playing the piano, travelling, and studying history and foreign languages. Readers can stay in touch on Bronwyn's website, www.bronwynnscott.com, or at her blog, www.bronwynswriting.blogspot.com—she loves to hear from readers.

**Ann Lethbridge** grew up roaming Britain with her military father. She now lives in Canada with her husband, two beautiful daughters, and a Maltese terrier named Teaser. Ann visits Britain every year to undertake research and also to visit family members. If you would like to know more about Ann and her research, or to contact her, visit www.annlethbridge.com

**Amanda McCabe**'s books have been nominated for many awards, including a RITA® Award and an RT Reviewers' Choice Award. She lives in Oklahoma with a menagerie of two cats, a pug and a bossy miniature poodle, and loves dance classes, collecting cheesy travel souvenirs and watching the Food Network—even though she doesn't cook. Visit her at www.ammandamccabe.com and www.riskyregencies.com

Born and educated in Scotland, **Marguerite Kaye** originally qualified as a lawyer but chose not to practise. Instead, she carved out a career in IT and studied history part-time, gaining first-class honours and a master's degree. She decided to pursue her lifelong ambition to write, and submitted her first historical romance to Mills & Boon. They accepted it, and she's been writing ever since. You can contact Marguerite through her website at: www.margueritekaye.com

# UNLACED BY CANDLELIGHT

Carole Mortimer
Bronwyn Scott
Ann Lethbridge
Amanda McCabe
Marguerite Kaye

First published in Great Britain 2014
by Mills & Boon, an imprint of Harlequin (UK) Limited.
Large Print edition 2015
Harlequin (UK) Limited, Eton House, 18-24 Paradise Road,
Richmond, Surrey TW9 1SR

Unlaced by Candlelight



ISBN: 978-0-263-25535-5



These five stories have been previously published in eBook
under Mills & Boon Historical *Undone!*

Harlequin (UK) policy is to use papers that are natural, renewable and recyclable products and made from wood grown in sustainable forests. The logging and manufacturing process conform to the legal environmental regulations of the country of origin.

Printed and bound in Great Britain
by CPI Antony Rowe, Chippenham, Wiltshire

CONTENTS

# NOT JUST A SEDUCTION

Carole Mortimer

If you enjoy NOT JUST A SEDUCTION
make sure to check out the other books
in Carole Mortimer's
*A Season of Secrets* mini-series:

NOT JUST A GOVERNESS
NOT JUST A WALLFLOWER

**Other recent titles by Carole Mortimer:**

THE LADY GAMBLES**
THE LADY FORFEITS**
THE LADY CONFESSES**
SOME LIKE IT WICKED†
SOME LIKE TO SHOCK†

***The Copeland Sisters*
†*Daring Duchesses*

**And in**
**M&B Regency *Castonbury Park* mini-series:**

THE WICKED LORD MONTAGUE

And don't miss the new *Dangerous Dukes*
mini-series from Carole Mortimer

MARCUS FIELDING:
DUKE OF PLEASURE
Online prequel

ZACHARY BLACK:
DUKE OF DEBAUCHERY
Already available

DARIAN HUNTER: DUKE OF DESIRE
Available this month

# *Chapter One*

*April, 1817*
*The London home of Lady Cicely Hawthorne.*

"I trust, ladies, that you have not begun to discuss the matter of our grandsons' future wives without me…?" Edith St. Just, Dowager Duchess of Royston, frowned down the length of her aristocratic nose as she entered the salon where her two closest friends sat on the sofa in cozy conversation together.

"We would not think of doing such a thing, Edith." Her hostess stood up to cross the room and greet her with a warm kiss on both of her powdered cheeks.

"Of course we would not." A smiling Lady Jocelyn Ambrose, Dowager Countess of Chambourne, also rose to her feet.

The three women had been firm friends since some fifty years ago when, at the age of eighteen, they had shared a coming-out Season, their friendship continuing after they had all married. After becoming mothers and then grandmothers in the same years, the ladies continued to meet at least once a week while their respective husbands were still alive and sometimes two or three times a week since being widowed.

The dowager duchess nodded her satisfaction with her friends' replies before turning to the young lady who had accompanied her into the salon. "You may join Miss Thompson and Mrs. Spencer at their sewing, Ellie."

Eleanor Rosewood gave a brief curtsy to the lady who was not only her step-great-aunt by marriage but also her benefactress before stepping lightly across the room to join the other companions quietly sewing in the window alcove. The ladies, much older than her nineteen years, nevertheless smiled at her in welcome. As they had for this past year.

If not for the dowager duchess's kindness, Ellie feared that she might have been forced to offer herself up to the tender mercies of becoming one of the demimonde after the death of her mother and stepfather had revealed she had not only been left penniless but seriously in debt. Edith St. Just, hearing of her nephew's profligacy, had wasted no time in sweeping into his stepdaughter's heavily mortgaged home and paying off those debts before gathering Ellie up to her ample bosom and making a place for her in her own household as her companion. This past year in that lady's employ had revealed to Ellie that Edith St. Just's outward appearance of stern severity hid a heart of gold.

Unfortunately the same could not be said of her grandson, the arrogant and ruthless Justin St. Just, Duke of

Royston, the haughtiness of his own demeanor a reflection of the steel within…

"Are you sure this is altogether wise?" Lady Cicely ventured uncertainly. "Thorne is sure to be most displeased with me if he should discover I have plotted behind his back to secure him a wife."

"Humph." The dowager duchess snorted down the length of her aristocratic nose as she took a seat beside the unlit fireplace. "We may plot all we like, Cicely, but it will be our grandsons' decisions as to whether or not they are equally as enamored of our choices of brides for them. Besides, our grandsons are all past the age of eight and twenty, two of them never having married, the third long a widower, and none of them giving so much as a glance in the direction of the sweet young things paraded before them with the advent of each new Season."

"And can you blame them?" Lady Cicely frowned. "When those young girls seem to get sillier and sillier each year?"

"That silliness is not exclusive to the present." The dowager duchess frowned. "My own daughter-in-law, but eighteen when Robert married her, was herself evidence of that very silliness when a year later she chose to name my only grandson Justin—to be coupled with St. Just! Which is why it is our duty to seek out more sensible women to be the future brides of our respective grandsons, and mothers of the future heirs."

Lady Cicely did not look convinced. "It is only that Thorne has such an icy demeanor when angry…"

Lady Jocelyn gave her friend a consoling grimace. "I am afraid Edith is, as usual, perfectly correct. If we are to see our grandsons suitably married, then I fear we shall have to be the ones to arrange matters. No doubts they will all thank us for it one day. Besides," she added coyly, "with the advent of my ball tomorrow evening, I do believe that I have already set things in motion regarding Christian's future."

"Indeed?" The dowager duchess raised steely brows.

"Oh, do tell!" Lady Cicely encouraged excitedly.

Ellie, listening attentively to the conversation while giving the outward appearance of concentrating upon her own sewing, was also curious to hear how Lady Jocelyn believed she had managed to arrange the securing of a wife for her grandson, the cynical and jaded—frighteningly so, in Ellie's opinion!—Lord Christian Ambrose, Earl of Chambourne…

# *Chapter Two*

"Tell me, how did you explain your…loss of innocence to your elderly husband on your wedding night?"

Sylvie's spine stiffened upon hearing that soft and cruelly mocking voice just behind her as she stood alone in the candlelit ballroom in the Dowager Countess of Chambourne's London home. A voice, and man, standing so near to her that the warmth of his breath slightly ruffled the loose curls at her temple and beside her pearl-adorned earlobe. So near that she could feel the heat of that gentleman's body through the silk of her gown…

She would have been foolish not to have expected some response from Lord Christian Ambrose, Earl of Chambourne, after arriving at his grandmother's ball some half an hour earlier and finding the countess's coldly arrogant grandson at that lady's side as he acted as host to her hostess.

Yes, Sylvie had known, and expected, when she had accepted the invitation to this ball, some sort of acknowledgment of their previous acquaintance from

Christian, but she had not expected it to be quite so cruelly pointed in nature!

She stiffened her spine and drew in a slow and controlled breath before turning to face him, her outward expression one of calm disdain. At the same time, her pulse gave an alarmed leap as she had to look up at least a foot in order to meet familiar moss-green eyes set in a face of such stark male beauty it might have been carved by Michelangelo. Arrogant dark brows above those moss-green eyes, high cheekbones either side of a long and aristocratic nose, chiseled lips above a square and determined jaw, raven-dark locks falling rakishly across the wide and intelligent brow.

She did not need to lower her gaze to know that Christian's black evening jacket had been tailored to fit like a glove over the wide expanse of his shoulders and muscled chest. His linen snowy white beneath a pale-silver waistcoat, black satin breeches encasing the long and muscled length of his thighs.

No, Sylvie did not need to look to know all of those things, having taken in Christian Ambrose's appearance fully upon her arrival earlier. And cursed herself for noticing that Christian had only grown more handsome—disturbingly so—rather than less, in the years since she had last seen him.

Four years, to be precise. Years that had seen Sylvie change to the coolly composed woman she presented to Society this evening, rather than that young girl of eighteen summers who had been totally besotted with this gentleman's rakish good looks.

That same young girl who had so trustingly given this man the innocence which he now dismissed so contemptuously…

To say that Christian had been disarmed to discover that Lady Sylviana Moorland, widowed Countess of Ampthill, was one of the guests at his grandmother's ball this evening would have been deeply understating the matter. He could not have been more surprised if that upstart Napoleon, presently and hopefully forever incarcerated on St. Helena, had arrived on his grandmother's doorstep brandishing an invitation!

Not that he had not been fully aware of Sylviana Moorland's

return to Society, now that her year of mourning her husband was well and truly over—indeed, it was closer to two years since Colonel Lord Gerald Moorland had been struck down at the battle of Waterloo. And having heard that gentleman's widow had returned to town at the start of the Season, Christian had taken the steps necessary to ensure that they were never in attendance at the same social function.

Steps that had been shattered this evening by his own grandmother, of all people!

Unintentionally, of course, for surely his grandmother was as much in ignorance of Christian's previous acquaintance with Sylviana as was the rest of Society.

If anything Sylvie was more beautiful than Christian remembered, no longer that young girl on the brink of womanhood but now fully matured into a beautiful woman. The gold of her hair was arranged in artful curls upon her crown, with several loose tendrils at her temples and nape. Brown eyes surrounded by long dark lashes, and as deep and impenetrable as the golden molasses they resembled in her heart-shaped face; a small and delicate nose, with full and pouting lips above a small and determined chin. Her body was no longer coltishly slender, either, but lush and sensual, the fullness of her creamy breasts spilling over the low neckline of her green silk gown.

A gown of the same moss-green color as Christian's eyes…Deliberately so?

The challenge in her dark gaze as she gazed up at him so

disdainfully would seem to imply so. "How unfortunate, my lord, that the passing of the years appears to have done nothing to improve your manners!"

Christian gave a hard and derisive smile. "Did you expect them to have done so?"

She eyed him coolly. "One might have hoped so, yes…"

"Why did you come here this evening, Sylvie?" He snapped his impatience with that coolness. "Or perhaps you prefer the grander Sylviana now that you are become a countess?" he added contemptuously as he saw the way she stiffened at his familiarity.

"I believe 'my lady' and 'my lord' are a more fitting address between two people of equal rank." She had drawn herself up to her full height of just over five feet. "And I am here this evening because your grandmother invited me."

Christian gave a derisive snort. "And are your invitations into Society so few and far between that you must needs accept this one?"

"On the contrary." That golden gaze raked over him contemptuously. "Perhaps you have not heard, my lord, but I believe I am considered to be something of a matrimonial catch this Season, and as such in receipt of more invitations than I could ever hope to accept."

His mouth twisted with disgust. "I had heard that your elderly husband left you a rich widow, yes. Which, no doubt, was your intention when you married a man so much older than yourself."

Her eyes widened. "How dare you—"

"Oh, I believe, Sylvie, that you will find I dare much where you are concerned!" His eyes glittered dangerously. "A first lover's privilege, shall we say?"

"No, we will not say!" All the color had now faded from her cheeks.

Christian gave a humorless smile. "What reason *did* you give your ancient husband when he discovered that there was no maidenhead for him to breach on your wedding night?"

It took every effort of will on Sylvie's part not to flinch at the

unmistakable disdain in Christian Ambrose's tone, and the hard censor of his moss-green gaze as it raked over her with slow contempt, from her blond curls down to her green-slippered feet, before shifting, deliberately lingering, on the firm swell of her breasts.

As if she were nothing more than a slab of meat on a butcher's block that he was considering the merits of purchasing!

As if this man had no recollection of once upon a time slowly removing every article of clothing from her body—much more than once!—before making love to her as if she were the most delicate, precious thing upon this earth…

Once upon a time?

For Sylvie it was a different lifetime!

Certainly she was no longer that innocent young miss who had believed, in her naïveté, that Christian Ambrose, a gentleman six years her senior—in experience as well as years—returned the deep love she had felt for him. That trusting young girl had disappeared long, long ago, upon the realization that she had been nothing more than yet another female conquest to the rakish Christian Ambrose.

In her place was Sylviana Moorland, wealthy widow of Colonel Lord Gerald Moorland, a coolly composed woman of two and twenty, who felt as cynical toward love as the gentleman now standing before her gazing down at her so disdainfully.

Sylvie drew in a deep, controlling breath. "I—"

"I believe it would be best if we were to finish this conversation outside on the terrace," Christian Ambrose grated harshly even as he grasped Sylvie's arm and pulled her toward one of the sets of open French doors.

She resisted that painful hold upon her arm. “Unhand me at once, sir—” She broke off her protest abruptly as Christian turned to focus the full fierceness of his icy-cold moss-green eyes upon her, eyes that had once caused her to melt with passion but which she now knew only too well to be wary of. “People are staring at us…” she substituted lamely.

“Let them,” he grated unconcernedly as he continued to pull her effortlessly across the candlelit room, through the open doorway and out onto the dark seclusion of the terrace.

# *Chapter Three*

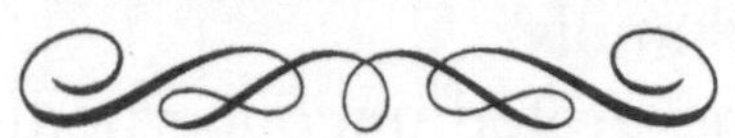

No sooner had they stepped outside into that shadowed darkness than Sylvie felt the steely strength of Christian's arms as he pulled her hard against him, the lowering of his head blocking out the brightness of the moon overhead as his lips claimed hers.

Not a gentle or exploratory kiss, but that of an experienced lover, demanding she return that same heat of passion. An experienced lover who knew exactly how to kiss and caress the woman in his arms until she was weak with arousal…

Try as Sylvie might to resist that seduction, and her determination never to fall for this man's rakish charms ever again, she found she had no defenses against the onslaught. Christian's tongue parted her lips before plunging possessively inside, his hands moving in a restless caress down the length of her spine before cupping beneath her bottom to pull her in so tight against him Sylvie could feel the hard ridge of his arousal.

Betraying heat flooded between her thighs, her nipples aching beneath the bodice of her gown as Christian deliberately rubbed his chest rhythmically against them, eliciting a want, an unwanted hunger deep inside her—

Christian wrenched his mouth from hers to lower his lips to the swell of her breasts, his tongue rasping, lapping, across that sensitized flesh before he tugged down on the bodice of her gown. One of those swollen orbs spilled out of its confinement to allow him to place his lips about her nipple.

Arousing a heat that none of Sylvie's late-night imaginings had even come close to replicating as she stroked the nubbin between her thighs, faster and harder until she reached a shuddering climax.

Sylvie felt that same climax rapidly building within her now as Christian continued to caress her nipple, harder, deeper, teeth biting, tongue laving as her back arched to press her breast deeper into that sensual delight.

She had no intention of ever falling in love with this man again, but that was no reason why she should not take the sexual gratification he now offered, in the same way he had once taken sexual gratification from her.

Sylvie parted her thighs and moved up on her toes so that she might rub herself against the hard ridge of Christian's arousal, perfectly positioning that hardness against herself as she stroked herself against him in a rapidly increasing rhythm—

She gave a groan of protest as Christian wrenched his mouth away from her breast even as he grasped her shoulders to steady her before he stepped back and away from her, his eyes a hard and glittering green. "I do not in the least mind paying for a woman's…services, but I prefer to know the price of those services *before* I bed her rather than be apprised of it afterward," he drawled contemptuously as he straightened the lace at his cuffs.

"Price…?" she repeated sharply.

He gave a mocking inclination of his head. "I have no doubts that a man of Ampthill's advanced years thought himself truly blessed when he took such a young beauty as his wife. I, however, am in no hurry to contemplate marriage," Christian drawled contemptuously, at the same time feeling a moment's regret as Sylvie set the front of her gown to rights. "Especially when I have already sampled your goods—"

He got no further in his insult as the palm of Sylvie's left hand made loud and painful contact with his right cheek. "I will allow you that one small lapse," he bit out harshly, a nerve now pulsing in that no doubt rapidly reddening cheek. "But be warned, Sylvie, that the next time I will retaliate in kind."

"You are as much a bastard as you ever were, I see!" Her eyes flashed.

Christian raised mocking brows. "Because I gladly took what you offered four years ago?"

Her eyes glittered darkly. "Because you took what you wanted before departing to enjoy the licentiousness of London and then returning to your regiment with not a thought for what might become of me!"

Christian studied her flushed face between narrowed lids. "Unless I am mistaken, you became the Countess of Moorland."

Her hands had clenched into fists at her sides, her breasts quickly rising and falling as she breathed deeply. "And you returned to your life of debauchery with not a thought to the fact that I was ruined. Used goods."

"Not so 'used' you did not marry within months of our parting. And to another earl, no less," he added. "Although well beyond the flush of youth." Christian's mouth twisted derisively at the thought of the gentleman who had been old enough to be Sylvie's grandfather rather than her husband. "But perhaps he was so grateful to have you in his bed that he chose not to question your lack of virginity?"

There appeared a look of such chilly contempt upon Sylvie's face that it took every effort on Christian's part not to flinch from that coldness. "You may insult me all you wish," she bit out. "But you will never talk of Gerald again in that tone. He was a gentleman. A man of honor. Of integrity. And you—you are not even fit to so much as lick one of his boots!"

Christian scowled his displeasure. Not because Sylvie had just roundly insulted him, but because her words made it very clear that even if she had not loved her aged husband, she had deeply respected and liked him. A respect and liking she made it equally clear she did not feel for Christian…

Did he want Sylvie's liking and respect?

Before this evening his answer would have been a resounding no. Before he had kissed her again, caressed her, suckled the fullness of her breast and felt the heat of her response to him, he would have said no. But now? How did Christian feel now that he had done all of those things?

Four years ago Sylvie had been the only daughter of the family living on the small estate neighboring his own in Berkshire. A young girl he had seen about the village for most of his life, even if his years away at school, university and latterly the army had meant he had never known her well.

But he had come home on leave from his regiment the summer of 1813, battle-worn and inwardly scarred and sickened from seeing too much blood and the death of many of his friends. And the young and beautiful Sylvie Buchanan, with her ready smile and innocently eager body, had been exactly the distraction Christian had needed to help him forget, if only for a few weeks, that he must soon return to that bloodbath.

Their first meeting had been completely accidental. Christian, strolling about the countryside several days after his arrival, had come upon Sylvie swimming in a curve of the local river.

Even now Christian could remember the warmth of that day and how the sun had turned Sylvie's long hair to rippling gold as it flowed out to float loosely in the water behind her after she had given a surprised shriek at espying him on the grassy riverbank and dipped below the water to just below her chin.

Far from leaving, as she had begged him to do, Christian had instead made himself comfortable on that grassy riverbank and laughingly dared her to come out of the water. A dare Sylvie had protested, her beautiful face burning hotly with embarrassment. Christian had persisted in his request at the same time as he informed her he was in no hurry to leave, his breath catching in his throat when, almost an hour later, she finally stood up in the water to reveal she wore only a wet and clinging chemise.

The water had rendered that chemise almost completely see-through, revealing all of her charms as she stepped fully from the water—pale and satiny skin, those high and tilting breasts tipped by rosy nipples, the slightly darker-blond curls nestled between her thighs, her legs long and slender—and all causing Christian's manhood to harden in a way it had not done in the last months of bloody battle, and which he had secretly feared it might never do again.

The relief of knowing that his lack of desire had only been a temporary aberration had allowed Christian to rein in his own needs and only kiss Sylvie lightly that first day, not wanting to frighten her with the depth of the desire he felt for her.

He had so enjoyed her company, her innocence of passion, that he had arranged to meet her at the same place the following day. And the day following that one. And the one after that. And as each day passed, their kisses deepened, became more passionate, needy, quickly advancing to caresses, and then finally the two of them had made love on that grassy knoll beside the river, the sunshine continuing to shine down on them as Christian made love to Sylvie a second time, and then a third, his hunger to possess her, to claim her, seeming never ending.

A hunger that Christian's response to kissing Sylvie again this evening had now shown him, no matter how he might wish it otherwise, had never completely gone away…

# *Chapter Four*

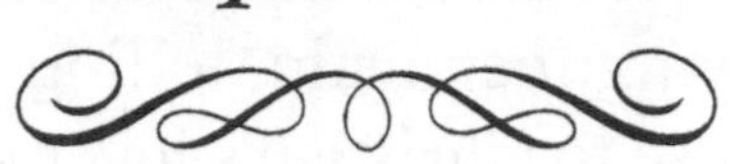

His mouth twisted disdainfully. "I believe I would far rather lick the honey from between your silken thighs than I would your husband's boots," he drawled suggestively. "Something, if my memory serves me correctly, that you would also enjoy?" He quirked one mocking brow.

Her breath caught in her throat. "You are disgusting!"

"Have a care, Sylvie." His eyes narrowed dangerously.

"And if I choose not to do so?" she dared.

Christian gave an unconcerned shrug. "Then you will suffer the consequences of deliberately challenging me."

Sylvie gave an involuntary shiver as she heard the steely edge beneath Christian's tone, knowing she should not have attended the Dowager Countess of Chambourne's ball this evening.

Recently returned to Society, and having only seen Christian Ambrose occasionally from a great distance, Sylvie had known that it was only a matter of time before the two of them were introduced by a hostesses at one function or another. That being so, Sylvie had decided that she would prefer to be in control of when and how that meeting took place, her years of being married to the gentlemanly Gerald having led her to believe she was now immune to Christian Ambrose's dangerous brand of sensuality.

Instead she had found herself in his arms within minutes of their having met again, telling her that if anything, her response to Christian's lovemaking was even more intense, more immediate, than it had been four years ago.

Because *she* was also four years older? And as such her physical desires had become that much more mature too?

Whatever the reason, Sylvie knew she should not have come here this evening. Should never have risked drawing Christian's attention to her. And she most certainly should never have allowed herself to respond to him on even a physical level! He—

"Why did you not wait for me, as I asked you to?"

Sylvie blinked up at him. "I beg your pardon?"

Christian's jaw tightened. "Four years ago. I told you I loved you and asked you to wait for me." And only thoughts of this woman waiting for him in England had kept him alive.

Her chin rose defensively as she recalled how his own household in the country, unaware of Sylvie's previous involvement with Christian, had been indulgently abuzz with the rumors of his return to his rakish behavior during his week's stay in London prior to returning to his regiment. Rumors that had put Sylvie's own importance in his life in its proper context.

She lifted her chin. "And when, after two months, you had not so much as written me a single letter, I had no choice but to accept that our affair was over."

He scowled. "There was a reason I did not write to you—"

"None that are acceptable to me, I assure you." Sylvie gave him a contemptuous smile.

Christian's jaw tightened as he remembered those weeks he lay suffering, when only thoughts of Sylvie, waiting for him at home, had prevented him from succumbing to the fatality of his infected wound. "And how long after I left did you wait before accepting Ampthill's offer of marriage?" His top lip curled back in disgust. "A week? Two? On the basis, no doubt, that an earl 'in the hand' was better than the uncertainty of the return of the one who had so recently gone back to the war!"

Sylvie gave a rueful shake of her head. "How dare you stand there and accuse me of inconstancy when you were the one who left without so much as a single glance back at the girl you had used to fill your hours of boredom whilst in the country!"

"I told you I loved you and asked you to wait for me, damn it!" His eyes glittered.

Sylvie forced herself not to wilt under the barrage of Christian's accusing tone, distrustful of that anger as she had good reason to be distrustful of the man himself. "I was eighteen years old, Christian, with all of the impatience of youth."

"So impatient you could not even have waited a few months?" Christian frowned as he recalled finally returning to England three months after he and Sylvie had last seen each other, only to be informed by her proud parents, when he rode over to their estate to pay his respects, that Sylviana no longer lived on their estate with them, but was now residing in Bedfordshire with her husband, Colonel Lord Gerald Moorland, Earl of Ampthill.

Christian had no recollection of the rest of his conversation that day with Henry and Jessica Buchanan, or of taking his leave some half an hour or so later. He had felt as if someone had punched him in the chest, rendering him both speechless and numb. He'd had no choice but to accept that Sylvie was now another man's wife, and as such, was far beyond his reach.

That numbness had lasted for several days, only to be replaced by anger and disillusionment. He had believed Sylvie was different from all those other marriage-minded chits he so frequently met in Society, that she actually cared about him, Christian the man, rather than his title. The fact that she had married an ancient earl in the few months of his absence showed Christian that had not been the case, that the title was everything to her.

And so had begun the months and years of debauchery he had embarked upon following his disillusionment. Those same years that had quickly earned him the reputation for being a rake and a dissolute, a man who cared naught for the softer emotions and everything for the pleasure of the moment.

"Obviously you could not," Christian answered his own question contemptuously. "And as luck would have it, you only had to suffer an old man's pawing for a year or two before you were conveniently left his widow and in possession of all his fortune."

Sylvie felt the color leech from her cheeks at Christian's deliberately insulting tone. An insult she did not deserve from this particular man. Not now, and certainly not four years ago.

She had been deeply in love with Christian. Even when she had been told of his behavior in London after he left her, she had tried to dismiss it as just rumors, malicious gossip that could not possibly be true. The months of silence that had followed those rumors had left her with no choice but to accept she had merely been a diversion for him during the weeks he spent in the country attending to estate matters.

"You know absolutely nothing of my marriage to Gerald—"

"I know enough to realize that an old man of sixty could not possibly have hoped to satisfy the physical demands of a young girl of eighteen!" His top lip curled back with distaste. "I know *you*, Sylvie," he added softly. "How to touch and arouse every silken inch of your body." He reached out to run his fingers lightly across the firm swell of her breasts revealed by the low neckline of her gown. "I have watched you, enjoyed you, time and time again, as you experienced climax after shattering climax. Did Moorland do that for you, Sylvie? Did he touch you in all the intimate places that I know give you such pleasure—"

"Stop it!" she protested, knowing and regretting that the heated flush to her cheeks and breasts revealed how much Christian's words had aroused her. Aroused her, but never again would she allow her heart to be broken by this man. "All this talk of the past achieves nothing—"

"And if it does not have to be the past?" Those long and caressing fingers dipped beneath the bodice of her gown to pluck unerringly at one roused nipple. "It so happens I am currently without a mistress—"

"And I am not so desperate for a man's intimate touch that I would ever consider accepting such an offer from you!" Sylvie glared up at him. Not on his terms, at least. Not on any terms that would endanger her heart or the independent life she now lived.

Those sculpted lips curved into a humorless smile. "All evidence to the contrary, my dear." He squeezed that roused nipple between thumb and finger, looking down at her dispassionately as she drew her breath in sharply. "Are you damp and ready for me between your thighs, Sylvie? Perhaps I should touch you there too and see for myself—"

"Leave me be!" Sylvie could stand it no more, slapping his hand away before stepping back.

"You are," Christian murmured with quiet satisfaction as he continued to regard her flushed cheeks dispassionately. "You will give me the name of the gentleman—

or gentlemen?—currently sharing the pleasure of your body and your bed," he said.

"And why would I wish to do that…?" She eyed him contemptuously.

"So that I may dispense with his, or their, services, of course." He shrugged those broad shoulders. "I may be considered an out-and-out rake by all of Society, but I draw the line at sharing my woman with another man!"

Sylvie gave an indignant gasp. "I have no intention of ever

becoming *your woman*!"

"Oh, but you will, Sylvie," Christian assured her confidently. "In fact, I intend calling upon you tomorrow so that we might…discuss the terms of that agreement."

Sylvie stared up at him for several long moments, knowing by the cold implacability of Christian's pale-green gaze that he meant exactly what he said. "I do believe that your arrogance has now become as large as your overinflated ego!" she finally snapped dismissively. "Now, if you will excuse me, I have a headache, and wish to go and make my excuses to your grandmother before taking my leave." She turned briskly on one satin slipper before marching away.

Christian watched between narrowed lids as Sylvie walked the length of the terrace before stepping lightly back into the ballroom, knowing he needed to delay his own return several more minutes if he was not to appear before his grandmother with an indecent erection tenting the front of his silk breeches.

And despite her protests to the contrary, he had every intention of having Sylvie satisfied on the morrow…

Once safely returned to her home in Berkeley Square, Sylvie went straight up the stairs, moving quietly into the candlelit bedchamber before nodding dismissal of the nurse and taking that lady's place in the chair beside the small bed, the tension leaving her expression as she gazed down at her sleeping daughter.

Sylvie felt a deep outpouring of love as she reached out to gently touch the abundance of dark curls framing those baby cheeks and small rosebud of a mouth, and knowing that if Christianna's eyes were open, they would be a beautiful, warm, moss green.

The exact same shade as her father's…

# *Chapter Five*

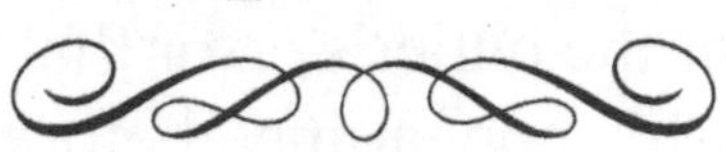

"What are you doing here?" Christian scowled darkly at Sylvie when he entered the drawing room of his London home the morning following his grandmother's ball, accepting that he owed his butler an apology for disbelieving him when that gentleman had entered Christian's darkened bedchamber a few minutes ago and informed him that Lady Sylviana Moorland, Countess of Ampthill, was waiting downstairs to speak with him.

Christian's mood was taciturn at best this morning, after the hours he had necessarily spent at his grandmother's ball following Sylvie's early departure, most of that time spent in fending off his grandmother's less-than-subtle determination to see him in the company of Lady Vanessa Styles, a young lady of one and twenty whom his grandmother had obviously decided would make him a suitable countess.

Having finally managed to escape those machinations shortly after midnight, Christian had spent the hours until daybreak at one of the more disreputable clubs, rebuffing the obvious attentions of the willing ladies there in favor of drinking copious amounts of brandy and winning at the gaming tables.

As a consequence he had not been best pleased to be awakened, only hours after falling fully clothed into his bed, and informed by his butler of Sylvie's presence downstairs in his drawing room. So certain had Christian been of the butler's error that he had not even bothered to tidy his appearance before coming downstairs, let alone change his clothes.

An oversight he deeply regretted as he saw the way Sylvie's tiny nose wrinkled with distaste as she took in his disreputable appearance—the crumpled clothes he had been wearing the evening before, the darkness of his curls in disarray, a growth of beard darkening his jaw. That jaw now tightened. "I asked—"

"I heard you," Sylvie spoke quietly, her own appearance immaculate as she perched, ladylike, upon the edge of her chair, several loose gold curls peeking out from beneath the yellow silk bonnet that was an exact match in color for her gown, her hands and arms covered by cream lace gloves.

Christian gave a wince as the brightness of those colors hurt his eyes. "And yet you did not answer," he bit out.

In truth, Sylvie regretted the need for her having to come here at all, let alone finding herself faced with Christian's disreputable appearance. His evening clothes were crumpled, as if he had slept in them. At the same time, the dark shadows below his eyes and the stubble on his arrogant chin gave the impression he had not been to bed at all. To sleep, at least…

She stiffened her spine. "Perhaps you would like to return upstairs and…see to your appearance before we commence our conversation…?"

He raised mocking brows as he threw himself down in the chair facing her own. "I am perfectly comfortable as I am, thank you," he drawled dismissively as he leaned his elbows on the arms of the chair and steepled his fingers in front of him. "And I believe we are already in conversation…?"

Sylvie drew her breath in sharply, having known the moment she saw Christian's rumpled appearance that she should not have come here today without first making an appointment. She had thought to put Christian at a disadvantage by doing so, and instead she once again found herself the one who was wrong-footed. "You put forward a suggestion to me yesterday evening—"

"If you are referring to becoming my mistress, that was not a suggestion but a statement of intent," he cut in, eyes gleaming through narrowed lids as he looked at her above those long, steepled fingers.

Sylvie was well aware of that. Just as she knew she had no intention of allowing this man to call at her home. The home where Christianna also resided…

"Perhaps your…other activities last night have now rendered that conversation obsolete?"

Those chiseled lips tilted in a humorless smile. "If you wish to know if I bedded another woman last night then just ask, Sylvie," he mocked. "I promise I will not lie to you."

"That will certainly be a novelty!"

Christian's eyes narrowed in warning. "To my knowledge I have never lied to you. Nor will I lie to you now."

Sylvie's cheeks warmed even as she berated herself for caring one way or the other whether or not Christian had gone to another woman's bed last night. In truth, it would be preferable if he had done so, would give her the perfect excuse to turn down his scandalous offer to her the previous evening. "Very well. Did you bed another woman last night?"

"No."

"Oh."

"Do not look so disappointed, Sylvie." He gave a hard laugh. "Why would I even consider the idea of bedding another woman after making love to you earlier in the evening?"

Her mouth firmed at his mockery. "You must know that you are not known for your constancy in regard to any particular woman."

He raised dark brows. "And is that to be a condition of our own arrangement? That, for the time of our… affair, I will occupy only your bed?"

"We do not have an arrangement—"

"As yet," Christian bit out decisively. "But that is your reason for being here today, is it not? So that we might thrash out the terms and conditions of such a relationship between the two of us?" The alcoholic fog and lack of sleep had now cleared enough from Christian's head for him to have considered all of the reasons Sylvie had chosen to call on him this morning.

She wished to reiterate that there would be no affair between them, now, or in the future? Something she could far more easily have told him in a note, or when he called upon her later in the day.

That she had decided to take another man as her lover? He was sure Sylvie knew him well enough to know that he would never accept such a decision.

Which only left the more obvious reason: that Sylvie had decided to accept his offer after all, but on her own terms.

And Christian was very interested in knowing what those terms might be.

"Well?" he prompted at her continued silence. "Is that not the reason you are here, Sylvie?"

# Chapter Six

Damn him!

Damn, damn, damn Lord Christian Matthew Faulkner Ambrose, the Earl of Chambourne, to the hell he deserved!

Because, having considered all of the options during the long and sleepless night, and out of a need to protect Christianna, that was precisely the reason Sylvie had called upon him this morning.

Christian had made it abundantly clear the evening before that, the two of them now having met again, he had no intention of quietly absenting himself from her life a second time. Not, at least, until he had taken what he wanted from her. As clear as he had made it that what he wanted was *her*, in his bed, for as long as it took him to tire of her again. None of which would have—should have—mattered in the least to Sylvie after Christian's despicable treatment of her four years ago.

And it would not have done.

If not for Christianna.

The man Sylvie had met yesterday evening was even

less the man she had thought him to be four years ago, the Christian from the past having at least given the appearance of warmth and caring. Last night he had been every inch the cold and arrogant Lord Christian Ambrose, the Earl of Chambourne, a known rake and a man who cared for no one—except a possible affection for his grandmother?—and neither expected nor wanted anyone to care for him. Even so, Sylvie had no doubts that he would care about his daughter if he ever learned of her existence. As he must surely do, if he were ever to actually see Christianna.

Which was precisely the reason Sylvie had decided to accept, and put her own limitations—some control—on the…relationship, Christian stated, no, demanded, there now be between the two of them.

That, and the fact that—despite everything that had once passed between them—Sylvie still responded physically to this man. Her heart, she was sure, was in no further danger from this man; how could it be when he had used her so shamefully in the past?

She rose briskly to her feet. "Being a young and wealthy widow, I have received several such offers as yours these past few months—"

"A young, wealthy and beautiful widow," Christian corrected softly.

Sylvie refused to allow herself to be moved by his compliment; Christian Ambrose was a silver-tongued devil bent on seduction, nothing more. A seduction that would take place under Sylvie's rules or not at all. "I obviously cannot vouch as to that—"

"I can," he bit out tersely. "If anything, Sylvie, you are more beautiful now than you were four years ago." And it was true, Christian acknowledged with a frown. There was a confidence to Sylvie now that had not been present four years earlier, an elegance in her carriage and demeanor that implied a coolness to her nature that Christian knew to be only skin deep; her responses to him yesterday evening had been every bit as fiery as he remembered from the past.

"Yes. Well." She gave him a scathing glance. "Several of these gentleman have been…pressing, in their attentions—"

Christian's eyes were narrowed. "Tell me the names of these other gentlemen and I will consign them to the devil."

She gave a shake of her head. "I only mentioned them at all in order to explain why I have decided to accept an offer of…protection, from one gentleman, a gentleman of my own choice, rather than continue to be plagued by many."

"And I am to be that gentleman…?"

Sylvie looked at him coolly. "Only if you are willing to accept the relationship under my terms."

His eyes narrowed. "And those terms are…?"

She drew in a deep breath. "One—there will be no other lovers in your life for as long as this…arrangement between us lasts, the arrangement becoming null and void if that should ever be the case."

"I believe I have already stated there will be no other women."

"No, you stated I should not be allowed other lovers but you," she recalled dryly.

He frowned grimly. "I give you my word there will be no other women for me, either, for the time of our own affair."

Her mouth thinned. "Two—we will meet a maximum of two nights a week—"

"Two?" Christian repeated, astounded. "I had it more in mind to spend every night together until we had sated our desire for each other."

"A maximum of two," Sylvie repeated firmly.

"Three," he stated stubbornly. "And let us hope that you will succeed in so satiating my appetite during those times that I have no strength left to so much as think of bedding another woman the other four nights of the week!"

Sylvie looked at him searchingly for several long minutes before nodding slowly. "Very well, three."

"Beginning with this one," he added softly.

Sylvie's eyes widened in alarm. Tonight? Christian wished to start bedding her this very night?

Somehow, in all her thinking the evening before, Sylvie had avoided actually dwelling on *when* Christian would require her to start sharing his bed. Just the thought of it being this night, in several hours' time, was enough to make her tremble. In trepidation, she hoped…

"Very well," she agreed. "Three—our times together will be spent here rather than in my own home—"

"Why?"

Sylvie avoided directly meeting that piercing green gaze. "It is enough that I prefer it should be so."

Christian's lids narrowed as he looked at her searchingly for several long seconds before murmuring. "It is not the usual way of things…"

"I am aware of that."

"The fact that you are here this morning, calling at the home of a single gentleman without so much as your maid in attendance, would be cause for gossip among the ton if any were to learn of it, let alone the knowledge that you are spending three nights a week here in my bed."

"Then we will have to endeavor to ensure that none of the ton learn the terms of our arrangement," Sylvie dismissed. "And I will not be spending the whole night here, merely a few hours."

His brow rose. "You intend sneaking out of my house like a thief in the middle of the night?"

Her jaw tensed. "Gentlemen do it all the time, so why should I not do the same!"

"Why would you even risk such a thing?" Christian pondered.

Sylvie's eyes flashed darkly as she looked at him with contempt. "Perhaps because I have no intention of sharing a bed with you in the home I shared with my husband until his death?"

Christian felt a harsh shard of jealousy rip through him at the thought of Sylvie sharing the home—and the bed—of another man. Especially that of the husband she had thrown him over for four years ago.

He rose slowly to his feet, his mouth curving into a hard smile as he saw the way Sylvie instantly took a step back and away from him. "Did you love him after all, then?"

She looked startled for a moment, and then that coolness settled on her face once more. "As I told you yesterday evening, Gerald was a man it was all too easy to respect and admire."

"I asked if you loved him!" Christian reached out to grasp the tops of her arms, his glittering gaze easily holding her own captive.

She moistened her lips with the tip of her tongue. "I have already told you—"

"That you respected and admired Gerald Moorland." A nerve pulsed in Christian's clenched jaw as he continued to glare down at her. "They are the emotions one feels for a favorite uncle, not a husband!"

Possibly because that was how Sylvie had always regarded Gerald, who had been a friend of her father's. That affection had grown exponentially when Gerald, finding her alone and sobbing in the garden during one of his visits, had demanded she tell him what ailed her, only to then offer her the respectability of marriage to him and legitimacy for her unborn babe rather than scandal for her whole family.

Sylvie had initially refused Gerald's offer, of course, claiming that a marriage between the two of them would be unfair to him, when she was still in love with the father of her baby, when a part of her had still hoped—prayed—that the rumors she had heard about Christian were untrue, and that he would either write to her or appear in person and that the two of them would then marry.

But Gerald had been tenacious, repeating his offer several more times during the next few weeks until, tired and heartsick at Christian's continued silence, Sylvie knew she had no choice but to acknowledge she had merely been a passing fancy for him, someone for him to make love to and with during the weeks of his leave from the army.

She looked up to meet Christian's gaze unflinchingly. "Any discussion of my feelings for my husband will not be a part of our arrangement."

Christian frowned down at her in frustration for several minutes, annoyed with Sylvie's stubbornness, but even more annoyed with himself for still desiring her so much he was willing to allow her to dictate the terms of their future relationship. Up to a point!

"I believe it is usual for gentlemen to shake hands at the successful conclusion of a deal," he murmured gruffly. "And for men and women to kiss," he added before his head swooped down and he claimed her lips with his own.

She tasted of honey, and smelt of violets, the fullness of her curves fitting perfectly against Christian as his arms tightened about her and he deepened the kiss, his erection rising to press against her as his tongue swept between the parted softness of her lips—

Sylvie wrenched her mouth from his, her cheeks flushed as she pushed away from him, her eyes bright as she looked up at him, her nose wrinkling with distaste. "You smell of cheap liquor and even cheaper perfume!"

Christian scowled his frustration. At eighteen Sylvie had seemed like an open book to him, her brightness and enthusiasm for life attracting him as nothing else could have done after so many months of battle and death. A brightness and innocence that had been deliberately designed to entice, Christian had realized after he returned to England and learned that she had married another man, another *earl*, in the three short months of his absence.

He found the confident woman who now stood before him, her every thought a mystery to him, totally frustrating and yet no less intriguing.

His mouth firmed. "What time will you come to me tonight?"

Her throat moved as she swallowed before answering. "Does eleven o'clock suit?"

Christian's brows rose. "You do not intend to join me for dinner first?"

She eyed him coolly. "For what purpose?"

He scowled. "So that we might engage in conversation before the bedding."

"Again, for what purpose?" She eyed him disdainfully. "The rakish life you have led these past four years holds no more interest for me than I am sure my own more sedate one does for you."

"Very well." Christian breathed his irritation with her coolness. "I will expect you here at eleven o'clock this evening. And I will endeavor to ensure there is no lingering odor of 'cheap liquor or even cheaper perfume'!" he taunted as she straightened her appearance in preparation for leaving.

Christian remained where he was for several more minutes after Sylvie's departure, knowing there was something about her acquiescence to becoming his mistress that was…not quite right. Oh, there was no denying her physical response to him the previous evening, or his own determination that Sylvie would become his mistress. But she had fought her own attraction to him last night, been determined that she would not give in to him, that she had no intention of ever becoming 'his woman'. Even under her own terms.

Something had happened to change her mind in those intervening hours, and despite what Sylvie said to the contrary, Christian did not believe for one moment that it had anything to do with those other gentlemen 'pressing' for her attention.

# *Chapter Seven*

"Would you care to join me in a glass of port?" Christian indicated the decanter on the table beside him as he remained seated in an armchair beside the unlit fireplace, looking across the room to where Sylvie stood hesitantly beside the door Smith had recently closed behind her, and looking ethereally beautiful in a gown of deep gold. "Or perhaps you would prefer a glass of wine?"

Sylvie was more than a little disconcerted to find herself in a room that was so obviously Christian Ambrose's private domain, serving as both a library and his study, if the book-lined walls and the cluttered desk in front of the window were any indication.

She was even more disturbed by Christian, his appearance impeccable and stylish this evening, in a dark-green superfine worn over a paler-green waistcoat and snowy-white linen, buff pantaloons outlining the muscled strength of his legs above shiny black Hessians. His dark curls looked slightly damp, as if he had recently bathed, the squareness of his jaw showing no evidence of this morning's stubble.

A pity his manners did not match that gentlemanly appearance. But no doubt his neglecting to stand up when she had entered the room was an indication of their arrangement.

"Sylvie?" he prompted softly at her continued silence.

Her spine stiffened. "Thank you, but no, I do not require any refreshment. I would much prefer that we just retire to your bedchamber and get this business over and done with."

Christian's eyes widened before narrowing. "You earlier refused conversation, and now you are also refusing to share a glass of wine with me?"

She nodded. "Because I do not believe either of those things to be a requirement of our arrangement."

Christian frowned. "You would prefer, perhaps, that I dispense with the niceties altogether and simply toss your skirts up now and take you where you stand?"

She gasped. "There is no need for crudeness!"

Christian sighed as he placed his glass of port down on the table beside him. "I freely admit I do not quite know what to make of the woman you are now, Sylvie…"

He had been angry with Sylvie four years ago for not waiting for him as he had asked her to do, but he'd had every intention of her enjoying their lovemaking tonight. Of perhaps realizing all she had given up in her youthful eagerness to become Gerald Moorland's countess…But he found her continued coolness, despite having agreed to become his mistress, completely baffling.

"There is nothing to know," she dismissed flatly. "We have an arrangement, I am simply making it clear that I am…willing to begin that arrangement."

Christian looked at her through narrowed lids for several moments before giving a rueful shake of his head. "I am used to receiving a little more enthusiasm from my lovers."

"No doubt. But I should perhaps tell you—warn you—that there have only been two men in my life, Christian." Her cheeks were flushed. "You. And my husband. I am not—I ask that you not expect me to have the physical expertise of your previous mistresses."

Christian drew his breath in sharply at her hesitant admission. "I do not believe I found you in the least wanting four years ago, Sylvie." The opposite, in fact—Sylvie's enthusiasm for enjoying all things physical had been its own aphrodisiac to his battle-numbed senses. "And it pleases me to know you have taken no other lovers since your husband died," he added.

She blinked. "It does?"

"Yes." Christian nodded. "Whatever thoughts you may have of this arrangement, Sylvie, I assure you it is not my intention to ever hurt you. On the contrary, it is my hope that we both enjoy our times together."

Sylvie's fear was that she might enjoy Christian's lovemaking too much, that she might fall in love with him all over again.

If she had ever stopped loving him…

She might only have been eighteen when the two of them were last together, but her love for Christian had been that of a woman, deep and true. Much as she had liked and respected Gerald, she had never felt a romantic love for him. Or for any other man. Mere hours after meeting Christian again, being in his company, she found herself here in his home, having agreed to become his mistress.

Oh, she had told herself earlier today that she acted out of a need to protect Christianna, to ensure that Christian never learned of the existence of his daughter, with all the accompanying complications that knowledge was sure to create.

But that excuse did not explain the excitement that had thrummed through Sylvie's veins earlier this evening—that still thrummed through her veins!—as she had dressed to meet her lover, deliberately choosing a gold gown that she knew flattered her fair coloring, its low neckline revealing the full swell of her breasts. Breasts which Christian had caressed and suckled the evening before…

And which Sylvie knew she had longed, ached, for him to caress again ever since.

"Will you join me here, Sylvie?" Christian held his hand out to her invitingly.

Her cheeks felt flushed, her heart beating wildly in her chest as she took a step toward him, and then another, and another, until she placed her gloved hand in his as she now stood beside his chair. "I— Should we not go upstairs to your bedchamber…?" Her heart skipped a beat as Christian instead pulled her in to stand between his thighs, holding her gaze with his as he slowly began to peel her lace glove down the length of her arm.

He smiled slightly as he glanced up at her. “There is no need for us to rush, Sylvie.” He slowly, leisurely, pulled the lace from each of her fingers before pulling the glove off completely and allowing it to drift softly to the carpeted floor as he raised her hand to his lips, his gaze holding hers captive as his tongue became a silky-soft caress against her fingertips before he sucked the length of one of those fingers into the heat of his mouth.

Sylvic’s breath caught in her throat as she watched that steady and erotic in and out pull on the dampness of her finger, her breasts full and aching beneath her gown, her body aching.

“I have waited too long for this to be in any hurry,” Christian murmured softly as he reached back and unfastened the buttons at the back of her gown before allowing it to fall down the slender length of her arms to the carpeted floor, revealing that she wore only a thin chemise beneath, golden curls visible between her thighs, swollen nipples tipping the fullness of her breasts. Christian slipped the ribbon strap of her chemise down her arms and allowed that to fall too.

“Christian…!”

“Let me look, love,” he groaned as he caught both her hands in one of his as she would have covered those bared breasts. “You are bigger here than I remember, Sylvie.” He watched as his fingertips skimmed her rounded breasts. "And your nipples are darker." He ran the soft pad of his thumb across her before lowering his head to suck first one, and then the other, into the moistness of his mouth, laving those tight buds with his tongue, gently biting with his teeth as he continued to caress, causing her nipples to swell and elongate in the heat of his mouth.

He ran his hand along the silky length of Sylvie's thigh, feeling the throb of her hidden nubbin against his palm as he cupped those silky gold curls to stroke her before entering her with first one finger and then two. He heard the catch in Sylvie's ragged breathing. She cried out in pleasure as she exploded in climax before collapsing against him weakly.

Christian rested his head against the fullness of Sylvie's breasts, feeling completely at peace as he enjoyed the feel of her fingers lightly caressing his hair. She continued to tremble and cling to him in the aftershocks of that climax.

A peace and completion he had not felt since last making love to Sylvie four years ago…

# *Chapter Eight*

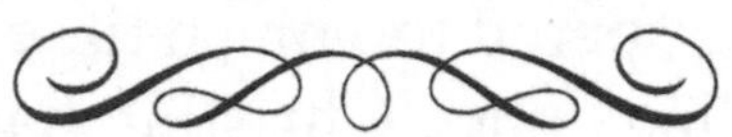

"Where are you taking me?" Sylvie gasped as Christian stood up and swung her up into his arms to carry her over to the door, the darkness of his hair tousled from her caressing fingers.

"Upstairs to my bedchamber—"

"But my clothes…? The servants…?" she protested weakly.

"We can collect your clothes later, and I instructed Smith to dismiss the household for the rest of the night once you arrived," Christian assured her with satisfaction. "Open the door, Sylvie," he encouraged.

Sylvie knew that Christian did not love her, that he had never loved her, but she appreciated that he had made love to her just now with tenderness as well as passion rather than the disrespect she had expected. A tenderness and passion that were irresistible to her…

"Good girl." He murmured his approval as she bent to open the door to allow him to step out into the deserted, candlelit hallway before striding purposefully toward the stairs, carrying her in his arms as if she weighed nothing at all.

A single candle burned in his bedchamber, the green-and-cream brocade curtains at the windows and about the four-poster bed suiting him perfectly, as did the heavy oak furniture.

Not that Sylvie spared too much time in appreciation of her surroundings once Christian had placed her in the middle of the bed, a mute shaking of his head halting her as she would have pulled the bedcovers over her nakedness, the steadiness of his gaze holding hers as he straightened to begin removing his own clothes.

Sylvie forgot her own nakedness as he peeled off his fashionably tight jacket and waistcoat. Followed by his neck cloth, and then he unfastened the four buttons at his throat before pulling his shirt over his head, leaving the darkness of his hair even more tousled as he sat facing her on the stool before the dressing table in order to remove his boots.

Sylvie's breath caught in her throat as his hands moved to his pantaloons, the unfastening of those six buttons revealing that he wore no undergarments. Christian removed his pantaloons completely to stand before her completely naked.

Sylvie's fingers curled into the bedcovers beneath her, her throat moving convulsively as she swallowed. She had forgotten just how beautiful he was, shoulders and chest wide and muscled, waist tapered above that proudly thrusting erection, his legs all long and muscled elegance.

"Do I still meet with your approval, Sylvie?" he prompted.

"Oh, yes," she breathed as she finally managed to uncurl her fingers from the bedcovers before moving up onto her knees and moving to the side of the bed where he stood, gaze heated as she gazed down at his proudly jutting manhood before reaching out to curl her fingers about that hardness encased in velvet. "Oh, yes," she repeated achingly.

Christian groaned low in his throat as he thrust slowly into her caresses. "Sylvie…!" he gasped achingly, his hands moving up to cradle each side of her face as her head lowered and her little pink tongue darted out to continue the seduction.

Satisfaction gleamed in her eyes as she glanced up at him briefly before parting her lips wide and taking him fully into the heat of her mouth. Christian caressed and plucked at her breasts even as he thrust into that moist heat, until he knew he was about to explode as the pleasure became too much even for his rigid self-control.

"No more!" he groaned before reluctantly pulling free of her, his cock a throbbing ache. "I want to be inside you when I come, Sylvie," he breathed raggedly. "But not quite yet," he murmured as he laid her back against the bedcovers before kneeling between her parted her thighs to gaze down in appreciation at those moist and swollen lips. He lowered his head, fingers lightly caressing her opening as his tongue rasped moistly around that pulsing nubbin without ever quite touching it.

"Christian!" Sylvie cried out, back arching restlessly even as her hands moved up to grip his shoulders tightly.

"Tell me, Sylvie. Tell me what you want." His hands cupped beneath the globes of her bottom as he breathed lightly on that throbbing nubbin, eyes gleaming with satisfaction as her nether lips pulsed and parted against the caress of his fingers.

"I need you to touch me there—" She broke off with a gasp as Christian gave her the lightest of caresses with his tongue. "More, Christian. Oh please, more…!" She raised her hips in restless invitation.

His hands tightened on her bottom as he lifted her into the rasping stroke of his tongue, holding her captive as he stroked time and time again until he felt her exploding beneath him in a trembling, shuddering climax.

Christian reared up onto his knees, taking his weight onto his elbows as he positioned his erection at her entrance before thrusting deeply into that hot and welcoming channel, paying great attention to one nipple to prolong Sylvie's orgasm even as the rhythmic convulsing of her inner muscles took him crashing over the edge of his own pleasure and he released, long and satisfying, inside her.

"Christian…?"

"Am I too heavy for you?" he murmured against the warmth of her throat, his body stretched out above hers.

He was a little heavy, but Sylvie was loath to relinquish their closeness just yet. "No," she denied even as she reached up to caress the heat of his shoulders, fingers lightly caressing down his muscled back. "I merely wondered—Christian?" Her voice sharpened in alarm as she felt and then traced the hard ridge of a scar running from his left shoulder across his back and down to his right side. "What happened to your back…?" she gasped as she attempted to sit up so that she might see his back for herself, only to find that Christian's weight pressing down on her made that impossible. "Christian?"

"It is an old scar," he dismissed lightly as his lips skimmed across her collarbone.

"But—" She stilled suddenly, eyes wide. "How old…?"

"Do we have to discuss this now, Sylvie?" he murmured indulgently as his lips continued that caressing assault on the creaminess of her throat. "I do not recall your having this need for conversation after our lovemaking in the past," he added teasingly.

"Christian, please…!" she pressed, needing to know—exactly—when he had received the wound that had left such a terrible and lasting scar upon his back.

A scar that she knew had not been there four years ago…

# *Chapter Nine*

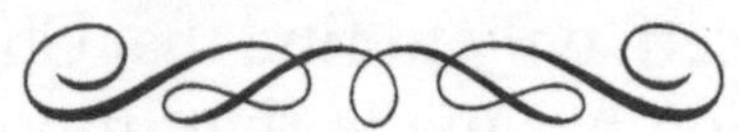

Christian moved up onto his elbow to withdraw gently from Sylvie before moving to lie down beside her, satiated and satisfied in a way he had not been since they had last made love together. "Does the thought of my scar repulse you?"

"Of course it does not," she dismissed impatiently, her face pale as she sat up and turned him slightly so that she might look at the scar for herself. "How—how did this happen?"

Christian shrugged. "A French saber."

Her face became paler. "When?"

Christian fell back onto the pillows. "What does it matter—"

"It matters to me!" she assured him fiercely. "Tell me, Christian. Please!"

He frowned. "It happened four years ago, two weeks after I left you and two days after I returned to my regiment." He smiled bitterly. "The wound incapacitated me, became infected, and I was out of my head with a fever for almost a week, and then weakened for many more." He shrugged. "It is the reason I was unable to write to you. The reason for my delay in returning to you."

That is what Sylvie had thought he might say. What she had dreaded hearing. "You were coming back to me?"

"Of course I was coming back to you!" He frowned. "How many times do I have to tell you that before you believe me? I had told you that I loved you and that I would come back to you as soon as I was able!"

Yes, he had. And, despite the rumors of his behavior in London after he had left her, Sylvie had waited and waited for his return, until the babe she carried meant she could wait no longer and she had accepted the offer of marriage made to her by another man.

And all the time she waited, Christian had been ill and fevered, cut down by a French saber. It was the reason he had not returned to England until it was too late; Sylvie had already been another man's wife, and the babe she carried accepted as a child of that marriage.

What had she done?

Christian frowned as Sylvie moved abruptly away to sit on the side of the bed, before standing up to cross the room and pull on his black brocade bathrobe he had draped across the chair beside the window.

"Are you leaving already?" He kept his tone deliberately neutral as he sat up, knowing he had agreed, accepted, Sylvie's decree that she would only stay with him for a few hours, but he had hoped, after the enjoyment of their lovemaking— Whatever he might have hoped, it was obviously not to be. "When will I see you again?"

She finished fastening the belt of the robe before looking up at him with dark and guarded eyes. "I—I will send you a note tomorrow."

His brows rose. "A note…?"

"Yes." She turned away. "I will leave your robe downstairs in the library after I have dressed, and then let myself out—"

"Give me a minute and I will come down with you." Christian swung his legs to the side of the bed.

"No! No," she repeated more calmly, the dullness of her eyes appearing like dark bruises in the pallor of her face as she refused to so much as look at him. "I— We will talk again tomorrow."

"Talk?" he repeated sharply.

"Yes," she sighed. "We will talk. I— There is something— I must

go!" She hurried to the door, wrenching it open before turning back to him briefly, her expression anguished. "Please believe that I—that I am sorry."

Christian tensed, stomach churning. "You are not ending our association already?"

"No! I— " She gave a shake of her head, tears now glistening in the darkness of her eyes.

Relief flooded him. "Then what are you sorry for?"

"For everything!" she choked. "I am sorry for everything," she repeated shakily.

"I do not understand, Sylvie…" He gave a pained

frown. "You are not ending our association and yet you are sorry. What—"

"Tomorrow, Christian. I will explain all tomorrow," she assured him dully. "Do not follow me now. I— It is for the best— Tomorrow," she repeated before stepping out into the hallway, the door to the bedchamber closing quietly behind her.

Christian had no idea what had just happened. One minute he and Sylvie had been lying satiated in each other's arms after the most satisfying lovemaking Christian had ever known, and the next she had run from him as if the hounds of hell were at her heels.

Tomorrow.

Sylvie had said she would explain all tomorrow.

And he hoped that explanation did not include the ending of their relationship, because having now made love with Sylvie again, that possibility was even less acceptable to Christian than it had been four years ago…

"The Earl of Chambourne to see you, my lady," Sylvie's butler announced from the doorway of her private parlor.

Sylvie ceased her restless pacing as she turned to him, the deep-brown gown she wore only emphasizing the pallor of her face. "Please show him in, Bellows."

After a sleepless and troubled night, Sylvie had written a note and had it delivered to Christian only an hour ago, requesting that he call upon her at his earliest convenience. She should have known, after the manner in which she had fled his home the night before, that

Christian's 'earliest convenience' would be almost immediately.

Quite what she was to say to him, how to explain, was still not exactly clear to her. She only knew that she owed Christian an explanation. For her behavior both the previous night and four years ago…

Christian gave the standing and unsmiling Sylvie a searching glance after the butler left the two of them alone. Her golden curls were fashionably styled, her brown silk gown also the height of fashion, and yet—and yet there was an air of fragility about her, a translucence to the creaminess of her skin, and a haunted look in the dark depths of her eyes. "Tell me," he demanded without preamble.

She gave a shake of her head, not of denial, but as if she was at a loss to know quite how to proceed. She closed her lids briefly before opening them again, her chin rising as if for a blow. "There is something that I wish—no, something I *must* tell you." She moistened her rosy-pink lips. "I have thought about this for most of the night, have considered all the consequences of—of my admission, but I can see no other way. No other honorable way," she added huskily.

Christian frowned darkly. "You are making me nervous, Sylvie."

She swallowed. "I assure you, that is not my intention. I— You see—"

"Mama? Mama, Nurse says I may not visit with you just yet, that you are too busy this morning!"

Christian had turned at the first sound of that trilling little voice as it preceded the opening of the door and the entrance of a little green whirlwind that launched itself into Sylvie's arms before turning to look at him curiously.

His eyes narrowed as he found himself looking down at a beautiful little girl of possibly three years old, dressed in a green gown, with dark curls and—and moss-green eyes…

His own dark curls and moss-green eyes?

## *Chapter Ten*

"Please say something, Christian," Sylvie choked, having just returned from taking a reluctant Christianna back to the nursery and her flustered and scolding nurse. The tears streamed unchecked down Sylvie's cheeks as she saw that Christian's face still bore an expression of shocked disbelief. "Anything!"

His throat moved convulsively as he swallowed. "What do you call her…?"

Sylvie gave a pained frown. "I— Her name is Christianna."

His breath left him in a hiss. "You named her for me?"

"Yes. Christian—"

"Dear God, Sylvie, she is so beautiful!" The tension leached from his body and he dropped down into one of the armchairs, his face pale, his expression tortured as he stared up at her. "Is she— Can she be the reason you accepted Gerald Moorland's offer of marriage four years ago?"

"Yes."

Christian gave a pained wince. "And did he know—"

"Yes, he knew. Oh, not who the father of my babe was, but I never tried to deceive him into believing the child was his," Sylvie assured huskily. "Please believe—I did not know what to do when I realized I carried your child, and although Gerald's life had been dedicated to the army, and he had never shown any inclination to marry, he nevertheless offered—Gerald was a friend of my father's—"

Christian looked at her sharply. "Your parents know—"

"No." She gave a sad shake of her head. "They have always believed that Christianna was a seven-month babe." Sylvie twisted her fingers together in her agitation. "Only Gerald knew she was not. And he was too much of a gentleman to ever reveal the truth to anyone."

"And—and did you grow to love him...?"

She gave a slow shake of her head. "Not in a romantic way. But he became my closest friend."

"You were not— It was not a physical marriage?" Christian prompted sharply.

Sylvie smiled slightly. "Gerald did not think of me in that way. He did not think of anyone in that way," she added softly as she saw Christian's incredulous expression. "He really was married to the army. Although I never had any doubts that he cared for both Christianna and me. For the short time he was alive after Christianna's birth, he was a wonderful father to her."

"I am glad of it." Christian nodded.

"You do not really mean that!" Sylvie groaned.

"Of course I do."

"How could you? Because of my lack of faith in you, in myself, I have denied you the first three years of your daughter's life!" Her eyes glistened with unshed tears. "And I am so sorry for that, Christian."

"Why did you not write to me?"

Sylvie closed her eyes briefly. "After you left me, there were rumors on your estate of the women you had been seen with in London before you rejoined your regiment—"

"They were untrue." He looked at her bleakly. "I did not so much as look at another woman. Why would I, when it was you I wanted? You I intended to return to? You whom I loved?"

Sylvie looked at him searchingly, seeing the truth in the bleakness of his expression. As she heard the past tense in his last statement. "I am so sorry, Christian. So very sorry that I ever doubted you." She turned away to stare sightlessly out of the window overlooking the garden. "I cannot bear to think of how much you must now hate and despise me!"

Christian rose abruptly to his feet to cross the room in three long strides before grasping Sylvie's shoulders and turning her to face him. "I could never hate or despise you, Sylvie," he assured her gruffly as he cupped either side of her face to brush his thumbs across her cheek and erase the tears. "How could I when I fell in love with you the moment I saw you swimming half-naked in that river four years ago? And it is a love that never died, Sylvie. Never," he assured her fiercely as her eyes widened incredulously, hopefully. "Yes, I felt angry and betrayed when I returned to England and found you had married another man. And I behaved abominably for the next four years—"

"So I believe." She smiled sadly.

"I am not proud of those years, Sylvie," he acknowledged. "How could I be? But I did not know how else to get through the pain of loving you and knowing you were so far out of my reach, that you belonged with another man. And all this time!" He gave a self-disgusted shake of his head. "Was the reason you agreed to become my mistress, but with that proviso that we meet in my home and not yours, because you wished to protect Christianna from me?"

"Partly," she acknowledged.

Christian looked at her closely. "And the other part?"

Sylvie released her breath in a sigh. "The other part was that I only had to see you again, to be with you again, to know, despite denying it to myself, wishing it to be the contrary, that I still had feelings for you."

He stilled. "As I only had to see you again the night of my grandmother's ball to know that I have never stopped loving you."

She gasped. "You believed I had married Gerald for his money and title—"

"And it made no difference to the love I still feel for you!" he admitted fiercely. "I knew that night that I wanted you back in my life—that I *had* to have you back in my life, in any way that you would allow!" He drew in a ragged breath. "How you must now hate and despise me because I tried to force you into my bed!"

Sylvie huskily gave a self-derisive laugh. "Did it seem last night as if I felt forced into responding to your lovemaking?"

"No..." Christian looked down at her searchingly. "And it was lovemaking, Sylvie. No matter how I might have behaved the night of my grandmother's ball, how much I tried to continue to despise you for believing you had married an old man for his title and fortune, once I held you in my arms again, kissed you, I could never do less than make love with you."

Yes, for all of those things, Sylvie knew that Christian's lovemaking the previous night had been every bit as tender and caring for her own needs as it had ever been in the past. "You did not know of Christianna's existence then..."

His hands moved to tightly grip her shoulders. "If anything, that only makes me love you more," he assured her fiercely. "You did what you believed you had to do to in order to protect our daughter when you accepted Ampthill's offer, what was necessary to protect both Christianna and yourself!"

"And by my doing so, you have missed the first three years of your daughter's life," she repeated sadly.

"But God willing I will not miss any more. Or that of any other children we might be blessed with?" He looked down at her uncertainly.

Sylvie gazed up at him searchingly, seeing only love burning in Christian's beautiful moss-green eyes. "What are you saying?"

"Asking," he corrected huskily. "I am asking what I should have asked you before I left four years ago. What, in my arrogance, I believed could wait until the next time I returned to England." He gave a self-disgusted shake of his head.

Sylvie swallowed. "And what is that?"

"That you do me the honor of marrying me," Christian pressed softly. "I had never loved until I met you that summer, Sylvie. Nor have I loved again since. I loved you then, and I love you still, and if you will consent to become my wife, I swear to you that I will tell you, show you, every day for the rest of our lives together how very much I love and cherish you!"

Tears welled in her eyes once more, but this time they were tears of happiness. "I realized last night that I have never stopped loving you either, Christian. I loved you then, I love you now. I will always love and cherish you."

He looked down at her searchingly for several long, disbelieving seconds, his expression turning to one of wonder as he saw that love shining in the darkness of her eyes. He fell to his knees in front of her. "Sylviana Moorland, will you do me the honor of becoming my wife? Allow me to love and cherish you for the rest of your life?"

"Oh, yes, Christian!" She threw herself into his arms. "Oh, yes, yes, and a thousand times yes!"

"You have made me the happiest of men," Christian choked as he stood up to take her gently in his arms and kiss her with all of the tenderness of a man deeply in and forever in love.

And ensuring that Sylvie became the happiest of women.

At last…

# *Chapter Eleven*

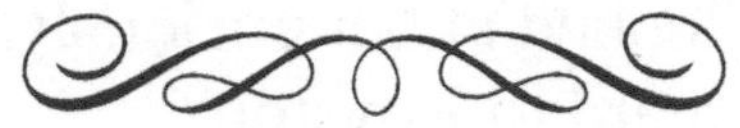

*The London home of Lady Jocelyn Ambrose, Dowager Countess of Chambourne.*

"—and the wedding is to be next month," Lady Jocelyn concluded gleefully to her two closest friends.

"But Chambourne is not marrying the woman you had chosen to become his future wife?" Lady Cicely Hawthorne said doubtfully.

"Well. No." Some of Lady Jocelyn's glee abated. "He did not care for Lady Vanessa at all. But he is to marry. Which, after all, is what we had all decided upon, is it not?" Both ladies turned to the silent Dowager Duchess of Royston for confirmation.

"Yes. Yes," Edith St. Just acknowledged briskly. "Although I agree with Cicely, in that it would be more of a triumph if Chambourne had decided upon the lady you had chosen for him."

Lady Jocelyn looked suitably deflated. "Perhaps one of you will be more success in that regard than I."

"I am not at all sure of any degree of success in regard

to Thorne," Lady Cicely admitted heavily. "Since his first wife died four years ago, he has shown a decided aversion to the very idea of remarrying."

"And yet he must, for he is in need of an heir, the same as our own two grandsons," the dowager duchess dismissed briskly.

Lady Jocelyn looked at her curiously. "How go your own efforts in regard to Royston?"

"Nicely, thank you." Edith St. Just nodded regally.

"You believe he will marry the woman of your choice?" Lady Cicely looked suitably impressed.

"I am sure of it, yes."

"How confident are you of that?" Lady Jocelyn challenged daringly, still feeling slightly stung in regard to her friends' reaction to her news of Chambourne's forthcoming marriage to Lady Sylviana Moorland, the Countess of Ampthill.

"So confident," the dowager duchess assured haughtily, "that I am willing to write that lady's name on a piece of paper this very minute and leave it in the safekeeping of your butler, only to be returned and read by all of us when Royston announces his intention of marrying."

"Is that not rather presumptuous of you, Edith?" Lady Cicely raised skeptical brows.

"Not in the least," the dowager duchess dismissed briskly. "In fact, call for Edwards and we shall do it now. This very minute."

Ellie, sitting in her usual place in the window beside Miss Thompson and Mrs. Spencer, could only watch with a sinking heart as Edith St. Just did exactly as she had said she would.

Could only wonder as to the name of the lady—and secretly envy her—written on that innocuous piece of paper, which was taken away by Lady Jocelyn's butler some minutes later…

As she knew beyond a doubt that it would not be her own name.

Despite the fact she had fallen in love with the arrogantly disdainful Justin St. Just several months ago…

* * * * *

# AN OFFICER BUT NO GENTLEMAN

Bronwyn Scott

If you enjoy
AN OFFICER BUT NO GENTLEMAN
don't miss the rest of Bronwyn Scott's quartet
*Rakes Who Make Husbands Jealous*

Available from
Mills and Boon® Historical Romance:

SECRETS OF A GENTLEMAN ESCORT
LONDON'S MOST WANTED RAKE

And as a Mills & Boon® Historical *Undone!* eBook:

A MOST INDECENT GENTLEMAN

**Other recent novels by Bronwyn Scott:**

HOW TO DISGRACE A LADY*
HOW TO RUIN A REPUTATION*
HOW TO SIN SUCCESSFULLY*
A LADY RISKS ALL**
A LADY DARES**

**Rakes Beyond Redemption*
***Ladies of Impropriety*

**And in**
**M&B Regency *Castonbury Park* mini-series:**

UNBEFITTING A LADY

Coming soon from Bronwyn Scott—
her new hot and sultry duet
*Rakes of the Caribbean*

PLAYING THE RAKE'S GAME

BREAKING THE RAKE'S RULES

**DEDICATION**

For my friends Leslie and Jim. Just because.

# *Chapter One*

*London, Fall 1839*

Some men thrived in peacetime. Captain Grahame Westmore definitely wasn't one of them. His army, the Queen's army, didn't need him anymore and four years of London life had left him restless for a change. That restlessness caused him to eye the file on Channing Deveril's desk with a mixture of suspicion and anticipation as he paced the league's office. Would the next assignment be the adventure he was looking for? He doubted it. His work for the league was starting to pale, not that he'd ever tell Channing. He probably didn't have to. Channing likely already knew.

"Go ahead, open it." Channing grinned and sat back in his chair, hands steepled in supreme confidence. Someone who didn't know Channing well would take that grin as a sign of complete unawareness to the restlessness plaguing him. But Grahame knew better. Channing was not given to obliviousness. It would be a mistake to assume otherwise. As the founder of the

League of Discreet Gentlemen, an underground organization dedicated to the pursuit of women's pleasure, Channing prided himself on perfectly matching his men to their missions. As a result, Grahame's senses were on high alert. What was he about to be matched with? Or more appropriate, to whom?

Grahame picked up the folder with healthy skepticism. Something was definitely afoot. Channing was far too smug this morning. He opened the folder and scanned the brief for pertinent information. Details could come later. He saw all he needed to make his decision. He slid the folder back across the desk and gave Channing his one-word answer. "No."

"No?" Channing arched a blond eyebrow. "Care to have a seat and tell me why? You'll wear me out with all that pacing."

Grahame took the chair. He could humor Channing in that respect, at least. He was *not* taking this assignment. "I'm a cavalry officer not a nursemaid."

"Ex-cavalry officer," Channing corrected. "And I think your skills in that regard make you the ideal candidate. I admit it's not our usual. We're escorts, not bodyguards, but when this opportunity came up in conversation I immediately thought of you."

Grahame sat up a little straighter, instantly wary. Now they were getting somewhere. "You didn't already commit me without my approval?" It was one of the rules of the league that no one be forced into an assignment. In their line of work, where assignments ranged anywhere from providing an innocuous escort to an opera or ball to more physically intimate engagements, consent was essential.

Channing gave an easy shrug. "I simply told the people in question I might have a man for them."

"Then you can tell them you were mistaken. I am qualified to lead men in battle, not play governess to a diplomat's spoiled daughter," Grahame replied firmly. Squiring a diplomat's daughter to her father's new post was not his idea of anything remotely positive. He knew the sort. He'd seen how diplomats traveled during his time in the military. He wouldn't just be moving a daughter. He'd be shepherding a household. She'd come with wagons of luggage, carriages of servants and an attitude to match. These daughters were the children of second and third sons, often raised with an eye toward privilege as granddaughters of earls and viscounts. As such, Grahame found them to be usually unsuited for the difficulties of travel.

"I must respectfully disagree with your assessment." Channing remained unfazed by his firm response. "You are not giving yourself enough credit. If you can organize a troop of men on horseback in the melee of battle, I would think moving one woman and her luggage would be easily done. Additionally, you're competent with a variety of arms and could defend her little cavalcade if necessary."

Now *that* pricked. "Competent? I am more than competent with pistols and saber." It was a point of pride that he was known in high military circles for his skill with weapons on horseback. He'd worked hard for that reputation, learning early on that without a title, perfection was his only route to respect.

Channing just smiled. "Exactly. As I said, you're perfect. Don't you even want to know where she's going?"

"It won't make a difference." There was only one place Grahame wanted to go, only one place that had any need for his unique skills, but it was a continent away and it would mean leaving Channing, something he was reluctant to do. It would leave Channing shorthanded at the agency. Channing had always been loyal to him. Now he had a chance to return the favor by staying.

"I think it will," Channing said quietly. Grahame tried not to shift in his seat. Channing's incessant smiling was making him nervous. He liked Channing Deveril immensely but Channing had an unnerving talent to literally read people like books, which was a good thing, Grahame reasoned, because Channing didn't read. It wasn't that he couldn't read, the man was certainly literate, he simply didn't. But that talent was deuced awkward when it was turned on him. It meant Channing knew something he did not and that made Grahame uneasy, indeed.

"All right then, tell me." The room had suddenly become fraught with an invisible air of anticipation. Grahame far preferred the foe he could see.

Channing pulled out another file from his desk. He pushed it toward him and spoke one word into the tense silence. "Vienna."

Of all the words Channing could have spoken, this was the one he couldn't resist. Vienna, home of the

Spanish riding school, the very place that had written two weeks ago and asked him to come for an interview on the eighteenth of the month. They thought perhaps they could use an instructor of his caliber on horseback and with his distinct specialty in sabrage, a gentleman's art to be sure.

Vienna represented everything he'd been chasing since he'd known what it was he hungered for—the chance to belong, the type of belonging that came with a sense of permanence and respect, not because of birth but because of skill.

Grahame blew out a breath and gave in to the urge to shift in his seat. He crossed and recrossed his legs. He wasn't like the others here: not like Channing, an earl's second son, or Jocelyn Eisley, heir to an earldom, or even the recently married and retired Nicholas D'Arcy who was at least the son of gentry. He, Grahame Westmore, was nothing. He'd earned his commission, not bought it. He'd fought for his leg up in the world every step of the way. To have been an English officer and to now be invited to the Spanish riding school in Vienna, was the best he could hope for, a dream, really, for a boy of his humbling beginnings.

"You know very well what that means to me," Grahame said slowly. "I would escort the devil himself in order to get to Vienna."

Channing nodded. "Then I'll take that as a yes. But you're cutting it pretty fine. They'll expect you to arrive on time if you're serious."

Grahame gave a tight grimace. He knew what it meant to escort the devil. There'd be hell to pay.

# *Chapter Two*

What the devil was going on down there? The sound of barked orders and the hurried march of booted feet on hardwood floors brought Elowyn Bagshaw to the balustrade overlooking the townhouse foyer. Below her, footmen carried boxes and trunks out the door, maids scurried to and fro with last-minute packing supplies. Everyone was organized and purposeful in their tasks, the chaos of moving minimized with efficiency and it was *all wrong*, every last bit of it, starting with the fact that they weren't moving.

At least not today. She should know. She'd been moving her father's household since she was fifteen. Boxes and trunks weren't scheduled to be loaded until Thursday and by all accounts, today was Tuesday. She knew exactly where to place the blame—Captain Grahame Westmore, a man she'd met only by letter. More like by note. The two lines he'd sent over yesterday hardly qualified as a letter.

The culprit stood with his back—his very wide, broad-shouldered back—to her, directing it all, looking for all intents as a man on a mission. There was a bridled urgency to the way he ordered the staff, as if it mattered how quickly this task could be done.

It had not been hard to pick him out. Her eyes had found him with little effort. Elowyn suspected he would be easy to spot in any room. His physical presence reeked of command. Captain Westmore was taller than most men, his hair longer, his shoulders broader and his stance wider. Attributes which were all emphasized by the absence of his coat. There were other attributes emphasized, too, like the firm, muscled contours of his buttocks encased in snug riding breeches. She'd always had a weakness for horsemen. There was nothing sexier than a well-made man in tight breeches.

Still, a delicious derriere and the fact the hall was emptying at an impressive pace didn't excuse his arrogance. It would have been nice if he'd seen fit to consult her before he started carting up her mother's china without so much as a by your leave. *She* was in charge here. He took orders, he didn't give them.

Elowyn started down the staircase, ready to do battle. It was not her first choice of introduction but he'd left her no option with his unorthodox barging in. It would be a long trip to Vienna if she didn't put him in his place. One should always begin as one meant to go on; it was *the* essential rule of establishing control in any relationship. If Westmore thought he could just walk into her home and start moving her things without permission, who knew what other presumptions he'd make?

A bit of naughty excitement trilled through her. There

were presumptions and then there were *presumptions*. He looked like a man who didn't let the difference stop him. Dear Lord, she hadn't even officially met him and her imagination was already running away with her. Now was not the time. There was business to take care of. When he'd written to say he'd call in the morning, she'd never equated that two-line statement with *this*.

Elowyn raised her voice to be heard over the noise. "*What* do you think you're doing, Captain?" The foyer fell silent, all activity freezing in motion at the sound of her challenge. Captain Westmore pivoted toward her and advanced, hands on lean hips, drawing her eyes to the core of his swagger—hips, pelvis and the place in between.

What had been impressive physicality at a distance was imposing masculinity up close. Elowyn took an involuntary step up the staircase to establish an equality of heights and tried to focus her gaze on the rugged features of his face instead of that one place a well-bred lady never looked on a man. It would have certainly helped if he'd been wearing a coat. Then again, the man fairly exuded raw sexuality. It was likely to find its way out regardless of how many coats he put on. Well, this was just fabulous. Her father had managed to hire the most dashing guard in London.

"What does it look like I'm doing, princess?" Westmore planted a booted foot on the bottom stair and gave her a gray-eyed perusal that suggested the answer to his question was less about moving boxes and more about something else altogether, something that sent a slow trail of heat straight to her stomach.

Elowyn met his gaze evenly. “It’s hard to say, since what it appears you’re doing isn’t scheduled for another two days.”

“There’s been a change of plan.”

*That was it?* There was no attempt at an apology, no effort to be conciliatory. Not even an explanation. This was not the attitude of a model employee.

Elowyn crossed her arms and stood her ground. Leave it to her father to also hire the most arrogant escort available. She was beginning to wonder if her father had even met Westmore. He wasn’t really her father’s type. “Since when do you make the plans, Captain?”

“Since the weather changed.” Again, the unrepentant stare. “My sources on the Channel coast say there’s a storm moving in. Unless you want to be holed up in an inn with your wagons stuck in a stable yard for a few days, we leave now and hope we can beat the weather.”

She hated being cornered. The captain had to know very well she wouldn’t want the wagons exposed to the elements and possible theft any more than they had to be.

Captain Westmore gestured to the room behind him, now empty of boxes. “I believe we’re packed. We’re just waiting on you, miss.”

She wanted to wipe that self-satisfied smile off his face. There was winning and then there was gloating. *He was gloating.* He thought he had the upper hand. The captain was about to get his comeuppance. “I believe you are mistaken. There are still the trunks in my room. I always have them loaded last so they'll be first off."

He raised a dark eyebrow. "Is that so?"

"I'm afraid it is." Elowyn gave him a sweet smile and moved past him, unable to resist a parting shot. "You would have known if you'd asked first." Round one to her. Elowyn stopped in the foyer to claim her victor's prize. She got to watch that derriere of his go up the stairs *five* times. She couldn't recall the last time she'd enjoyed moving quite so much.

# *Chapter Three*

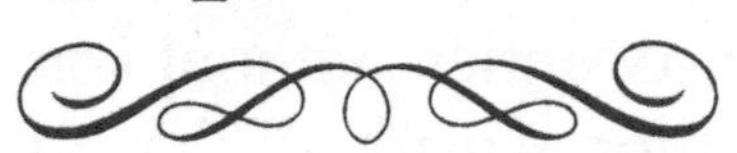

Grahame couldn't recall the last time he'd enjoyed ruffling someone's feathers quite so much. He whistled a little tune atop his big bay stallion, Aramis, as London disappeared behind them. Miss Bagshaw had shown a surprising amount of fire this morning when faced with his dictatorial orders regarding an early departure.

True, it would have been easier if she'd meekly acquiesced. Meek acquiescence was always easier but a lot less fun. It was also true that she lived up to his expectations, or down, depending on how one looked at them. She was a diplomat's daughter, haughty and used to getting her own way. When she'd stared him down with green eyes, hard as emerald shards, he knew he'd been right on that account. But she'd done more than stare in anger. She'd also stared in interest.

He'd not been oblivious to the gaze that had followed him up the stairs. Over the years, he'd come to know when a woman wanted him. He'd also come to know when things could be allowed to progress that far. This was *not* one of those jobs. This was not escorting a notorious widow to a ball or accompanying a lonely woman to the opera while her husband was out of town. Elowyn Bagshaw fit into neither of the usual categories. She was a diplomat's daughter.

It was a pity, really. Her demeanor suggested she was a passionate woman by nature, a woman who had not reached her mid-twenties without some experimentation. The realization wasn't all that surprising considering her extensive travel and the fact other countries had more lenient outlooks on female sexual purity—outlooks he personally favored. He could well imagine all that carefully coiffed chestnut hair of hers falling over naked shoulders, candlelight limning her curves in provocative shadows as she sat astride her lover. Of course, her lover would have to be a man who could take that attitude of hers in hand or she'd never respect him. Respect was just as essential in bed as it was elsewhere.

Grahame shifted uncomfortably in the saddle against the pressure of a growing arousal. His little fantasy had brought on a rather awkward erection. It was not a pleasant way to ride. He turned in his saddle and surveyed the road behind him for distraction, anything to keep his mind off more prurient subjects. The five wagons of goods stretched out at decent intervals and were keeping up but the going was slow. Caravans were always slow. At this rate it would take two days to reach Dover. It would put their arrival on Thursday night. They could sail on Friday, just ahead of the reported storm front.

Grahame drummed an impatient hand on his thigh. When he had thought of all the inconveniences that would manifest themselves on the journey to Vienna, he'd not counted celibacy among them. He'd been hired for her safety, not her seduction. Never mind that she had a siren's own body and a caramel cascade of Rapunzel-esque hair that would drive any man mad. She was not in the job description and he'd do well to remember it. A woman like her never would be. Single women of her background had expectations of their men like titles, wealth, social standing, none of which he had to offer. Elowyn Bagshaw was off-limits.

The captain was technically off-limits but that didn't stop her eye, or her maid's, she noted, from wandering to the coach window on frequent occasion to view the masculine scenery. Elowyn had come to the conclusion long ago that she was a woman who liked men and there was no point in pretending otherwise. However, there was always a point in being judicious with one's behavior. Her first lover, a French *vicomte* of incomparable charm, had chosen her, but *she* had chosen the other two—an Italian count and a Russian prince, both of whom had understood the discretion and sophistication required of a successful physical affair. They'd also understood the need for brevity in such circumstances. Nothing lasted forever. She preferred it that way. Control was essential. Brevity was essential. Possession, however, was not. In fact, possession, in most cases, had a tendency to undermine the other two.

Elowyn glanced back out the window. Would the captain understand that? He was a man of the world. He'd seen much of Europe with the military. With his rank, he'd have been invited to balls and parties. He would have met women who would have welcomed a short dalliance with a strong, attractive officer. Yet she did not have the impression it was a world to which he'd been born.

Outside, the captain kicked his horse into a trot. Elowyn bit the knuckle of her thumb. If he was half as good in bed as he was on that horse, he'd be magnificent. "Do you think the captain is out of bounds, Annie?"

Her maid looked up from her knitting with a knowing smile. "He's a fine figure of a man, miss. The way he hauled those trunks downstairs this morning drew more than a couple of eyes."

"That wasn't my question." Elowyn grinned and nudged Annie's toe playfully with her boot. "Do you think he's open to a little sport?"

"Of course. He's a man, isn't he? Which of them isn't?" Annie laughed. "The question is who with? I don't think you can expect him to make any opening overtures if he's a man of honor and if he's not, then you're better off without him, no matter how well he rides."

Elowyn tapped her index finger against her lips in thought. That had been her assessment, too. "Then it's up to me to make the first move." That suited her just fine. Making the first move gave one a certain modicum of control from the very start, the power to define the course of the relationship and set the rules. Although, she supposed that hot stare he'd given her on the steps could have counted as his opening salvo.

She was already mentally choosing possible gowns. Tonight at supper would be the perfect opportunity to make her intentions known, but not before she had a little payback for the upheaval he'd caused this morning. She didn't want to reward him for usurping her authority. If she was too easy he'd never respect her and she'd give away the control she valued so much in a relationship. By her estimate, they had two more hours before they'd stop for the evening. Just enough time to plan a perfect welcome reception for the captain.

She was all regal authority when she descended from the coach into the noisy yard at the inn. Elowyn had taken great efforts to appear as perfectly pressed and coiffed as she had that morning. She and Annie had put her traveling case to good use those last two hours to ensure she captured the captain's eye. A tired and mussed appearance drew no one's eye. He was over by the horses, holding their heads and talking with the driver. Ah, good, he saw her. She had his attention now. It was time for step two, a little harmless revenge.

Elowyn marshaled her troops with a gesture of her hand, the merest tilt of her head, issuing orders that left no misunderstanding as to who was in charge of this little expedition. "I'll need those two trunks. Annie, follow them up so I know the trunks get to my room. Then I'll need a bath set up right away and my sheets on the bed." She turned to the driver, "Christopher, see that the horses are rubbed down and have an extra ration tonight. We want to leave early in the morning."

That did the trick. Orders about the horses had infringed on his territory directly. The captain was by her side immediately. His hand took up proprietary residence at the small of her back, sending hot spears of excitement through her, his quick-silver eyes glinting with displeasure, but not entirely. Not too far off limits then, Elowyn thought smugly. He could be swayed with the right inducements.

He propelled her toward the common room, his head bent toward her, his mouth close to her ear in a way that suggested familiarity and intimacy to onlookers, a lover's gesture, his words for her alone. But his words were not lover's words. "What the hell do you think you're doing?"

Elowyn gave him a coy smile. "That is the burning question of the day, isn't it?"

# Chapter Four

Grahame knew very well what she was doing. He had no doubt her show was for his benefit, a payback for usurping her authority this morning. But payback or not, it was garnering the wrong kind of attention from the wrong kind of men as they made their way across the crowded inn yard, and it made Grahame uneasy. Not every eye in the place belonged to a gentleman he'd classify as reputable, or even as a gentleman, for that matter. "You're a bit spoiled, I'd say."

"You're a little close, I'd say." Elowyn tossed her head and tried to move away but he held fast. He knew what these men were thinking. A man who couldn't stand up to a woman wasn't a man at all. If he backed down, it would be nothing short of blood in the water. Elowyn would be fair game for any man there. He knew what Elowyn was thinking, too; she could handle them. She'd be wrong.

He ushered her through the door to the public room, regretting his decision to pass up the inn in the town an hour back in lieu of this one. This inn was well positioned for staging tomorrow's journey and it was an inn he knew, at least he thought he did. He didn't recall it having such a rough clientele the last few times he'd stayed here.

"Two trunks? Is such excess really necessary?" He kept his voice low at her ear, hoping to prove to those about them she belonged to him. She smelled good, like lemongrass and wildflowers, even after a long day in a coach. Grahame shot a hard look at the two men lounging near the door who hadn't quite taken the hint yet. Lucifer's balls, crossing that yard had been nothing short of charging through a battlefield facing enemy fire. He gave his eyes a moment to adjust to the dim interior only to discover it was very much a case of "out of the frying pan and into the fire." The room was noisy and crowded, full of rough working men, not all of whom, Grahame guessed, were legally employed. "We'll hardly be here twelve hours."

"One is for bedding," Elowyn said as if that excused the need for two trunks.

"In case you didn't know, one usually uses a man for that."

"Are you always this audacious?" She snapped.

"Me? I'm not the one announcing to all and sundry I will be naked in my room shortly."

Emerald eyes met his, burning with green fire. "I have done no such thing."

"You most certainly did when you called for a bath." He paused and arched an eyebrow. "Unless I'm mistaken and you intend to bathe with your clothes on?"

She looked at him as if he were the most ridiculous man she'd ever met. "You know very well I don't intend to bathe in my clothes." It was said a tad too loudly. Too late, she realized her mistake. Color rose becomingly in Elowyn's cheeks. "I hadn't thought of it quite like that."

His grip relaxed. She was starting to understand. "I assure you, my dear, *they* most certainly did." He gave a nod past her shoulder to indicate the overpopulated tap room beyond. "I don't find the notion unappealing and I'd wager last month's salary these men don't, either."

The innkeeper hurried over, drying his hands on a towel. "Captain Westmore, my apologies for the clientele. There's a cockfight in the next town over. We're full to the rafters but I've got your rooms and a parlor set aside for dinner."

Grahame smiled. "It's good to see you, Horace. I remember your wife's cooking fondly. I am sure all arrangements will be satisfactory." The cockfight explained it. Those with money would have taken rooms closer to the event. The knowledge, though, was merely a consolation prize. It wasn't going to make his job any easier tonight when it came to protecting Elowyn, who clearly had no idea she needed protecting. Beside him, she gave a huff at being pointedly ignored in the exchange with the innkeeper and mounted the stairs with a final order. "My maid will be coming with my trunks. Please direct her to my rooms."

Grahame watched her go with a chuckle. The innkeeper shot him a considering glance. "I'd say the chit's a bit spoilt. If you want my advice, best take that one in hand before it's too late or she'll walk all over you."

Grahame grinned. "Horace, I was just thinking the same thing." He was also thinking dinner would be very entertaining. Miss Bagshaw had not liked being thwarted in her show of power and she would not let it pass without comment. Grahame found himself looking forward to what that response might be. She'd chosen competition and challenge as her flirtatious weapons today and used them to her advantage.

She'd chosen wisely. He liked strong women, women who weren't afraid to stand up to him or put off by his more earthy approaches. The simpering miss was not for him. He had no use for women who portrayed themselves as nothing more than pretty dolls. He was starting to have no use for his self-enforced rules of celibacy, either. Just because Miss Bagshaw had not hired him to seduce her didn't mean he couldn't. It just meant he wasn't being paid for it—a concept that held some novelty in itself. He couldn't recall the last time he'd been part of a real seduction, not the paid fictions he played out nightly for London's more adventurous women. A real seduction. It could be fun. And why not?

Oh, Grahame didn't kid himself. There were legitimate reasons as to why not—her father's trust that he'd behave as a gentleman, although her father hadn't even bothered to meet him. The man had simply taken Channing's word, an agreement between gentlemen. That was the other reason, his loyalty to Channing. He had no desire to bring scandal to Channing if word of this dalliance ever reached England. But even that was doubtful. If he had to lay money on it, he'd bet Miss Bagshaw was a woman of discretion, and secrets on the road were far easier to hide, especially in foreign countries where no one knew your language, let alone your name. Hmm. It seemed the reasons for resisting were shrinking.

Salvos had been fired from both sides now. It wasn't as if he were forcing the issue. He could argue he was merely responding accordingly to opening maneuvers. If there was one thing Miss Bagshaw had proven she could do today, it was that she could play the game men and women had played since the beginning of the world, and she could play it well. Fortunately for her, so could he. It was time to cast off any notion of celibacy and see where the game led.

# *Chapter Five*

It was time to make her intentions clear. Elowyn swept down the stairs, fully confident she could tempt the captain. Exactly how far she could tempt him remained to be seen but that was half the fun. After all, what thrill, what *challenge* was there in a chase to which she already knew the conclusion?

Elowyn paused briefly outside the private parlor and smoothed her skirts. One must go fully armed to the hunt, and she'd done just that. She'd dressed carefully for her campaign in a gown of crushed gold silk embroidered with muted green and orange leaves at the hem. She straightened the topaz necklace at her throat, a gift from her Russian prince. She tightened the barrette in her hair. She'd opted to wear her hair loose tonight, caught back at her nape with a simple gold barrette due to time constraints. Her hair had taken longer than she had estimated to dry it and there had been no time to put it up. Satisfied that all was in place, Elowyn squared her shoulders, lifted her chin and put on her smile. It was the same ritual she went through before meeting her father's important guests when he entertained. Although this promised to be far more exciting. Let the negotiations begin.

The captain was waiting for her. He rose when she entered and came forward, taking her hand with a small bow but not before she'd seen the gleam of male appreciation in his eyes or the way his eyes had lingered on her bodice. "I am in the presence of a veritable autumn goddess. May I say you look lovely?"

Oh, he was very good at playing the gentleman officer. He pulled out her chair and she took a moment to surreptitiously run her eyes up his long legs as she settled her skirts. He, too, had taken pains with his appearance. He'd changed into dark trousers, a snug-fitting jacket of forest green with matching waistcoat and a clean, blindingly white shirt and cravat. In her opinion, other than tight riding breeches, there was nothing sexier on a man than immaculately pressed and starched shirts.

"I trust everything meets with your approval?" He took the chair across from her, the merest of smiles hovering around his lips.

"Yes, it most certainly does." She gave him a look akin to the stare he'd given her on the stairs that morning. Two could play this game. She knew very well he wasn't asking about her room. "And yourself, Captain? Does everything meet with your approval?"

"Most assuredly." He held her gaze a tad longer than what was polite before he reached for the bottle of wine and worked the cork. He poured her a glass. "I propose we dispense with the formalities. Call me Grahame. I don't think I can stand being called Captain all the way to Vienna."

Elowyn sipped from her glass. "Then I must insist you call me Elowyn." The move to first names was promising progress, indeed, although not unexpected if she'd read the signs right.

"It's a beautiful name, quite original. Tell me about it." He sliced bread for them from the loaf already on the table. Their meal would come later. "I'm guessing it's Cornish or maybe Welsh?"

"Cornish. It means Elm tree. My mother's family is from Cornwall. Elm trees are known for being difficult to split. Strong wood. How about you, *Grahame?* You must have had an interesting life with the military?" She was eager to steer the conversation away from where it was headed. Talk of her mother always made her sad, a cautionary reminder of what became of a woman who surrendered her control. Elowyn didn't want to be sad tonight; she wanted to be happy; she wanted to feel alive. And she was interested in the origins of Captain Grahame Westmore far more than she was interested in her own. She'd had hours to hypothesize about him in the carriage today, and she'd arrived at certain conclusions but he seemed just as reluctant to discuss himself as she did about herself.

"I think my life is no more interesting than any other soldier's." Grahame smiled over his wineglass and took a drink in an attempt at deflection. She wasn't fooled.

"I'll reserve comment on that for later," Elowyn offered coyly. She wanted to call him a liar on the spot. She had a fair amount of experience with the military. Officers were generally gentlemen, literally, because of the cost of buying the commission. She did not think that was the case here. Whoever he was, Grahame Westmore was not a gentleman's son, even if he had a gentleman's manners when he chose to use them. He'd given himself away today at the house when he'd gone up personally for her trunks, proof that certain nuances escaped him. That made him all the more exciting as far as she was concerned.

Horace bustled in with their plates and a second bottle of wine, "Just in case you and the missus are in the mood for celebrating." He set it down on the sideboard and Elowyn raised an inquiring eyebrow in Grahame's direction while Horace laid out a pot of *crème fraîche* alongside an apple pie. "Fresh baked this afternoon, especially for you, Captain. The wife knows how much you like her apple pie."

"Give her my compliments." Grahame drew in an exaggerated breath that made his chest expand. "It smells delicious." Yet another giveaway, Elowyn thought. No gentleman she knew would be on such close basis with an innkeeper. No gentleman she knew would lie about a wife, either.

"The missus?" she inquired the moment they were alone. That explained the fancy manners, the desire to move to first names.

"I think it best considering the circumstances." Grahame sliced into the massive beefsteak on his plate surrounded by potatoes and carrots. She was dying to do the same, but things needed to be settled before they ate. She didn't pretend not to know which circumstances he referred to. There were fifty *circumstances* just outside the door in the tap room. She'd seen them when she'd come down for dinner.

"I appreciate the concern, but I have handled worse." Cossacks in the Russian Steppes, for instance. She gave him a polite smile and took a bite of tender baby carrot.

Grahame set down his knife and fork. "I am not talking about your ability to handle a drunken diplomat looking for a quick paw in the corner. I have no doubts about your aptitude in that regard." It was time to dispel his doubts about her *aptitude* in other regards. Elowyn leaned forward over her plate, putting her cleavage on display, and fixed him with a smile designed to bewitch while her hand slid beneath the table and under her skirts. She gave a flick of her wrist. The next instant, a knife jutted out of the center of Grahame Westmore's steak.

"Lucifer's balls!" Grahame roared, pushing back from the table in alarm.

"His balls are fine. I'd be more worried about yours." Elowyn stood and reached over the table to yank the knife out of the meat before retaking her seat. "As I said, I can handle them. Besides, Grahame, it's not nice to stare."

"It sure makes things more interesting, though," Grahame retorted as he pulled himself back up to the table.

* * *

Interesting hardly began to cover it. He'd never wanted a woman more. She'd just pulled a knife on him in the middle of dinner and he was still aroused by her. What the hell was wrong with him? He watched her reach beneath the table and resheathe her blade, his body eager to discover what else what up her skirts.

She resumed eating as if nothing had happened. "I understand you're out of the military now, so how do you spend your time? Do you take missions like this one often?" It was a casual enough question if it were being asked of anyone else. But she had no idea he worked for the League of Discreet Gentlemen, that he'd spent his last four years selling pleasure to women rich enough to pay for that most elusive commodity.

"No. This is my first assignment." Graham took a bite of steak.

"Then you're a virgin."

Grahame was entirely unready for the comment. He choked. The meat he'd just swallowed popped back out on his plate. He took a quick gulp of wine. "I beg your pardon?" He hadn't been a virgin since he was fourteen and a half and a Seven Dials whore had given him a free one. He was lucky he hadn't caught the pox.

"This is your first time." She smiled coyly as she sipped her wine. He could watch her sip wine all night. Perhaps that's why Horace had brought the second bottle.

"And you?" Grahame tried to regain his aplomb. It was rare he was taken by surprise. He usually saw quips coming. The women in London had rather limited imaginations when it came to word play.

"No, this is definitely not my first. More like my fifth. Move, that is." She gave him a seductive glance that ratcheted up the temperature in the room. He was glad he'd already decided to forego celibacy. His morals wouldn't have stood a chance against her otherwise.

"I'm sure the move this morning was rather unorthodox." Not like this dinner wasn't. Barging into her home without an introduction was looking like a minor infraction compared to Elowyn pulling a knife at the table.

"Is that your idea of an apology?" She slid her hand up and down the stem of her wineglass in a manner reminiscent of a hand sliding on a stem of another sort. It was giving him ideas about what to do with the *crème fraîche* besides putting it on pie, well, on apple pie, at least.

"I was unaware an apology was needed." But he was aware he was driving her crazy as much as she was driving him. She wanted compliance and he would not give it to her. Whether by accident or design, they'd fallen into a most scintillating game of tease and denial, a game he'd played many times before with his clothes off, but never on, never like this. *Scintillating* wasn't quite strong enough. The word erotic came to mind. This was foreplay at its most refined level where it was hard to determine exactly who was seducing whom.

"It must be nice to live in your world where everything is so obviously divided into black and white." Her hand moved to the topaz at her neck, drawing attention to the cleavage on display.

"I am to understand diplomacy is more gray, then?"

She gave a short laugh. "One hundred times grayer. Everyone's got an angle. One never knows if one is looking at the real person or a carefully cultivated image. What's your angle, Grahame?"

He sat back in his chair, starting to enjoy this. "Maybe I don't have one."

"Of course you do." Green eyes challenged him. "You just admitted it when you said you didn't take jobs like this. So why now? There must be something you want badly to travel all the way to Vienna."

A future, a career, a chance to start over. There were so many things he wanted, so many things he hoped Vienna could give him. Elowyn rose and went to the sideboard to retrieve the second bottle. He followed her with his eyes, catching the sway of her hips beneath the silk, mentally outlining the curve of her derriere, how it would feel cupped in his hands, how easy it would be to simply come up behind her and press her forward onto the high, flat surface of the console. Did he dare? Their games tonight indicated such a move would be welcome.

Grahame was on his feet without thinking. She would let him know if it was too much; after all, she was the one with the knife. His hands were at her shoulders, his thumbs massaging the column of her neck. He could feel her pulse race in welcome. "What if I said I wanted you?" he whispered hoarsely at her ear, breathing in the smell of fresh-washed hair and woman aroused. "What if I said I wanted to take you, right here, right now, just like this?" He pushed his hips against the soft curve of her bottom, his erection evidence of his intentions.

Her answer came without hesitation. "I would say yes."

# *Chapter Six*

Elowyn trembled. THIS was by far the most erotic thing she'd ever done, the most decadent, the most exposed, the most *everything*. It had not escaped her that Horace could come through the door at any moment and discover them.

She could hardly think about that when all her senses were coalesced around Grahame—around the press of his phallus, long and ready against her buttocks, the warmth of his hand at the back of her neck, pushing her forward onto the sideboard until he had her positioned for him.

Grahame was the center of her world now. He had her skirts up and she shivered at the delicious decadence of cool air on private skin. She felt him shift behind her, heard the rustle and slide of his own clothes as he took himself in hand. Elowyn braced her weight with her arms. When penetration came it would be swift and fierce. She was ready for it.

His phallus was hot and naked behind her, brushing against the cleft of her bare bottom but it was his hand that cupped her, his fingers that entered her. "Are you ready for me?" His voice was harsh with desire at her ear.

"So ready." Her desire matched his in breathlessness. She moved on his fingers, hardly able to keep herself from doing anything else. His fingers withdrew and pressed against the skin hiding her pearl until she thought she'd scream from the exquisite touch. She squirmed and he held her, one strong hand on her neck, holding her down, her cheek flat against the cool wood of the sideboard. He came into her then, swift and sure, his phallus sliding into her depths until she was certain it touched the very edges of her womb.

She gasped. This was a fantasy come to life, this man deep-seated in her, her body flowing around his. She could feel her own heat, her own slickness as he started to move—back and forth, back and forth. She was a wanton, indeed, to enjoy such feral sex, but enjoy it, she did. She could hear Grahame with his rough love words at her ear as he rocked into her. "You're so wet, so tight, your cunny is sweet heaven." He nuzzled her neck with his mouth. His hair had come loose, tickling the bare skin of her shoulder, soft and loose, an antidote to the coarse hair that pressed against her bottom.

"Scream for me, Elowyn," he urged in a rasp, evidence that his release was nearly upon him. "Go ahead, no one will hear, they're too busy with their own fun."

He surged into her, hard and insistent, his thrusts becoming shorter, faster and stronger. She had no choice but to give over to the pleasure they elicited. She was vaguely aware her own arms had failed, that he was holding her up, as the threshold of her climax approached and she let herself go, crossing over into the shattering oblivion of desire replete. She did scream then, in joy, in release, in freedom. She soared with new wings in those moments, but not alone. Grahame was with her, his groan primal and rapturous as his body tensed and pulsed with hers.

How long had it been since a climax had taken him so thoroughly? Grahame bent over the basin in his room and splashed another round of cold water on his face, trying to cool down his heated body. Even now, everything seemed surreal, existing in fragmented scenes in his mind. He'd helped Elowyn restore herself; he'd escorted her upstairs. He'd done all the things protocol demanded in such situations and yet the sharp edge of clarity that accompanied his release had not ebbed.

He searched for reasons. Perhaps it was the spontaneity or the potential publicity of the act which had worked so strongly upon his senses? But that theory was full of holes. He'd had public encounters several times and never had the edge lasted like this. Spontaneity, too, was something to which he was all too well accustomed.

There were other explanations he could put forward. Maybe it was the novelty of having chosen this interlude for himself? There was no contract expecting him to perform. Perhaps the freedom had spurred him on? Or perhaps it was the woman herself; a beautiful, well-bred woman had wanted him for himself, not for his notoriety, not for the fulfillment of some need to impress her friends or any of the other reasons London's ladies sought him for their paids. Elowyn had no inkling of who he was or what he could do to a woman and she'd wanted him, anyway. It was heady knowledge for a man of his humble origins to think a woman of her quality would freely choose him, that he could belong.

There was the old ghost again. Grahame faced himself in the mirror over the basin, staring hard at the primal reflection. The military had made him rugged but it had made him ragged, too. He traced the thin line running toward his shoulder, one scar of many that had contributed to the man he was today—a leader of men, a lover of women. But still, deep inside, that man harbored the needs of the boy who had never wanted more than to belong, somewhere.

The military had been such a place for him. The camaraderie he'd built with his men had filled that need until they'd been scattered, proving that even the hard-forged bonds of shared misery and loss were temporary. There'd been a sense of belonging at Argosy House with Channing and the boys, where he was accepted among them, even if he hadn't been of the same birth. They'd formed bonds based on laughter and escapades and they, too, were free to scatter as the world beckoned. D'Arcy had already gone. He wanted more than that, more than temporary friendships. He wanted an unbreakable bond with someone, something that could not be torn apart by distance or circumstance.

It was his ultimate fantasy, a fantasy he played out

nightly with London's women, the fantasy that he belonged in their world. Tonight that fantasy had deepened dangerously. He could not have Elowyn Bagshaw any more than he could have any of the other women. With Elowyn the end was so obviously near. When they reached Vienna, all would be over. There wasn't even an illusion, a hope of permanence.

Grahame jerked, startled by the sudden knock on his door. "Come." He reached for a towel in a belated effort to address his shirtless dishabille, his hair still damp from his ablutions. Chances were it didn't matter. His visitor was most likely Christopher, come to report on the horses and the wagons. Still, he knew he'd grabbed the towel because he hadn't given up all hope.

"Hello, Grahame, it looks like you were expecting me." The sultry voice at the door sent a shot of white-hot desire to his groin. Her eyes flashed to his crotch where a new arousal stirred. Dammit! His trousers were undone. He'd forgotten and it was too late to do anything about it now except to let her watch the effect she had on him come to life.

His eyes drank in the sight of her—the white, satin robe belted at her waist, the fabric hugging the full curves of her breasts, the chestnut hair spilling seductively over one shoulder. Then it hit him—she'd crossed the hallway dressed like that.

"Shut the door, Elowyn. I can't have you traipsing around the hall like that," Grahame growled. "Have you forgotten the guests downstairs?"

Elowyn shrugged and stepped inside, holding up a

white, ceramic ramekin in her hand. Grahame recognized it as the one from dinner, the one placed next to the pie they'd never gotten around to eating. "I came to tell you, if you're in the mood, dessert's on me."

Good God, the woman was a temptress! He could see her in his mind's eye, a naked Elowyn streaked with *crème fraîche* and laid out before him. Her eyes roamed low, a wicked smile on her lips as she watched his arousal complete.

Maybe he could not have her forever; maybe she could no more fulfill his need to belong than any of his other attempts, but he could have it tonight, and the next and the next and perhaps that would be enough. It was the only deal he could make with himself that would preserve his sanity as he stood there, half-dressed and fully aroused. "Now that you mention it," Grahame drawled. "I think I could do with a piece of pie."

Elowyn dipped her finger into the pot and licked it with a flick of her tongue. "I thought that might be the case."

# *Chapter Seven*

Elowyn was ready for him. He'd taken just enough time to put on a shirt before crossing the hall. Grahame shut the door soundlessly behind him, taking in the terrain out of old military habit. Her room was a far sight cozier than his chamber. She and her maid had taken efforts here with sheets and pillows from home. Candles and the firelight added a seductive element, or maybe that was just her. Grahame was starting to think any room would be more seductive with Elowyn in it.

"You're a quiet mover for such a large man." Elowyn stepped into the light. She loosened the belt of her robe, offering him a tantalizing glimpse of skin and shadow.

"I can be. Stealth comes in handy in the military."

"And in dining parlors, too, apparently." Elowyn ran the tip of her tonguc over her lips.

Elowyn shook her hair free from the single tie that held it. The chestnut hues caught the light of the fire, dancing like a veritable autumn flame. She held his eyes, her mouth curving into a knowing smile. With a shrug, the robe began to slip—first one shoulder, then the other until the robe pooled at her feet, leaving her entirely naked to his gaze. The fact that she did not mind his rather blatant perusal registered somewhere in his brain. And why should she? Elowyn was marvelous naked.

High, firm breasts with pink nipples played peek-a-boo beneath the long curtain of hair draped over them, not unlike Botticelli's Venus, he thought. Her skin was pale, too, porcelain-smooth in its perfection, a perfection so different from the tanned roughness of his own. Grahame stepped forward, his body aching to worship this goddess of autumn and flame. It was time to do his part. But Elowyn stopped him with her eyes and an infinitesimal shake of her head. Apparently, her part was not yet done.

"Have a seat." She gestured to the chair pulled close to the fire. Grahame sat, hardly able to look away from his Venus. The firelight played across her body, adding grace and mystery to her every move. She stood in front of him, the ramekin in her hand, and Grahame's mouth went dry. She meant to do it. She meant to seduce him. Elowyn tossed her hair back over her shoulders so that nothing obscured his view now. With deliberate slowness, she scooped up the *crème* with her fingers and began to draw her hands down her body, circling the areolas of her breasts, then the breasts themselves with the *crème*. She cupped and lifted each breast, running her thumbs across her nipples for him, her neck arched in delight, a little moan on her lips until

Grahame thought he'd come in his chair. Yet he could not look away.

Always, the trail of her hands led downward, past the flat of her abdomen and the curve of her hip, a map to her pleasure, a key to her expectations until they rested on the auburn mons of her triangle. The silent invitation was not lost on him. She wanted his mouth on her in the most intimate of ways.

Elowyn stepped back and lay on the bed, legs parted, her inner femininity exposed to him. Her hand moved between her thighs with the last of the *crème* and Grahame forgot all else. Her voice beckoned, a goddess calling to her supplicant. "Now you may come and feast."

Grahame shed his shirt, his hands moving swiftly to the waistband of his trousers, nuisance that they were. He hadn't spent much time with them on tonight.

"No, leave the trousers." Elowyn gave the languorous command from the bed. "We'll take them off later." As long as his erection didn't get there first. The way he felt right now, he wouldn't be surprised if his cock simply burned a hole through the fabric and ripped its own way out. He couldn't ever remember being this thoroughly aroused.

Grahame braced himself over Elowyn, reveling in the ease with which he fit between the cradle of her legs, but that would come later, much later if he understood correctly. She was all temptress beneath him, her eyes glowing green embers, her body smeared with *crème*, awaiting his ministrations. "Has anyone ever told you what a vixen you are?" He didn't let her answer. He didn't want to know. He wanted to believe this had been inspired by him alone. Grahame bent his head to her breast, and began to lick.

Death by licking. Elowyn had not thought such a thing possible until now, but it must be because she was certain she could not stand much more of this exquisite torture before she would simply shatter into millions of tiny pieces.

She arched and cried out under Grahame's mouth as he nipped at the tender skin of her breast. She had not realized how sensitive she could be there. Nor had she realized what she was asking for, what her body was apparently capable of, when she'd begun her game. She wished she'd used less *crème*, or perhaps more *crème* as the case may be. This exquisite torture was indeed worth dying for and a most pleasant way to go, too.

Grahame's hot mouth drew a searing trail to her navel. He kissed her there, his tongue tickling the tiny crevice until she bucked. "Easy now." Grahame's voice was a low rumble, his hands framing her low on her hips, readying her for his next destination on his seductive journey down her body. Never mind, this sensual adventure had been hers at the start. It was his now. Somewhere between picking up the pot of *crème* and lying down on the bed, he'd usurped the game and made it his own. It seemed he was very good at usurping.

He looked up at her from the apex of her thighs—his eyes the color of hot mercury, all liquid and silver in his desire. She was not alone in this any more than she had been downstairs when they'd joined so swiftly, so frantically. Her want was his want. There was potency in knowing that this wild, competitive madness between them was shared.

His head dropped, his tongue lapping up the last of the *crème* on the insides of her thighs, each lap a flirtation, a promise of more as his mouth angled closer to the prize. He claimed the seam of her first, licking upward to her hidden pearl. His hands held her firm as he pleasured her, the restraint adding its own titillation to the act until she was entirely at sea, lost to all worlds but the one of pleasure. She was vaguely aware her hands had wrapped themselves in the darkness of Grahame's hair, her one anchor in this world of shattering sensation. But she was acutely aware for all the pleasure this act brought her, it wasn't enough.

"Trousers, Grahame. Take them off, now." Urgency was evident in her voice. She had not planned this. She'd meant another interlude of pleasuring him as he had her, but there was no more waiting, no more time for games.

Grahame shoved the trousers down, a grin on his face as he rose above her. "I thought you'd never ask, princess." He was huge and hard against her leg as he levered into position, a testament to his own desire. He thrust deep. There was no question of readiness, no need to play the gentleman with a tentative testing of the waters. These waters were primed and boiling, as they had been downstairs.

But this was different. This was no hurried, erotic coupling. This time she could see his face, she could watch her lover as he took her, as he moved in and out of her body with long, sure strokes. She tightened her muscles around him, watching pleasure pass over his face in response, watching it linger in the brackets about his mouth, in faint lines at the corners of his eyes as climax approached. His eyes! Almost too late she realized they were shut, those silver gateways to his mind, shut against her in this intimate moment. She would not have it, could not have it. She wanted him with her in all ways, not just in physical synchronicity when the pleasure took them.

"Open your eyes, Grahame." Elowyn gave the command with the last ounce of her reserve. "I want to see you when I fall apart."

His body tensed, his eyes flashed open with a final thrust, revealing far more than she had anticipated. Her one thought as release swamped her was a vague realization of what she'd done. She'd hoped for a glimpse of his mind; what she'd gotten was a sliver of his soul.

# *Chapter Eight*

Opened eyes! The little minx had no idea of what she'd done, of what she'd asked. He'd broken his cardinal rule. Eyes shut was his impenetrable wall, the one place where no one could reach him without his permission. Yet he'd let *her* in simply because she'd asked. Grahame shifted his body to adjust his position and she stirred beside him, lifting her sleep-tousled head in question.

"Go back to sleep," Grahame admonished softly. "Tomorrow will be a long day. We don't stop until we reach Dover."

Elowyn settled back to sleep, snuggling against him, her body soft and warm. His arm tightened about her. He should have been gone hours ago to his own bed. No good could come of lying here, holding her and pretending he wasn't a poor woman's son and she wasn't a gentleman's daughter, or pretending he wasn't a paid escort who'd spent the last four years in London pleasuring the ton's finest ladies on command. She could justify a fling with a dashing cavalry captain but the rest? Elowyn would die if she knew. She would feel betrayed, as if tonight had been nothing but another game to him. Grahame vowed in the darkness she would never find out. They would part ways in Vienna and that would be the end.

Perhaps it was the need to impress her so she might never guess he was more (or less) than what he seemed that drove him the next day. He was the perfect captain, all military precision with his orders and organization. Maybe it was simply the weather and his own urgency to cross the Channel. His deadline loomed. A delay in Dover would ruin his prospects at the riding school.

As if in ill portent, the sunny September skies that had met them that morning steadily darkened to gray as they journeyed toward Dover. By the time his little caravan pulled into Dover, he was certain. Bad weather was imminent. He would have to act quickly in order to avoid delay.

Grahame helped Elowyn down from the carriage with mannerly correctness. No one watching them would guess he'd spent the night in her bed. Perhaps that had been part of what had driven him, too. He had her reputation to protect, even if it was just among her retainers. But a show of polite distance didn't mean his body was immune to her presence. She looked stunning in a dark blue traveling costume cut in the fitted military style, the jacket nipped in tight at the waist, her hair piled up under a matching hat.

Elowyn's eyes went to the sky. "It seems you might have been right about the need for an early departure." She turned to him, her eyes holding his for a long moment, searching for something. He could guess what that might be—encouragement, direction, expectation. What were they to be to one another after their mad night?

He'd found the willpower in the early light of dawn to leave her bed before she awoke, and they had not spoken beyond the exchange of what was necessary to get underway. But he did not think what might be interpreted as aloofness on his part would deter Elowyn. Nor did he think she would misunderstand it. She was a woman of the world. She would know it was necessary in order to preserve an outward show of propriety. Most of the retainers with them, those who'd driven the wagons, would return to London after the household goods were loaded onto the boat. She wouldn't want them carrying tales back.

The inn at Dover was high-end, the best that could be had for their situation and circumstance. There'd be no cockfighting crowd here. It would be safe enough to leave Elowyn in charge. "I will go down to the docks and see what the news is."

"I will come with you," Elowyn said firmly. "Annie can oversee the unloading of what we need."

Grahame gave a wry smile. "Let's rephrase that, my dear. Of what *you* need. I only need my valise. I doubt unpacking my items is a chore that requires any specific skill. And no, you are not coming to the docks." Not after her show in the inn yard yesterday.

"I want to make sure the storage will be acceptable

for my items," Elowyn persisted. He would have to be strong here.

"Your household needs you here to organize things. There is much to do and I cannot be in both places at once," Grahame answered with equal firmness. "When I return, we'll discuss my news over dinner and decide what to do from there."

Elowyn seemed to weigh his words. She gave a short nod and flashed him a private smile. "All right. I'll have dinner waiting. You can think about that while you're down touring the docks." His groin tightened, his body recalling what she'd done with dessert.

"I shall lick forward to it, Miss Bagshaw."

Her eyes danced and he realized too late what he'd said out loud. "I believe the word is *look*, Captain. Perhaps tonight, I'll be the one doing the licking."

Good Lord, he was rock hard in the middle of an inn yard. Maybe a storm on the Channel wasn't bad news after all if it meant he could stay holed up at the inn with Elowyn.

Grahame had bad news. She could tell by the speed with which he'd ridden into the yard and dismounted. Elowyn stepped back from the window in her room on the second floor. He was going to tell her they'd have to wait, that they were too late to cross until the storm passed. She hated waiting. The journey was long enough as it was without being stalled in port.

"Grahame's back." She shot a worried look at her maid. "It doesn't look good. I'm going downstairs to meet him." He was back too soon. She'd hardly had time to get her trunks upstairs, let alone order that dinner she'd promised.

She didn't get out the door before Grahame knocked. He'd certainly moved fast, which made her worry all the more. "You're back awfully quick." She tried to smile as she opened the door.

"How fast can you be ready to leave?"

Elowyn did not miss the underlying urgency to the question, but that did not mitigate the presumption that she *would* leave.

"Leave?" That was not the news she'd been expecting. "We just got here. Annie just got the pillows on the bed."

"Will forty-five minutes be enough?" Grahame was already striding through her room like a storm, tossing a traveling bag on the bed and riffling her trunks. That made her mad. One night of mutual pleasure did not give him permission to barge into her room like he had her house.

"What do you think you're doing?" she demanded.

Grahame threw something lacy on the bed. "Be careful with that! It's French silk." Elowyn snatched the delicate garment up from the bed and hugged it to her chest.

Grahame grunted. "That's no good. Do you have anything warmer? Flannel, maybe?"

Heaven help her, she had a mad man in her room. Elowyn crossed the room and grabbed his hands. "Stop it. Tell me what's going on? You're making no sense."

Grahame paused his rummaging and looked at her, appearing altogether surprisingly sane. "Our boat leaves in forty-five minutes on the evening tide. If we're not on it, we wait, quite possibly for a week until I can make other arrangements." Desperation lay beneath his tone. She could tell the prospect of making those arrangements disgusted him. More than that, it upset him.

"Our boat isn't scheduled to leave until tomorrow." Elowyn sent out a challenging probe.

"Captain Anderson isn't going to wait. He doesn't want to chance the weather. He has a private mail pouch that has to get through." That wasn't all. There was more. Something he wasn't telling her.

"He'll be back. We'll go in a couple of days when he returns."

Grahame shook his head. "Anderson isn't scheduled back in Dover for another month. If we stay, we'll have to find another boat." She knew how onerous that would be. It would have to be a big boat, one that could hold the cargo of a household. Anderson's boat had been perfect.

Elowyn blew out a sigh. The situation was becoming impossible. "New boat or not, we can't possibly have all our things loaded in forty-five minutes. It will take that long to get the wagons to the docks." Not even the amazing Grahame Westmore could magically whisk the wagons down to the docks in time.

"I'm not talking about taking your things, Elowyn," Grahame began slowly. His grip tightened on her hands. "Just you. You and I can cross tonight and continue on. Annie and Christopher can bring the other things later and travel at their leisure. Christopher is more than capable of seeing the goods transferred and the drivers returned."

Something moved in Grahame's gray eyes. For reasons she could not guess, he needed this. He needed her to go with him now. Yet how could she leave all this responsibility?

Annie stepped forward. "You needn't be concerned on this end, miss. We can handle everything here. Christopher and I have moved with you before. Think about your father. He'll worry if you're late and there's no way to get word to him."

She did think of her father. Annie was right. He would worry himself sick. He would think of her mother, how she'd been late on that last trip and what it had meant. He had not worried back then, thinking her delay a natural consequence of travel in winter and that she was likely tucked up in a cozy inn. To this day, he still blamed himself. If he'd gone out searching for her earlier, he might have been in time. Elowyn could not put him through that doubt again.

Her decision was made. "We'll go. I'll be downstairs shortly." Was that relief in Grahame's eyes? Again, she had the sensation that he needed this beyond simply fulfilling his job for her father, beyond adherence to Captain Anderson's desire to leave early.

Grahame gave a tight smile. "I'll make the necessary arrangements with Christopher." He glanced about the room. "No trunks, just the one bag. It's all there's time for."

She drew a deep breath and looked about the very nice

room with a fire and her good sheets. Neither of which she'd get to enjoy. "Quickly, Annie, help me pack." If she stayed busy there'd be no time to think about what she'd just done. There was no question of who was in charge now. She'd given up control of the trip when she agreed to travel alone through Europe with Captain Grahame Westmore.

# *Chapter Nine*

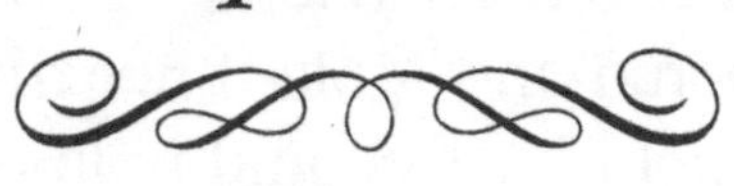

And his horse. She got to bring a valise. He got to bring his horse! "How is it that I only rate one bag?" Elowyn tried a halfhearted attempt at humor down in the hold where Aramis was stabled. But it was hard to be funny while the water rolled and pitched beneath her feet. They might be ahead of the storm coming down out of the North Sea, but it certainly didn't ensure smooth sailing.

Grahame gave a little chuckle and stroked Aramis's dark mane. She allowed herself a moment's jealousy, imagining those hands on her. She could use a little stroking about now. She'd been in difficult spots before but that didn't mean she liked them, or excelled at them. "If this ship goes down, you'll be glad he's here." Grahame crooned to the big stallion. "You're a fabulous swimmer, aren't you, old boy?"

That was too intriguing to let pass. Elowyn scooted forward on the bale of hay she sat on. "And we know this how?"

"He and I swam to shore after a transport we were

on sank off the coast of Crete. The Mediterranean was a bit warmer that time of year than the Channel would be, though." He smiled, letting the effort crinkle the corners of his eyes as he looked at his stallion with unmistakable affection. "Aramis and I have been through a lot and I've had no truer friend."

Grahame sobered and looked her direction. "If the worst happens, get him free and hold on to his bridle. He'll get you to land. Do you have your knife?"

Elowyn lifted her skirt to reveal the sheath on her calf.

"Good. You can cut your skirts off if you need to. They'll drag you down."

"Is all this really necessary?" She did not care for such grim talk, especially from the indomitable Grahame Westmore. She had no doubt that if strength of will could keep a ship together, he would be the man to do it.

Grahame shrugged. "A crisis is always better when you have a plan. But no, I don't think you'll need it. Ships have crossed safely in far worse weather. Odds are we'll be fine. Captain Anderson has no death wish. He wouldn't have set out not feeling certain it was the best choice."

Elowyn managed a smile. "I'll try to find reassurance in that somewhere." The boat lurched and she braced herself with a hand to the wall.

"You can go up. Anderson has his cabin set aside for you," Grahame replied as he steadied Aramis.

"No, I'll be fine here." No matter how bad the night got, she would be safe with him and his swimming horse. That might have been the moment she fell for him, right there in the dark hold of a storm-tossed ship. All else might be turmoil around them, but he was a literal pillar of strength—confident and sure, never wavering in the long night.

So sure of that strength was she, Elowyn actually slept, her head braced against the wall, her body curled on the hay bale. She didn't sleep well, of course, there were limits after all. She awoke once to find a blanket had been draped over her, another time to find a makeshift pillow beneath her head, and every time to see Grahame standing at Aramis's head, a reminder that she was safe.

It was Grahame who woke her in the morning with a gentle shake. He knelt down beside her rough bed and brushed back her hair, his voice soft at her ear. "We'll be in port momentarily, my dear. We made it. Aramis will have to demonstrate his swimming skills another time."

Elowyn smiled and sat up. "Ouch." She put a hand to her neck. "I'm stiff everywhere." And now that the ship had stopped rocking, she was hungry, tired and must look as rumpled as she felt. But she did not dare complain. Grahame would not be impressed with complaints. He'd provided her every comfort at his disposal: a blanket, a pillow, even a bed of sorts, while he'd gone without, standing sentinel for her and Aramis all night.

"Stiff everywhere?" Grahame teased. "And I thought I had it bad. I am only stiff in one spot."

Elowyn laughed and swatted at his shoulder. "You're incorrigible."

"I'm alive, my dear, and I want to celebrate it." He kissed her just as Captain Anderson came down the stairs. It was time to unload Aramis and get off the ship. Elowyn didn't have to be asked twice. Not because she'd had her fill of sailing but because a warm bath and a room awaited her in Ostend and she had every intention of enjoying them both with Grahame.

Traveling light had its benefits. True, she wouldn't have her own sheets tonight, but on the bright side, all they'd had to do was walk Aramis off the ship and go straight to the inn. There was no waiting while trunks were loaded and wagons arranged. The result was that half an hour after leaving the ship, her bath was ready.

Behind the dressing screen, she slipped off her robe and sank into the water. Ah, it felt good. This was heaven, right here in the tub next to the fire. The innkeeper had thought she was crazy for wanting a bath so early in the morning. But this was absolutely divine, or at least it would be. She smiled to herself. She was missing one thing. She could hear him moving around in the room beyond the screen. Elowyn called out, "Grahame, come join me. I hear warm baths work wonders for stiffness of all kinds."

"I wouldn't want it to work too well." Grahame came around the screen, already pulling his shirt off. "For the record, I do think this is a trick to see me naked."

"It seems to be working." Elowyn laughed. She was feeling decidedly giddy, a combination of elation and lack of sleep. She leaned her head back against the rim of the tub. "Stand over there." Elowyn gestured a bubble-covered hand toward the foot of the tub. "I can see you disrobe better that way."

"Brazen wench." Graham grinned and bent to pull off his boots. "How is this? Can you see me now?" he teased.

Elowyn sent a splash of water his way. "Yes, I can. There's just not much to see, *yet*." Although there was. Grahame was bare-chested, showing off the tanned, smooth musculature of his torso in all its glorious planes and ridges. Certainly, she'd felt the power of his body when he held her, but to see the proof of it so boldly on display was another thing entirely. There were scars, too, reminders that this power had been tried and tested. Her hands wanted to trace those scars. She wanted to hear those stories.

Grahame's hands dropped to his waistband, his eyes a wicked gleam of silver as his gaze held hers. "I hope this will change your mind, a little something for the girl who hasn't seen anything good *yet*."

He was a consummate flirt beneath that officer exterior of his. She wondered how many people ever saw him like this. More important, how many women saw him like this? It wasn't a very ladylike question to want to know but it was driven by curiosity. She knew so little about him, technically, and yet she felt she knew him in ways she'd never known her other lovers, or had *wanted* to know them. She'd been happy with the physical level of those liaisons. She'd not even been tempted to take them further.

That was not the case with Grahame. Physical intimacy had simply whetted her appetite for more emotional intimacies. She wanted to know him and there was danger in that. Nothing could come of this beyond momentary pleasure.

Grahame pushed his trousers and smalls down past his hips too slowly for her tastes. She let out a breath and blew bubbles in the water while he grinned at her impatience. "Good things come to those who wait, my dear."

They most certainly did. There at last, he stood before her entirely naked. Last night it had been too dark. There'd been no time to study him. But now, in the morning light, she wanted to study every glorious inch of him, although her eyes had a will of their own. They wanted to rest on the long, jutting phallus and the other manly accoutrements of him. He was absolutely, splendidly male. "You make my mouth water."

Grahame laughed and slid into the tub behind her, making the water rise and slosh as he wrapped his legs about her and pulled her close, that envious phallus pressing up against her bottom in the suds. "I'll taste better when I'm clean, I promise." Grahame dropped a kiss along Elowyn's jaw and nibbled at her ear. "Mmm. You taste better already."

# Chapter Ten

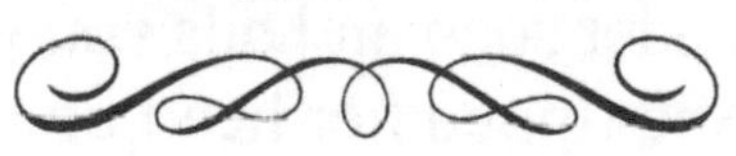

"It's the soap," Elowyn murmured, settling into him. She reveled in the feel of his body, the strength of his legs and the ease with which his arms wrapped around her. She closed her eyes and let her head loll against his chest. "It's lavender. It's good for relaxation." Not that either one of them needed to relax. They were both bone-tired after their night crossing.

"You pack the most interesting items." Grahame's voice caressed her ear. She heard him pluck the wash-cloth up from under the water. He was washing her, moving the cloth over her breasts and belly. "You had a few minutes to grab essentials and what did you grab?" He repeated the languorous washing pattern, sluicing warm water over her body. "You grabbed lavender soap, lavender oil and a white, satin dressing robe."

"All of which I've used less than twenty-four hours later," Elowyn argued. "I think that's the ultimate test of what is practical. Those items are small and hardly take up any room. You make it sound as if that's all I brought. I brought other things, too—undergarments, a spare dress, a hairbrush, toiletries, a nightgown."

He interrupted her with a laugh. "Let me guess, you brought that French-silk thing."

"I most certainly did and you'll be glad to thank me for it later. In fact, you should be thanking me now. Without my lavender soap and oils you wouldn't be having this bath." She tipped her head up to catch his eye.

"Well, you may have a point." Grahame looked down at her and smiled. Her stomach flipped. She really ought not to like him so much. He was arrogant and usurping. He'd upset her plans on two occasions now by barging into her house, into her room and demanding unscheduled departures. *And he'd been right to do so.* If they'd not left when they had, they'd have been cooling their heels in Dover for an indefinite period of time. It was hard to find fault with such a man.

"Would you like me to wash your hair?" Grahame murmured. His hands were busy kneading her breasts, his thumbs brushing her nipples into erect peaks. The warmth of pleasure was starting to build at her core ever so gradually.

She managed a drowsy response. "It will take too long to dry."

Grahame nipped her ear and pulled on the lobe with his teeth. She loved that, just the right hint of fierceness. "I'm not talking about the hair on your head." His hand dropped into the water between her legs, the bar of soap running up and down her inner thighs. Then came the cloth, washing, rinsing, massaging, pressing intimately around her furrow, her pearl, until her core was pulsing with want.

"How do you know what to do? You know my need before I do." Elowyn was barely cogent, drowsiness and need demanding her reserves for themselves. He knew just how to touch a woman to make her scream, to make her beg, to make her boneless in the bathtub. She had no idea how she would rise up out of the water without help.

His voice was a low litany at her ear, guiding her toward completion and she did as she was told. Her body had decided for her; it was her only choice. "Lean against me, Elowyn. Slide down a bit, yes, like that. I can take you where you want to go." He rubbed his thumb across the source of her bliss, once, twice more and she was there at the promised destination. She pushed back hard, sloshing water out of the tub as the intensity of release hit her.

Slowly, she came back to earth. The water was cooling and it was time for his pleasure. "If you stay in here much longer, you'll wrinkle." Elowyn said coyly.

"Where shall I go?" Grahame played along.

She rose first, amazed she'd found the strength. "To bed, Grahame. You've had a long—" she paused and cast a glance downward "—night."

Grahame laughed and put a hand to his chest in mock disappointment. "You wound me! A long night, indeed. Perhaps I will wait and hope for better compliments."

She gave his phallus a contemplative look. "I wouldn't wait much longer if I were you. Wrinkles are starting to settle in." Elowyn handed him a towel that had been set to warming by the fire. "This should help." She watched him stand in the tub and wrap it kilt-style about his hips.

"I might never let you wear anything else," she said appreciatively. "Now, lie down. It's time you let *me* pleasure *you*."

He shouldn't allow himself to enjoy this, shouldn't allow himself to let the intimacy she wove like a spell seep into his bones any further than it already had. But he was helpless to halt it. He let Elowyn strip away his towel. He let the scent of lavender fill his nostrils when she opened her vial. He let her pour the oil on his skin, warmed by her breath. He let her put her hands on his back, his shoulders, his buttocks. *He let her.* The words played in his head like a mantra.

When had a woman last pleasured him? When had a woman *ever* captivated him so entirely in bed and out? She had risen admirably to the occasion yesterday, taking the need for a premature departure from Dover in stride. The princess who had needed two trunks for a single night had met the challenge of packing a single valise for interminable days on the road, proving her versatility and her fortitude. She'd given up clean sheets and gowns because he'd asked it. He'd been selfish to ask it of her. He knew full well his personal agenda to reach Vienna had driven his decisions. Nonetheless, she'd not questioned his motives *and* she'd been brave. She'd been terrified on the boat, but hadn't given voice to it; that's how he knew she'd been brave. Facing terror without complaint was the ultimate test of bravery, and she'd passed admirably.

He was about to be selfish again, taking the pleasure she offered with no real hope of anything coming from it. A woman like her would never want a man like him, not if she knew who he really was. But that didn't stop Grahame from giving himself over to her ministrations, his body finding its own relaxation in her touch, his muscles casting off their strain. Her hand slipped between his buttocks and cupped his sac. He gave a groan. Even relaxed and tired, his body roused to her willingly.

"Roll over," she whispered. Any number of fantasies raced through his head. Would she?

She straddled him, massaging his chest as she had his back, her hands moving ever downward until she gripped the very root of him, her hand slick with oil. She stroked him hard and firm, her thumb rubbing the tender tip of him. Her other hand squeezed his sac. "You like that?"

"Yes, dammit, I like that," Grahame managed. What man wouldn't? She was looking up at him from her place at his thighs, her hair spilling over her shoulders. He thought he might spend right there in her hand.

"Shall I put my mouth on you, Grahame?" Her voice was all sultry persuasion.

"Would you like to?" The power of speech was rapidly leaving him. He would be reduced to caveman—like grunts any moment if she kept stroking his head like that.

She gave him a wicked smile. "I would like to very

much." She parted his thighs, and bent to him, taking his manhead in her mouth, her tongue licking and swirling him into boneless compliance until his body could stand the exquisite torture no longer. He watched her sit up just in time to take him in her hand and catch him as he spent, coating her fingers in his seed. He'd never done, never seen, anything as intimate as what she did next.

Elowyn held his gaze, a courtesan's smile on her lips as she lifted her fingers and licked them one by one, sucking on the tips in mimicry of how she'd sucked on him. She ran her tongue along the last finger. "You're right. You do taste better after a bath."

"I don't deserve you," Grahame sighed, settling her against his side. He wanted nothing more now than to sleep. The sleepless night and the exhausting exhilaration of his climax had taken the last of his strength. Even the insatiable Elowyn was drowsy. They would sleep, then they would eat and then make their plans. But sleep had not quite subdued Elowyn yet.

"How many women have you had, Grahame?" She idly traced the areola of his breast with a finger, both of them too spent to do more.

"That's hardly a ladylike question." Grahame tried to demur with a playful scold. It was the question he least wanted to answer at a time he least wanted to answer it. He'd arguably had the most personal sexual experience of his life, a moment of intimacy that had been solely about him and his pleasure.

"Tell me, Grahame. I know there have been others," she cajoled.

Too many to count, actually, but he couldn't tell her that or why. "There's been enough to know there's never been one like you." It wasn't truly an answer but it would have to do. There never were good answers to those questions. At least this answer was true, far too true. This glimpse of what life could be like with Elowyn Bagshaw beside him was far too tempting, far too close to the fantasy he hungered for in his heart. But like all fantasies, it could be shattered with a confession or two. That's how he knew it wasn't real.

# Chapter Eleven

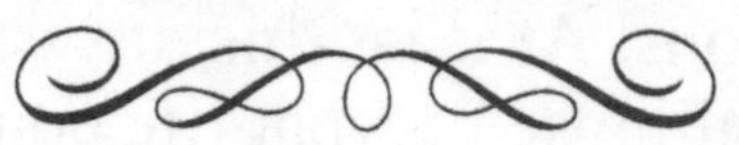

Life with Grahame Westmore was one giant adventure. The longer the adventure lasted, the more convinced Elowyn was she didn't want to give it up. Neither did she know what to do about it. Nothing lasted forever. She would genuinely miss him when it was over. But she'd miss her principles and her control more if she prolonged this beyond what was prudent.

She'd not thought things would progress this far. She'd waited, fully expecting the novelty of the road would wear off amid the dirty, dusty realities of travel. She'd waited, thinking the sensual edge he roused so thoroughly, so regularly, would dull after nights in his arms. But neither had happened. If anything, the sensuality between them had grown, enhanced by long conversations throughout the day. Theirs was no longer the physical joining of strangers but the intimacy of lovers who knew one another. Although she had begun to wonder lately if there were a stronger emotional attachment on her part, especially since she was certain he was keeping a secret, suggesting perhaps that the intimacy didn't run as deeply for him.

She was conscious, too, that the journey bore the stamp of the surreal. From the moment they left Ostend and headed south for Vienna, this adventure was a time apart, not truly part of the real world. Their world was no longer about schedules and the demands others made on her time. There was no household to organize, no entertainments to attend. There was only her and Grahame. He was the sole focus of her world and she of his. It wasn't normal. Reality didn't work that way.

Reality was full of items that competed for that time and attention. When they reached Vienna everything would change. She would have her father to look after, a house to coordinate, new people to meet. And Grahame would do what? She didn't know. He'd probably go back to England. His job would be over unless she could induce him to stay. Perhaps she could appeal to her father to get him a position with the British consulate there. The closer they got to Vienna, the more such plans dominated her thoughts.

"Watch out for the branch!" Grahame called, breaking into her thoughts just in time for her to avoid a collision with a low-hanging tree limb. Elowyn pulled her mare, a purchase in Ostend, to the left and smiled apologetically.

Grahame pulled Aramis up alongside her. "You were wool-gathering. Is everything all right?"

No, everything wasn't all right. They were two days out from Vienna. She was going to lose him and she didn't have a coping mechanism in place. Usually when it was time for an affair to end, she merely began to distance herself but she didn't want to employ such tactics with Grahame and waste the time they had left.

She couldn't confess to any of it. He wouldn't want her to cling to him and feel pushed into a corner where his honor demanded him to do something contrary to his wishes. Most of all, she didn't want to compromise their last two nights together.

"I was thinking we'll be there soon." She could say that much, at least.

Grahame gave her one of his boyish grins. "I'd wager you're already dreaming of a hot bath."

"Among other things." She didn't think she'd ever bathe without recalling their intimate bath in Ostend and the pleasure that followed. Elowyn eyed the gray sky. "Perhaps what I should be thinking about is where we're going to shelter for the night. It looks like rain." Again. There'd been plenty of rain on this trip and plenty of mud.

"There's a village five miles ahead if the last road sign is to be believed, but I don't think the rain will hold off that long." A fat, heavy drop fell on Grahame's nose in concurrence. He wiped it away. "There was an abandoned barn a mile back." He raised his dark eyebrows in question. "What do you think? The barn or the village?" The drops were starting to fall with more frequency. The village meant an inn, a dry bed. Elowyn curled her fist in her glove, feeling the press of the gold ring she'd worn on her fourth finger for the sake of validating Grahame's presence in her room whenever they encountered inns. But they'd be soaked to the skin before they reached it. An abandoned barn wasn't much better. It meant they were at nature's mercy, dependent on the quality of an old roof. But there would be absolute privacy, a chance they would reach it and still be relatively dry. A barrage of cold raindrops decided it. "The barn."

The barn was in better condition than the last one they'd taken shelter in. The roof was tight and they were able to find a corner that wasn't wracked with draught from the cold wind. Elowyn set up "house" as she privately liked to think of it. After multiple nights on the road, she had her routine. While Grahame settled the horses into the vacant stalls and searched out clean hay, she set up their belongings—their two tin cups and eating things, acquired along the road when it became apparent they wouldn't always have an inn at their disposal. She went outside to gather firewood. There'd be a fire pit to make and food to lay out—cold meat pies from the little town they'd passed through that morning and a jug of ale.

Elowyn shook out their blankets and reached for Grahame's valise. He'd be wet when he came in and he'd want his dry shirt. Normally, his spare shirt was on top but today she had to hunt for it. There it was! Elowyn pulled out the shirt and a folded letter fluttered out, too. She bent to pick it up. The heavy paper felt expensive in her hand. She should let it be. This wasn't her business but resisting curiosity had never been her strong suit.

Elowyn opened the letter and read, her eyes drawn immediately to the letterhead at the top. The Spanish Riding School! And here she'd been worrying about a job for him. She read a little further, noting the date of the interview just three days away. Her mouth tightened into a grimace. The date explained the urgency both in London and in Dover. He couldn't wait. He'd lose his chance.

This was the reason he'd taken on the job of escorting her to Vienna. This was his secret. There was another secret, too, one that hit Elowyn full force with its layers of implications. He was staying in Vienna. The affair didn't have to end when the road ended and yet he'd chosen to let her believe it would. They were just two days away from the completion of their journey and he'd not brought up any plans for future continuation. Worst of all, he'd known all along. It seemed patently unfair that he'd known from the start he'd be staying when she'd assumed the exact opposite. It just went to show how little she knew about him.

In regular cases that would be fine. The less she knew about someone, the easier it was to control the relationship without emotional attachment getting in the way. But it hadn't worked that way with Grahame and now she was standing in a leaky barn feeling betrayed. She had to be fair here. She'd broken her own rules and this was what she got for her efforts.

Tears smarted in her eyes. There was only one reason why he hadn't told her. He didn't want to continue the arrangement beyond arrival. If he told her about remaining in the city, he obviously thought she'd try and extend the affair. And he'd be right. She probably would have. She would have leaped at the chance.

Elowyn tucked the letter back into the bag. It wasn't his fault. He never suggested he wanted more than a fling on the road. In the beginning, it was all she'd wanted, too. Things had changed for her and she'd wrongly assumed things had changed for him, too. She'd misjudged him and by extension, she'd misjudged them.

She'd just lit the fire when Grahame entered the little alcove, looking wet from his efforts with the horses. "The rest of the barn isn't as snug as our corner here," he said, reaching for a blanket and stripping out of his wet coat. He looked around. "I must say, you'd have made an admirable army wife. I wouldn't have expected it."

Usually, she would have said something saucy in reply to his teasing. Tonight, she simply handed him his shirt, still too numb from her discoveries. Grahame shrugged into his dry shirt with slow movements, finally sensing something was off. "What is it, Ell?"

She hadn't meant to confront him. She'd meant to have one more night and then distance herself in the morning, but seeing him so easy and free as if nothing was wrong, as if her heart wasn't starting to break just the tiniest of bits, had prompted a more direct response. Elowyn met his gaze evenly. "I know about Vienna. I saw the letter in your bag."

# Chapter Twelve

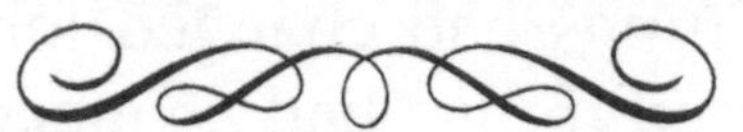

The revelation caught him off guard. His face became a stoic mask as he lowered himself down by the fire. She pressed her brief advantage. "Why didn't you tell me, Grahame?"

"It doesn't change anything." His gaze was riveted on the flames.

"I disagree. It has the power to change everything. Is that why you said nothing?" She tried to stay cool. Yelling and fighting were not viable substitutes for a controlled, adult discussion. "When we arrive in Vienna, it's over?"

"It has to be," Grahame bit out tersely.

"Care to explain why? I'm a big girl, Grahame. I can take it." It was a lie. Whatever he told her, it was going to hurt. She knew that much already.

"No, I wouldn't care to explain it," Grahame growled. He glanced up from the fire and his features seemed to soften. "I'm not all you think I am. I'd prefer to leave it at that. My pride demands it."

"What about my pride? It demands a little something, too," Elowyn shot back, unwilling to settle.

He gave her a look of exasperation. "It's not you, it's me."

Elowyn snorted. "*That* doesn't make it better." She wanted to stay angry; it was easier to distance herself from him then. But her anger was slipping away. She'd expected him to be harsh, to laugh at her notions of what their affair had meant; perhaps she'd expected him to even tell her she'd been foolish in her assumptions. But he'd done none of that. Instead, he mirrored her own frustration.

Something flickered in his gray eyes. "Believe me when I tell you I wish this could all be different."

"If wishes were horses…" Elowyn flashed a sardonic glance to where their mounts were stabled. "What do you suppose that makes us?" Oh, yes, the edge was starting to wear off indeed, the anger all but gone now. Was she going to despise herself for this in the morning?

Grahame's eyes were solemn and sad. "Two people who found happiness for a short while. But Ell, it can't last. I can't make you happy forever."

"Let me be the judge of that." Suddenly, she knew her own mind. She went to him, kissing him on the mouth, her hands working the shirt he'd so recently put on. She couldn't control him, or the outcome once they reached Vienna, but she could control tonight. Tonight she wanted him one last time.

Elowyn reached for him, her hand seeking his phallus, but he stalled her. "No, tonight, let me take you."

He wanted her! Her heart soared with elation, his words further proof that she'd not misread the solemnity in his eyes just now. He truly did wish things could be different. It wasn't that he didn't want things to continue in Vienna, it was that he felt they *couldn't* continue. There was still a secret, only not the one she'd thought. There was hope in that, she thought. It wasn't over, not yet.

Grahame moved over her, pushing up her skirts and settling between her legs. The primal need to conquer had come upon him suddenly, brought on by the questions and disclosure. He wanted her to belong to him, even if just for tonight. Time was running out for his fantasy and he would not let it go easily, not without a few more memories. He thrust in hard, finding her slick and ready. Did he imagine it, or did her arms tighten about his neck more fiercely? Did her legs clasp him more firmly, unwilling to let him leave her body? Was it possible she felt it, too, that the end was near and nothing could stop it? Had she understood his subtle plea?. More important, would she honor it and not push him for more?

It was simple sex, man on top, nothing fancy, nothing that would have dazzled the tonnish ladies with his prowess, and yet when they'd climaxed together beneath their rough blankets, beside their little fire in a rickety barn, rain pounding on the roof, Grahame felt like a king. The restlessness he'd felt in London had been resolved. He needed nothing more than this. This was it. Elowyn was it and he couldn't have her.

"Why did you cross the Channel with me?" Grahame murmured into the darkness. The fire had burned low and now they lay beside it, wrapped in blankets, savoring the afterglow of their lovemaking. It was a risky question given their other disclosures tonight, but he needed the answer.

What did she see in him? How badly was it going to hurt to let her go? And always, the question, would it hurt more to tell her the real reason it had to end? To see her turn away from him in disgust? He'd not intended to let things get this far, and clearly from her reaction earlier tonight, she had not intended it, either. But here they were, both of them seeking a physical affair that had spun out of control and now they were at sea, trying not to drown in their attraction.

Elowyn took her time swallowing, gathering her thoughts. He could see the silhouette of her throat working in the firelight. "I couldn't bear for my father to worry." She stared into the fire. "My mother froze to death en route to one of my father's postings. A wheel had come off her carriage. When she didn't arrive on time, no one worried. Carriages were always late. The roads weren't made for fast travel. There were constant delays—it was what was expected. By the time my father went looking for her, it was too late. I couldn't put him through that again."

He was surprisingly disappointed to hear that. He supposed he'd wanted a confession that she'd come for him, that she couldn't resist him, although in the long run, this answer was much better. It proved that maybe some detachment still remained after all.

The fire sparked and popped. Elowyn picked up a long stick and poked the wood about, rearranging the kindling. "But that wasn't the only reason." She shot him a look and worried her lip. "I couldn't make you stay. You needed to cross the Channel. I don't know what for, but it was there in your eyes. You couldn't wait and I didn't want to make you. You would have stayed. You wouldn't have left me in Dover with wagons and servants to manage. Your honor as a gentleman, as an officer, wouldn't allow it."

Would his honor allow her to believe that statement? It was Grahame's turn to look away, uncertain about how much to say. He wasn't a gentleman, never had been by birth or by deed. The goodness she assigned to him was overwhelming and even a bit shaming. He should tell her. It would be the final wall he needed to keep her from him. She would pull away from him once she knew. He wouldn't have to be the one to end the relationship. She would end it for him. Now he was torn. Did honor demand he tell her, or did honor demand he keep his secret and face the end of this relationship like a man?

"Well, Grahame?" Elowyn prompted gently. "I came. That's your answer. Now you tell me, what did I come for?"

A droplet of juice from her meat pie lingered on her lips. Grahame leaned forward, catching her chin between his thumb and forefinger, ready to employ an age-old strategy. "You came for this, because we can't get enough of each other and we both wanted to know how it was going to end." He covered her mouth softly with his, his tongue licking the seam of her lips. A kiss could stop a lot of things, in this case, even time.

# Chapter Thirteen

Sex was not an answer, no matter how good it was. But she'd let it be a sufficient substitute last night. As a result, in the light of day, nothing had been resolved. Grahame was still determined it all had to end, just for different reasons than the ones she had supposed. It didn't help that she didn't know what those reasons were. This was their last day on the road. They were running out of time. It was small consolation that last night's revelation had not been a rejection, that his decision to hide his post in Vienna had not been out of a need to break with her. But it made no difference if he still meant to end things.

Elowyn could not get past that one thought as she folded their blankets and put away their things. The rain had stopped in the night and the morning was bright. It would be a good day for travel. They would make decent time. The thought should have filled her with relief. The day after tomorrow she'd be with her father. She'd be in circumstances more suited to her upbringing. She was the granddaughter of an earl, the daughter of a third son. She did have some station in life—not enough to stifle her, but enough to give her comforts. And all she wanted was Grahame Westmore.

Last night's intimacy had sealed it. She could no longer argue the excitement was in the adventure of sex, or the games Westmore could play with her body. Even ordinary sex was riveting, fulfilling, beyond anything she'd imagined because it wasn't simply sex as it had been with her other lovers. Those interludes were pale shadows against what she shared with Grahame.

"Are you ready?" Grahame came to collect the valises and blankets to tie on behind the saddles. His hair was tied back, his coat was dry and brushed, but his boots had lost their polish miles ago. Their clothes at least would be glad to see Vienna, even if their owners weren't. Even Grahame seemed subdued this morning.

*No, you silly ninny. I am not ready. I want to stay in this rickety barn with you forever and make love next to a dying fire.* She didn't dare say it. If she could persuade him to stay it would mean missing his interview. She couldn't do that to him, so she lied. "Yes, I've got everything."

Outside, Grahame threw her up on her horse before mounting Aramis. How she loved watching the strength of him in motion as he swung up on the big beast. How many more chances would she have to see him do that? Or to feel his big hand on her leg as he tossed her up? It was going to be a long day if she insisted on that train of thought. Emotionally, she could not afford to spend the day remembering every detail of their time together, or thinking of all the “lasts.” What was she willing to do about it?

Elowyn let the question occupy her mind during the early miles of the morning. They rode in silence, an awkward quiet springing up between them, proof that she was not the only one grappling with the dilemma. Grahame might have made a decision, but he wasn’t happy with it. She would take encouragement from that.

“I imagine you will be glad to see the city tomorrow,” Grahame said after the silence between them had grown stifling.

“I never wanted to leave London,” Elowyn replied honestly. It was one of her secrets, the one thing she kept buried deep inside her. In all her years of travel, she’d never admitted as much to her father.

Grahame looked at her and she could see the words had surprised him. “I would have thought a diplomat’s daughter was used to moving.”

“Being used to it doesn’t mean I like it,” Elowyn sighed. “This time, I thought we might stay. London is the hub of the empire now. There’s plenty of diplomatic work to do without leaving England. We’d been there five years. I thought this time it would be different.” Elowyn shrugged. “But I was wrong. Britain wanted my father well-positioned for negotiations when the Treaty of Unkiar Skelessi expires so there are no surprises like last time.” The secret clause between Turkey and Russia had led to eight years of British unrest where Russian allegiances were concerned.

"What about you? Are you looking forward to Vienna?" She turned the conversation back toward him.

"I'm excited about the opportunity but I, too, will miss England and my friends."

"And your family," Elowyn supplied. "You've not mentioned them in all the time we've talked, but they must be sad to see you go."

"No. I don't have any family. I never knew my father, and my mother passed away several years ago." Grahame's eyes had gone granite hard in their grayness. She had trespassed into forbidden territory, a reminder that no matter how far they'd come together, there were still areas off-limits like this one, like the one last secret he held.

"I'm sorry. I didn't know," Elowyn answered tersely. Let him hear the scold in her words. She should have known that much about him. He should have told her. The thought halted her. She was right. She should have known. Knowing the basics of his family was harmless enough. Unless it wasn't…

Elowyn studied his profile, straight and strong. Did his last secret have to do with his family? Was there some kind of embarrassment he was loath to share? Was it potent enough that it could not be tolerated? The reference to his father asserted itself, conjuring up images of illegitimacy. Her own father would resist such a match. He'd always fancied her married to a foreign prince or high-ranking Englishman. To date, she'd defied him with her discreet, temporary affairs; they were a chance to remind herself she had control. She decided the course of her life, when so often she felt she didn't.

Road traffic was picking up, making it difficult for extended private conversation. There was no chance to probe further. Elowyn noted they were passing wagons, other riders and families on foot dressed in their best.

"What do you think?" she said to Grahame, the first words they'd spoken since his mention of his family. Perhaps returning to lighter conversation would lessen the tension between them. "There's something going on up ahead."

Grahame nodded in agreement. "I bet a shilling it's a fair." He called out in German to a man on the roadside with his family. "What's happening today?"

The man grinned and gestured down the road. "It's the beer festival!"

It was the perfect distraction whether they wanted to go or not. The road passed straight through the village where booths were set up in a field, pennants and flags flew gaily and the smell of food filled the air. "I think we are duty bound to stop," Elowyn suggested as traffic clogged the street. She was desperate to reclaim Grahame from wherever he'd retreated. Even if she was fooling herself, she'd be glad to fool herself a little bit longer.

Grahame grinned and the tension disappeared. Perhaps he, too, was eager to prolong the illusion. "I do believe you're right. A fair is exactly what we need." A celebration of sorts, a chance to say farewell without doing it in Vienna. That wasn't where they should say goodbye. But that went without saying. They were getting pretty good at avoiding the things that needed to be said. Soon it would be too late for anything except regrets.

They found a place to stable the horses and began to stroll the grounds, a perfect excuse to keep her arm tucked into Grahame's. They spent the morning looking at livestock and admiring the horses, the early afternoon eating hot sausages and taking in the vendors, all the while the sky remained blue overhead. Grahame bought her a green ribbon he said matched her eyes and tied it in her hair, his hands lingering at her shoulders. In the late afternoon, a space was cleared for games. Men began to gather, boasting and joking as targets were set up for knife throwing. The old question of the morning reasserted itself. *If she was not willing to give up Grahame, what was she willing to do to keep him?* Elowyn smiled, an idea coming to her.

"I think I could beat you," Elowyn said in low tones as they wandered over to the gaming field.

"That's hardly fair. A gentleman is honor-bound to lose." But a competitive spirit sparked in his eyes nonetheless.

Her next words were bold. "But you're no gentleman, are you, Grahame? That's the secret, isn't it? The one thing that keeps you from continuing our affair?" The look on his face said she was close. The pieces were starting to fall into place. He didn't think he was good enough for her.

"Why does it matter so much to you?" Grahame blew

out an exasperated sigh. "I've asked you to leave this alone. It can't matter in the end."

The end being tomorrow, Elowyn thought. "It matters, because I've found a man worth keeping."

He raised an eyebrow at that. "For how long, Ell?" Until you decide it's over? Is that what this is about? You don't like that I've decided it needs to end? Is that how it was with the others? You chose? What do you want?"

She let the comment slide, all but the last part. They'd arrived at the knife throwing. She put down coins for the entrance fee and faced Grahame. "What I want is your best throw and then I'll want your secret, you stubborn man."

Grahame hefted one of the knives laid out at the booth while Elowyn marched up to the throwing line. Folks had begun to gather. He smiled in spite of himself. Elowyn knew how to draw a crowd. She was magnificent. Even now after days on the road there was a regal quality to her as she stepped up to throw. She stood there, proud and defiant, staring down the target with deadly intent. A few onlookers called friendly advice but she paid them no attention. That was when Grahame realized he was going to lose. Elowyn only knew how to win, even if the prize was something she wouldn't want.

She threw her three knives in rapid succession, one of them hitting the bull's-eye, the other two close enough it didn't matter. Elowyn turned to him with a confident smile. "It's all yours, Captain." The crowd cheered.

They wanted her to win. Maybe he did, too. Maybe the truth needed to come out.

Maybe.

His first throw matched hers.

His second throw matched hers.

His third throw went wide, just wide enough to make a difference in her favor. The crowd roared. Someone took up the chant, "Kiss! Kiss!" Grahame obliged. He swept a triumphant Elowyn into his arms, wanting to remember her like this always with her cheeks flushed, her hair falling down, her eyes on fire. He kissed her for the crowd. He kissed her for all he was worth and wasn't worth because very soon it would be over. She would know his secret and she would be done with him.

Not as soon as he thought. The crowd saved him. One man clapped a friendly hand on his shoulder. "Captain, is it? You'd better redeem yourself for the lady right over here." The man gestured toward the horse and rider obstacle course and the crowd surged, sweeping Grahame along with them. He caught sight of Elowyn among them, but she was of no help. She merely nodded and laughed along with the rest of them.

Aramis was already there, waiting for him. Grahame threw a censorious look at his newfound friend, who merely shrugged. "We all figured you were probably cavalry when we saw that big stallion of yours."

It was hard to be angry when spirits were riding high. Grahame swung up on Aramis. If he was committed to this, he might as well win it. Elowyn waved from the crowd and he lost himself in the moment at the sight of her. It occurred to him in a flash of insight this might be one of the best days of his life. His woman was cheering for him. Something primal surged in him as he kneed Aramis forward. He would ride for her and he'd win for her. Who he was might stop him from claiming her, but it couldn't stop him from loving her. Right now, that was enough.

He watched the first four competitors take the field and studied the course. It was classic, designed to test the skills of both horse and rider. The first test was about balance, a line of rope loops through, which the riders were expected to cut through with their sabers. The second was a set of poles the rider and the horse were to weave through, testing the horse's flexibility. Finally, there was the double test of the horse's steadiness and the rider's strength, the stuffed dummies that were to be stabbed.

The fifth rider did well, only missing one of the dummies. Then it was his turn. He saluted the judges, turned Aramis in a tight circle, readying him for the course. With a kick of his heels, Aramis was off. Grahame leaned low over Aramis's neck as the first task approached, saber leveled. The rope loops gave. He was through the first task. He urged Aramis on, not letting the horse slow as they came up on the weaving poles. He worked the reins, kneeing the horse subtly, in and out, while the crowd cheered, loving the speed. He would need that speed for the dummies so his saber wouldn't stick when it struck straw.

Grahame steadied his arm and plunged into the first

dummy and withdrew. He had to rely entirely on his knees for keeping Aramis on course, his hand occupied with the saber. He plunged again and again, taking the final dummy in a round of rambunctious applause from the audience.

Elowyn was in his arms, kissing him soundly the moment he dismounted. The judges were congratulating him; strangers in a town he'd never met were pounding his back. Tonight, he was Captain Grahame Westmore, and tonight he belonged.

The prize was a bottle of champagne. Grahame grinned and took the bottle from thc judges. "Shall I open it here?" he asked the crowd gathered about him. They cheered him on and he took out his saber one more time and turned the flat of the blade against the bottle. The cry of "sabrage!" broke out through the crowd in surprised delight. Elowyn's eyes were alight in awe. Grahame slid the blade along the body of the bottle and broke the neck away, the bubbling foam covering his hand while everyone clapped. He drank first and passed the bottle to Elowyn, who charmed the crowd with a healthy swig of her own. She passed the bottle on and that was the last he saw of the prize. They were swept up with the crowd toward the dancing floor and the trestle tables set up for eating.

Overhead, stars came out. Lanterns were lit. There were beer, sausages and potatoes until neither he nor Elowyn could eat another bite, and there was dancing! Country dancing, where no one cared how many times you danced with the same partner. He danced all night with Elowyn, watching her eyes burn with green fire, watching her hair come loose, watching her smile at him as if she were the happiest woman in the world and he knew he had to tell her. It was not fair to let her fall in love with an illusion.

The crowd was thinning, the musicians tiring as he led her to the inn where the innkeeper was all too glad to have chamber set aside for the day's champion and his wife. Elowyn collapsed on the bed, arms outstretched in weary happiness. "You were magnificent today! No wonder the Spanish riding school wants you."

When he said nothing, she sat up and fixed him with a puzzled stare. "You're still dressed. Aren't you coming to bed?"

"I will, if you want me to."

"Of course I want you to."

Grahame cut her off gently. "I owe you my secret. That was our wager today." He didn't want to hurt her but she had to know. "I have to tell you who I am and you may not want me after that." He shook his head to silence her protest. She had no business protesting what she didn't know.

Elowyn sat up in bed, all seriousness. "All right, then tell me."

Grahame began to pace. "I am a captain, but I didn't buy my commission. Mine was a field promotion for valor and leadership during battle. That's all true, but I'm not a gentleman born as you may have guessed. I have no title, not even a brother with a title. There's no grandfatherly baron on my family tree, no pretensions to the gentry at all. I'm a kid from the slums who enlisted in the army as soon as he was able. I worked my way up from there." He studied her, watching her take in the first salvo.

"You're truly a self-made man, then. That's more than admirable, Grahame," Elowyn said with quiet fortitude.

"There's more, Ell. Think about what that means. Being self-made means I work for a living. I will probably always have to work for a living. I can't offer you the things you're used to. Your father will see that right away. He will not find me suitable for any kind of association with you."

She pleated the blanket between her fingers, thinking. "He doesn't decide for me."

"Then there's more you need to know. I can't have you making decisions without all the knowledge." Grahame ran a hand through his hair. "I have to tell you the rest. After I returned to London, I needed work. A half-pay officer doesn't have a salary that will keep him in London, so I started escorting rich women to their entertainments. They were grateful."

"How grateful?" Elowyn had stopped pleating the blanket and fixed him with a hard stare.

"They would give me gems, necklaces, bracelets, expensive jewelry." Lord, it was hard to say the words. It had never bothered him before, but he'd not cared for anyone's opinion the way he cared for Elowyn's.

"Did you have sex with them?"

"Some of them, yes. All right, a lot of them." Grahame shook his head, trying to dispel the memories. "I was part of a group that called themselves the League of Discreet Gentlemen. We pleasured women who were unable to find pleasure in their own relationships." He blew out a breath. "I know it sounds bad." He waited. He waited for her ultimate rejection, her revulsion. Her green eyes were narrowed like a cat's.

"Well, Grahame Westmore, that certainly explains a lot of things." He could not tell by her tone how angry she was.

"What things?" Grahame ventured tentatively.

"Why you are so damn good in bed." Elowyn rose off the bed and came to him. She circled him, her hand caressing him as she went, her hips swaying seductively. "As for being bad, I would have to disagree. I think there's a bit of nobility in your calling. It is a great thing to give a woman pleasure. What it doesn't explain, though, is how you ended up with my father's commission."

Grahame coughed uncomfortably. "A mix up of words, I imagine. Your father was looking for an escort, just of a different sort." Channing had known that and exploited it.

Elowyn smiled. "Imagine that. Well, we don't have to tell him." She sobered, her hand pausing on his chest. "It also doesn't explain us. I need to know, was I a game? Was I just another woman in need of your skills?"

Grahame covered her hand with his. Everything depended on these next simple words. "No. You were not, *are* not a game, which is why you had to know who I was, what I was. I could not bind you to a fiction of a man and have you discover too late what you'd chosen."

"And what will I have chosen?" Elowyn's eyes glinted in challenge. She was not going to let him go. He would treasure that later. Right now, he had to make her see the futility of her tenacity.

"Ell, I am a man of no background and no significant wealth. I work for a living. I will probably move several more times and you hate moving. I can give you none of what you crave. But God help me, I'm the man who wants to bed you tonight one last time before I deliver you to your father and say goodbye tomorrow." If she would not let him go, he would have to stand firm and let her go, even if it killed him to do it. He would not be able to respect himself otherwise if he dragged her down to his level. But before that, he'd give them a night to remember.

# Chapter Fourteen

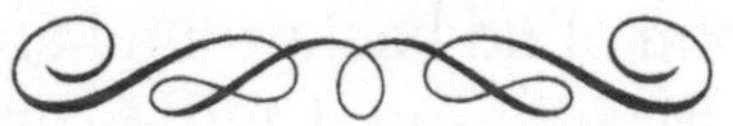

It had been a week and Grahame Westmore had proven to be as good as his word, damn him. Elowyn looked out the front room window yet again. It had a view of the busy street and she'd found her eyes going to that view several times a day as if she expected to see Grahame striding up the front steps and declaring he'd made a mistake, that he'd been wrong when he'd decided there were more important things for her to have besides love.

She rather thought he'd overestimated those things and underestimated her. For that matter, he'd underestimated what he did have to offer. For starters, he wasn't without resources. He *did* have an income. They'd have her dowry. They would hardly be paupers the way he made it sound. But there had been no convincing him of that. She'd hoped a week's separation would have done the convincing for her. Perhaps that was why her eyes were ever drawn to the window these days.

The housekeeper bustled in. "Miss, will you want to go over the menus for the week?"

Elowyn turned her gaze from the window. She stared at the housekeeper, one thought demanding all her concentration. This was *not* control, the thing she valued so highly in her life. Deciding what to eat, which china to eat it off, who to invite to dinner, what dress to wear, none of it was really control. In the end, she moved when her father said move. She'd been deciding the small things all along, making temporary decisions. Even her relationships mirrored that pattern.

"Miss?" The housekeeper queried. Elowyn was sure she must look strange but she didn't care. There was an important discussion going on in her head right now and if she deviated from listening to it for even a second, she would lose the thread. She loved Grahame Westmore. He loved her. If she really wanted to take control of something as significant as the direction of her life, she would not let his concern over society's reaction stand in her way. Instead, she'd walk out this door and go straight to him.

Elowyn rose. "If you'll excuse me. I have something I need to do. I'm going out."

Grahame leaned against the stall door, exhausted and dirty. He'd just finished putting away the last horse of the day. The school was training a new group of horses for the king of Spain. There were grooms, of course, to do the menial work of grooming and stabling but Grahame had insisted he and the group of Spaniards working with him do it themselves as a way to build trust between horse and rider.

Maybe tonight he'd be tired enough to sleep, really sleep, without dreams. He only dreamed of one thing: Elowyn. He would wake hard and aching. Some nights he reached for her before he'd realize she was gone. His damnable respect was becoming a double-edged sword that was cutting only him. Perhaps he'd been wrong to let Elowyn go. It wasn't that he didn't value what they had. He knew how rare real happiness was and he'd meant it when he'd told her they'd found happiness for a short time. He'd seen too many unhappy women, women who'd come looking for him to provide them a type of happiness to know the difference. Maybe that was what scared him the most. What if he and Elowyn lost their happiness? It would be far worse to know what he'd lost then never to have had it at all.

A few men passed by the stall and stopped to invite him to go out with them. He smiled, thanked them and waved them on. He was not fit company for anyone tonight. By turning Elowyn free, he'd done the best he could for her. Right now, she was probably getting ready for a splendid night in a sparkling mansion near the Belvedere. In his mind's eye he could see her putting on a silk gown, her maid putting up her hair. A loose curl would dangle in tantalizing temptation at her neck. Tonight, whether she meant to or not, she would dazzle some poor unsuspecting soul who had no idea what he was getting himself into. She couldn't help it. He could almost hear that sultry voice of hers.

"Grahame Westmore, are you waiting for me?"

His imaginings must be getting stronger because that voice sounded very real. Only it wouldn't be his name, of course. His name. Wait. Grahame turned slowly.

Elowyn stood there, just feet away, looking far too fresh for the stables, even pristine stables like this one. The horse in the stall gave him a hard nudge with its nose, pushing him forward as if even it knew Elowyn was his destiny.

"Hello, Ell." Maybe not so fresh, now that he had time to study her. Her cheeks were flushed and she was out of breath. That only made his blood pound harder. "You've been running."

"Yes, damn you, and it's all your fault." Her eyes sparkled and there was no malice behind her words. "I have something to say." She put her hands on her hips, her face set in earnest. "I want you, Grahame Westmore, for better or for worse, for now and for always. I don't care about the money, I don't care about moving, I don't care what anyone thinks. I've had a week to think it over and for the first time, I know my own mind."

He couldn't let her do this. Grahame opened his mouth to remind her of all the reasons they needed to exercise restraint but the words never came. Elowyn crossed the distance between them in two strides and sealed his mouth with a kiss. She had him up against the stable wall before he knew what was happening. His body knew, though. It had gone hard at the sight of her and her rough play was exciting it beyond measure now.

"You've spent too much time talking me out of this.

Now it's time for me to talk you into it," She said between kisses, her hand slipping to his trousers.

"Ell, you know what I can offer you is not what you're used to. You know the man I am." He had to try but his words sounded weak, even to himself. All he wanted was to seat himself in her and be done with it, be done with all the worry, all the doubt.

"Yes, I do." She stopped her kisses for a moment and met his eyes. "You are the man I love."

There was no fighting that. There was no desire to fight that. If he was truly brave, he'd reach out and seize what she was offering him with both hands; it was his dream, his fantasy. He'd found someone to belong with if he would take it. Grahame dropped a kiss along her jaw. "Then I guess there's only one question left. Elowyn Bagshaw, will you be my wife?"

Elowyn's arms went around his neck. "I think the question is will you be my husband?" She laughed up at him but his answer was serious.

"There will be difficulties," Grahame warned.

She gave him a soft smile. "Of course there will be. Sex is easy, Grahame. Love is hard."

He pressed his hips against her, letting her feel his arousal. "Damn right it is." Then he kissed her for all he was worth, which was substantially more than what he'd been worth a few weeks ago, not financially by any means, but by more important means. He was valued by this extraordinary woman and that was worth its weight in gold.

He held all he'd ever need in his arms and he was

a happy man at last. He'd always believed some men were made for peace, others for war. Today he'd learned there are others who are made for love and he was one of them.

* * * * *

# ONE NIGHT
# WITH THE HIGHLANDER

Ann Lethbridge

If you enjoy
ONE NIGHT WITH THE HIGHLANDER,
discover more about *The Gilvrys of Dunross*
in these associated books by Ann Lethbridge:

THE LAIRD'S FORBIDDEN LADY
HER HIGHLAND PROTECTOR
FALLING FOR THE HIGHLAND ROGUE
RETURN OF THE PRODIGAL GILVRY

**Other novels by Ann Lethbridge**
**in Mills & Boon® Historical Romance:**

MORE THAN A MISTRESS
LADY ROSABELLA'S RUSE
HAUNTED BY THE EARL'S TOUCH

**And in Mills & Boon® Historical eBooks:**

PRINCESS CHARLOTTE'S CHOICE
(part of *Royal Weddings Through the Ages*)

**And in**
**M&B Regency *Castonbury Park* mini-series:**

LADY OF SHAME

Look out for
CAPTURED COUNTESS
by Ann Lethbridge
Coming soon

# *Chapter One*

"Bad news, my lady?"

Startled from the perusal of her letter, Annabelle, Lady Merton, realized from the post office clerk's avid expression that she had revealed her shock. Folding the note she should have known better than to open in public, she forced a pleasant smile. "Not at all."

Bad did not begin to describe the news. Disastrous came closer. The bank, deeming the case against her dead husband's family hopeless, had refused to extend her further credit, and the lawyer was politely asking how she intended to settle his fees.

She couldn't. Her stomach fell away in a sickening rush. She was destitute except for a few remaining jewels. She'd be lucky if their sale kept her and Mother for as much as a month. What on earth would she do now? A cold hand clutched at her heart. There was nothing she could do. Except marry. Something she had hoped to avoid. Keeping her smile cool, she tucked the letter in her reticule and turned to leave.

The shop doorbell tinkled merrily. A broad-shouldered man wearing a greatcoat boasting several fashionable capes strode in with a decisive air.

Her heart lurched. An odd kind of tumble she'd experienced only once in her life. Joyful recognition. A sweetly painful sensation that stole her breath.

Gordon McLaughlin of Carrick. The last person she had expected to see in the sleepy village of Barton Sidley, even if it was but a few miles from the Scottish border. He'd been a well-looking young man at twenty. At closer to thirty, he was spectacularly handsome. He'd grown into his large nose and dark heavy brows. Broadened out to stand monument-square on long athletic legs encased in dazzlingly shiny black Hessians. With eyes the bright piercing blue of a clear winter sky.

Her heart clenched and her body hummed with sensual appreciation. As it had when they had first met. Before she fully understood those sensations. And it seemed the sparks were still there, hot and ready to be reignited.

Shaken by this second shock following on the heels of the first, she lowered her face beneath her wide-brimmed bonnet and edged around his large form. Fresh air and daylight lay not three yards away. Two yards. A few feet and she would be outside on the pavement. Yet even as she made to scuttle past, she sensed his attention. A searing intensity arcing across the space between them.

"Annabelle?" The soft Highland burr sounding out the syllables of her name was just as she remembered. A recollection so sharp it could have been yesterday. She had met him only once, at the local assembly. Against all propriety, she had slipped away from her mother to meet him outside in the courtyard. Her lips tingled at the memory of his gentle kiss. The scent of his spicy cologne. The feel of his strong arms holding her close. Heat stung her cheeks as she remembered how she'd reveled in his stolen kiss that night. How wicked she'd felt at deceiving her mother. And how very womanly, in his embrace. So foolish. So young and heedless. A youthful romantic adventure that had come to nothing.

"I mean Mrs. Jenkins?" he said, correcting himself, bringing her mind back to the present.

Bracing herself, she looked up, squaring her shoulders against whatever emotion she might see in his face, whether it be derision, disdain or simply coldness. A false smile curved her lips, a tight little grimace, even as her gaze roved his face. "Lady Merton now, Mr. McLaughlin."

The only expression she read was surprise. She almost sagged with relief. Though why she would care about his good opinion she didn't know.

His bow was of exactly the right depth and elegance to recognize her superior rank. "Lady Merton. I was unaware you had married again. Please, accept my sympathy for your earlier loss."

She clenched her hands tighter around the strings of her reticule. At any moment he would recall hearing her name. He would recollect what he knew of the infamous Lady Merton. And she would see revulsion instead of warmth.

"My first husband died many years ago," she said calmly enough. She dipped a curtsy, intending to hurry on, like a coward. To avoid the embarrassment of small talk. Of trying to pretend they were friends.

He shifted. A small move, but it effectively blocked the path to freedom, to cool fresh breezes that would drive the heat from her face.

"I had not heard you were in the neighborhood," he said. "Are you visiting your family?"

If forcing herself on her mother could be called visiting. And based on the news Annabelle had just received, she would be less welcome than she'd expected.

"Yes," she said flatly. "I am visiting."

He looked a little nonplussed.

Good manners required she say more. "I called in for the mail on my way to see my mother." She offered a tentative smile. "And you? Are you visiting Mrs. Blackstone and her niece?" she asked, recalling it was because of Mrs. Blackstone's niece, Lady Jenna, he had come to Barton Sidley that first time. He'd brought the girl, too. An elfin, sad-faced child he had escorted to her aunt after her father died. A curiously independent little creature who must be twenty by now.

He frowned. "Mrs. Blackstone passed away a few days ago. I am charged to bring Lady Jenna back to Carrick Castle."

A feeling of disappointment hollowed Annabelle's chest. What? Had she thought he might have returned on her account? After all this time? That really was being foolish. "I'm so sorry. Poor Lady Jenna, she must be devastated by the loss of her last family member."

"Her aunt had been ill for some time. Quite frankly, I do not think she should have been left to manage here alone."

Annabelle hesitated, trembling inside with fear of rejection. Cowardice, when she had resolved never to let what people thought beat her down. "May Mother and I call on Lady Jenna? To offer condolence? If she is receiving, that is?"

He looked pleased. "I am sure she would be delighted."

Then he must not have heard the gossip. Yet. Her heart lifted.

"I am just returned from America," he said, filling the growing silence.

The smile on her lips seemed to have a life of its own. She was probably grinning like one demented. "America? Were you there long?"

He gave a short laugh. "For more than five years. Looking after my father's business interests."

America. So faraway. It sounded wonderful. "But now you are back."

His face sobered. "For a while."

Other questions hovered on her tongue. Married? Children? Happy? *Patience,* she cautioned herself. These were all things she would learn on the morrow. "Mother and I will come in the afternoon. If you would be so good as to let Lady Jenna know."

He bowed. "She will look forward to it. Feel free to bring Lord Merton, if he accompanies you."

The mention of her husband brought the evils of her situation back in a rush. "Lord Merton passed away earlier this year," she said, keeping her voice emotionless. "Good day, Mr. McLaughlin. I look forward to seeing you and Lady Jenna tomorrow."

No amateur in the ways of the world herself, she took a small step toward the door, forcing him to stand aside and bow his farewell. "Until tomorrow, Lady Merton."

She did not miss the spark of interest in his eyes.

Was she wrong about him? Had he heard, and decided to try his luck? But surely he would not knowingly expose his precious cousin to a woman with her reputation? Edinburgh's wanton Black Widow.

Gordon could not help but watch the sway of her skirts at her quick firm step as she departed the shop. Or the proud tilt of her head on her slender neck. She'd been lovely as a girl of eighteen, with dove-gray eyes and hair the color of amber. A spirited girl. All laughter and passion. As a woman she had new depth. A new reserve. And secrets. But the passion between them remained. Held in check. Controlled. But there nonetheless, as it had been the first and only time they met. Like last time, he had only to look at her to want her.

And she was a widow.

Available. His body tightened in anticipation. Attractive widows were fertile hunting grounds for a man who wanted the satisfaction of mutual pleasure without ties.

More than one of his liaisons had thrown their caps at him over the years, but he'd never had the wherewithal to support a wife, let alone a family, in the way he thought he should. Finally he'd saved enough money to leave his father's business and strike out on his own.

Gordon thrust his inconvenient lust to the background. "Do you have a package for me?" he asked the hunched, balding clerk behind the counter. "Gordon McLaughlin."

"Yes, sir. Arrived on the mail." He reached beneath the counter and produced a bulky package. "From London." He eyed it with interest.

As he would. In this quiet backwater in the north of England, the death of one of its prominent citizens and the subsequent arrangements would be of interest to all. But this package had no relevance in the death of Jenna's aunt. Mrs. Blackstone had been her brother-in-law's pensioner. This package was Gordon's own personal business. His father had demanded he see Lady Jenna back to Carrick Castle the moment he stepped off his ship from Boston. Impatient at the delay, Gordon had sent word to his man of business to forward the contract to him here.

Once he signed the papers he would be the owner of his first merchant ship. He hefted the parcel in his hand and wandered out into the street, surprised when he caught himself glancing up and down, seeking sight of the lush figure of Lady Merton, like some randy youth.

But lust didn't completely cover the things he had felt on seeing Annabelle, though there was no mistaking its presence. There was also a sense of words unspoken. Promises not kept. Even a sense of loss.

He was imagining things. Had to be. All he felt was unrequited lust. Not something he couldn't control. Yet he found himself looking forward to meeting her again on the morrow.

Blackstone Manor lay about half a mile from the village. It was a fine day for a walk along a country lane. The scrub-covered foothills of the Cheviots, while not as rugged, reminded him of the hills around his home in Scotland. He felt a twinge of regret. With his plans set in motion he was likely to see as little of them in the future as he had these past few years. His father would likely be less than pleased with his decision. It was not an interview he looked forward to with pleasure.

Unlike seeing Lady Merton again. The passage of years had certainly added to her feminine appeal. His palms tingled yet with the desire to explore her lush curves. And if the flush on her creamy skin and the answering warmth in her gaze spoke true, she, too, had felt the pull of desire.

And she'd been widowed twice. He stopped, staring unseeing at a flock of sheep in the field on the other side of a stone wall. Two husbands. Envy for those unknown men twisted sharply in his gut. It would be another five years of hard work before he could think of supporting a wife.

Inside he froze, shocked that he was even thinking about the idea. He wasn't. He was thinking about how he would break the news of his departure to his father.

He'd let thoughts of a pretty woman distract him from an unpleasant duty. And now there was no time left for contemplation.

Nestled at the edge of a forest that marched up the hill behind it, Blackstone Manor was typical of the stone houses hereabouts. A pony and trap tied to the fence indicated Jenna had a visitor. There had been several visits of condolence since he arrived two days ago. Groaning inwardly at the thought of another round of stiff conversation, he passed through the gate in the fence surrounding the neat little garden, and entered the front door.

The housekeeper took his hat. "Lady Jenna asked me to tell you that Mrs. Tracey is sitting with her in the front parlor." She jerked her head toward the closed door. "There is a cup laid for you."

From that he gathered he was to rescue Jenna from the vicar's wife. He glanced regretfully down at his package. He would far rather go through the papers and make sure all was in order, but he could hardly leave Jenna in the lurch. He strolled into a room with closed drapes and black crepe adorning the pictures. Only one candle had been lit. Poor Jenna. She felt bad enough about losing her aunt without being forced to be reminded of it in such a gloomy way.

And he was glad he had decided to join them when he heard the relief in Jenna's voice as she made the introductions and he made his bows.

He sat down and Jenna handed him a cup of tea. "How very kind of you to call on Lady Jenna in this sad time," Gordon said with a smile.

"I am not one to be found lacking in my duty, Mr. McLaughlin. Lady Jenna tells me she is to return to her cousin at Carrick Castle."

"Yes," he said calmly, trying not to show annoyance at the woman's obvious prying. "My mother anxiously awaits her arrival. Since my sister married last year, she has been lacking female company."

Jenna gave him a smile, her heart-shaped face lighting up with pleasure. "I look forward to seeing her, too."

"I met Lady Merton in the village," he said, by way of filling an awkward pause in the conversation. "You knew her as Annabelle Dawson, Jenna. She plans to call tomorrow."

Mrs. Tracey's lips thinned in disapproval. "You surely will not entertain that…that woman here, Lady Jenna."

Jenna bristled at the admonition in the woman's tone. Gordon did a bit of bristling of his own. He held his temper and replied before Jenna's quick tongue doused them both in hot water. "Lady Merton is the daughter of your husband's predecessor," he said mildly. "Is there a problem?"

The woman's eyes gleamed. She glanced over her shoulder as if she expected the subject of their discussion to appear from nowhere, then leaned forward. "Both of her husbands died under very mysterious circumstances. In Edinburgh they call her the Black Widow."

Gordon's jaw dropped.

Mrs Tracey nodded, clearly satisfied by his reaction.

"The first one died of a supposed fever, but now there is talk that it might have been something in his food or drink. And the night Merton died, there were unexplained comings and goings, according to neighbors. My brother, a magistrate in Edinburgh, says it was a havey-cavey business, indeed. He is sure Lady Merton knows more than she admits, and so do her servants."

Their visitor sat back with a jerky nod. "And her no better than she should be, by all accounts. Not the sort of woman you should be admitting to the house, Lady Jenna."

Gordon felt his blood growing hotter by the second. Anger at the insinuations made his hands clench. But now he recalled why the name Merton had sounded familiar. One of his correspondents had regaled him with stories of the seductive Lady Merton. Rumors of a stable of young men at her every beck and call. Bile rose in Gordon's throat at the things he'd heard as he now tried to associate them with Annabelle.

Jenna's eyes had narrowed to slits of glittering green. "I met her the first year I arrived here. She was very kind."

Mrs. Tracey snorted, one of those scornful sounds made by those of a righteous disposition. "You must think of Lady Jenna's reputation, Mr. McLaughlin. A young lady of her breeding must not be exposed to a whiff of scandal."

Gordon put down his cup to free his hands so he could put them around the gossiping woman's throat. Thinking better of it, he picked it up again. "I thank you for your advice." He drew in a steadying breath. "It was most kind of you to call on Lady Jenna, but I must say she is looking a little pulled. The last few weeks have been hard on her."

Jenna's startled eyes swiveled to his face.

He gave her a concerned smile. "The doctor advised plenty of rest. Is that not so, dear cousin?"

Quick to get the message in his eyes, she put the back of her hand to her forehead. "Oh, yes. Oh dear, I am quite exhausted."

Mrs. Tracey put down her cup with a tight smile. "Indeed. Mr. Tracey said only the other day you were sterling in Mrs. Blackstone's hours of need. Most creditable. Which is why…" She glanced at Gordon and pressed her lips together. "Enough said. A word to the wise is all that is needed." She rose to her feet.

Gordon got up and Jenna started to rise.

"It is all right, Jenna," he said with great solicitation, "I will see our guest to the door. So very kind of you to come all this way, Mrs .Tracey," he murmured, ushering her out of the room. "Much appreciated."

Behind him he was aware of Jenna's attempt to suppress her laughter.

Fortunately for him, the housekeeper was already in the hall with their visitor's wrap and, once their guest was garbed, opened the door with a flourish. And closed it behind her with a bit more force than was necessary. "Gossipy old crone."

Gordon raised a brow.

"That's what my mistress always called her," the housekeeper said. "And she knew people, Mrs. Blackstone did."

Yes, Mrs. Blackstone had been no one's fool. Gordon returned to the parlor.

Jenna was laid out on the sofa with her hands crossed on her chest.

Gordon's heart dipped. "Jenna? Are you all right?"

She sat up, grinning. "Practicing my die-away airs for my come out next season. Really, Gordon, you do tell some bouncers."

He grinned in turn and sat down. But the woman's poisonous words lingered in the air, reminding him of his duty. "Shall I drop Lady Merton a wee note telling her you will no be at home tomorrow?"

Jenna glared at him. "Certainly not. That would make us as bad at That Woman."

He grimaced. The things he had heard did not reflect well on Lady Merton. He just hadn't realized the source of gossip was his Annabelle. *His Annabelle?* She had never really been his. "They do say where there's smoke..."

"There's fire." Jenna wrinkled her nose. "What do you think?"

He didn't want to believe the rumors about Annabelle. He wanted to remember her as the girl he'd met years before. And yet...He took a deep breath. "I think people are innocent until proven guilty."

Jenna nodded approval. "I, too, think she deserves the benefit of the doubt."

The way his heart leaped at the knowledge that he would see her again clearly meant his reasons had not been completely altruistic.

# *Chapter Two*

Annabelle hesitated ON the doorstep. Was Mother right? Should she have sent a note pleading illness? The reason Mother had given to disguise her embarrassment after hearing the gossip about Annabelle that was circulating in Barton Sidley.

If Merton's family had their way, the scandal would continue to grow. For all that she had kept her word to him, everything her husband had promised had fallen apart. With Merton's will being contested before the courts and her personal jewelry all but gone, she and Mother were on the brink of destitution. Yet like her mother, Annabelle still had her pride. So she would visit her mother's neighbor to offer condolences.

The thought that Gordon might also be there had not influenced her one jot.

Firmly, she rapped on the door with its black crepe-adorned knocker, and braced for what might come when it was opened. The door swung back. The housekeeper, a pleasant plump-faced woman, stepped back without expression. With a quick indrawn breath Annabelle stepped over the threshold and handed the woman her calling card.

"Lady Jenna is expecting you, my lady. If you would follow me, please."

Perhaps Gordon would not be here. Annabelle's heart dipped. Why had she thought he might be? It was Lady Jenna she had come to see. Indeed, it would be better if he was absent. She would not have to deal with all the disturbing feelings rushing through her veins. Or suffer the painful squeeze of regret in her heart. Regret for something that never could have been. Her family had needed her to marry well. No matter the leanings of her heart, a charming but penniless second son would have been impossible.

The housekeeper opened a door to reveal Lady Jenna and Gordon in a small snug room that looked out over a walled garden and the forest beyond. A bright sunny room painted cream and white. Books, cushions and bric-a-brac were scattered about in comfortable disarray. On the sofa sat Lady Jenna. Annabelle had forgotten how tiny she was. Her smile was warm, lighting her green eyes, and the sunlight turned her hair to a fiery halo around her face.

Gordon rose from the adjacent armchair, his extraordinary blue eyes fixed on Annabelle's face. Flames in ice. Blatantly sensual. The heat of that look drew her in, warmed her skin and left her trembling and breathing hard.

A shock hit her hard. He knew about her past indiscretions. Someone had told him.

Color rushed to her face in a hot painful tide. Spine straight, she swept into the room. "Lady Jenna. Mr. McLaughlin. How kind of you to receive me."

She lifted her chin, refusing to acknowledge her awareness of him as a predatory male.

Lady Jenna bounced up off the sofa. "No. It was kind of you to call. May I offer you tea?"

Annabelle glanced at Gordon. His expression was now unreadable, but his eyes did not warn her away. "Yes, thank you. I must apologise for coming alone. Mother is unwell." Sickened by her daughter's reputation.

"Nothing serious I hope," Lady Jenna said. "I will send some of Aunt…" she swallowed. "Some of Aunt Blackstone's calf's foot jelly home with you. It works wonders on the constitution." Lady Jenna gestured to the sofa. "Come. Sit down beside me. I hope you do not mind that I decided we should take tea here rather than the drawing room, where it is dark and cold."

Annabelle glanced around at the worn comfort. "It is a charming room."

"And my aunt was not one for sitting around weeping over what cannot be undone," Lady Jenna said rather defiantly.

"No indeed," Annabelle agreed, sitting down beside her hostess, feeling like a fraud. Mother was right. She should not have come. But it would only make her look worse if she fled.

"Are you staying with your mother long?" Lady Jenna asked.

"A few days only," she said, her heart dipping as she recalled the weight of her worries back in Edinburgh. "And you?"

"I go to Lady Carrick," Lady Jenna said. "To prepare for my come out in the spring." She smiled. "It was delayed when my aunt took ill. Not that I minded. She was always so very good to me."

How wonderful it must be to look forward to the future with such unaffected happiness. "Do you go to Edinburgh or London for your Season?"

Lady Jenna smiled as she poured the aromatic brew into the cups. "Edinburgh, I believe. I need a husband right away. Until I am married, I cannot go home to Braemuir, and I have been away far too long." She gave a bright little smile. "The prospect of a fine estate and a title should hurry things along, don't you think?"

Annabelle's felt the stirring of compassion for the young woman, but what could she say? She had followed much the same path. "I am sure there will be many fine, eligible young men only too delighted to make you an offer."

She turned to Gordon. "And what about you, sir. Are you planning to set up your nursery?" There now, that sounded casual enough. The sort of thing a married woman might say to a young man with whom she held a passing acquaintance. Her breath sat like a hot hard lump in her throat as she awaited his answer.

"I am no married as yet, Lady Merton," he replied, his deep burr a gentle caress to her ear and his smile a delicious shiver down her spine. Nor do I expect to remain in Scotland for any length of time," he continued. "My business concerns are in America."

Not staying. She felt an unaccountable stab of disappointment.

"Yes," Lady Jenna said, deftly adding milk to the cups. "And now he is stuck waiting for repairs to his carriage, or we would have been on our way yesterday."

"The roads around here are abominable," he said.

"Then what is bad luck for you is good luck for me," Annabelle said lightly, hoping it sounded like formality and not a fervent truth. "For I would have missed you altogether." Again her gaze strayed to his face, to the strong bones of cheek and jaw and the piercing blue eyes. Their glances met and lingered, and she felt herself blushing all over again.

"Sugar?" Lady Jenna asked.

"One lump," she said, her voice breathless.

Having added the sugar, Lady Jenna handed Annabelle her cup. "I know you will have sugar, Gordon."

"As much as the cup will hold," he said with a shamefaced smile at his cousin.

"I see you still have a sweet tooth," Annabelle said, and winced as she realized she'd made it clear she remembered him all too well. He'd piled knob after knob of sugar in his tea at the assembly. She had teased him about it. And he had laughed. It was how their conversation had started. Then he'd asked her to dance. A country dance, but the way he'd looked at her had been enough to quicken her heart. To make her ignore her mother's warnings and steal outside to meet him. She had been lucky no one had caught them that night. Or perhaps not. If they had been caught, they would have had no choice but to marry. She kept her gaze fixed on her cup and stirred slowly,waiting for the sting in her cheeks to fade.

"Yes," he said.

She looked up startled. Confused.

He smiled then and it was the familiar boyish smile she'd seen too often in her dreams. She tried not to look at his mouth. To focus in on those finely carved lips that had brushed her own so long ago in a shadowy courtyard beside a fountain.

"Yes, I still have my sweet tooth," he murmured in that deliciously deep voice.

And she knew he wasn't talking about sugar. She sipped at her tea to ease the dryness in her throat, and turned to Lady Jenna, presenting her shoulder to Gordon, putting him out of the direct line of her sight so as not to be tempted to gaze at him like a mooncalf. "What will happen to this house when you leave?"

Lady Jenna shrugged. "I believe it is to be sold off. Mrs. Blackstone's brother-in-law inherits everything. He never wanted this house, but was quite happy to let her stay here as long as she wished."

Merton's relatives were not nearly so generous. "I wonder if he will be asking a high price?"

Lady Jenna looked intrigued. "Were you thinking of buying it then?"

It would be perfect for Mother. But with the settlement in doubt, that was out of the question. "Idle curiosity, I'm afraid. Mother likes to keep her finger on the pulse of what goes on in the village."

"Your father was sorely missed by everyone hereabouts."

"And Mrs. Blackstone was very kind to Mother after he passed away."

"She was a dear, wasn't she?" Lady Jenna said, and the brave facade seemed to waver. Her eyes misted and she pulled out a handkerchief. "Oh, dear. I do apologize. I am not usually such a watering pot."

Annabelle put down her cup. "Not at all. Your grief does your aunt great honor. Perhaps I may call on you again before you leave."

"We are leaving the day after tomorrow," Gordon said. "I am promised the carriage for then."

"And if it isn't convenient for you to call tomorrow, perhaps we will meet in Edinburgh next season, if you will be there?" Lady Jenna said.

Lady Carrick would never allow it, of course, but Annabelle smiled and nodded. "I shall look forward to it with pleasure." She rose to her feet.

Gordon also stood. "I see you walked here alone, Lady Merton."

Was that censure she heard in his voice? "Our maid stayed to attend my mother," she said calmly. "And besides, it is only a few steps from here to Ivy Cottage."

"I will walk you home."

The tone of command in his voice and the set of his jaw said he would not take no for an answer. Most likely he intended to use their time in private to warn her away from his family. And he would be in the right. She should never have suggested this call. Once she had left him at the post office, reason should have returned. She should have written with excuses, as Mother had advised. But it seemed where he was concerned Annabelle's willpower was lacking.

Just as it had been when she was a girl. The moment she had seen him, good sense flew out the window. Now it was time to face reality. "I am glad to accept your escort, Mr. McLaughlin." She couldn't do him too much harm in the time it would take him to walk her to her front door, and she would assure him she had no intention of drawing his cousin into her sphere.

With a smile, she leaned down and patted Lady Jenna's small hand. "All things pass in time," she said softly. "The pain eases and leaves only the happiest of memories."

Once more Lady Jenna's eyes glittered with unshed tears. "Thank you," she said huskily.

Gordon escorted Annabelle from the room.

He could not believe it. After all these years, he was strolling down a country lane in the sunshine with Annabelle's hand in the crook of arm, accompanied by the twitter of sparrows. Fortunately, it hadn't rained for days, and the rutted lane between the dry stone walls merely mired their footwear in dust.

Though if there had been puddles, he might have had an excuse to carry her over them. He glanced at her from the corner of his eye. Where he had been stunned by her beauty yesterday, today he could only admire her aplomb. Her dignity. At least his mind held that sort of admiration. Another part of him was occupied by the base urge to investigate the rumors of her wantonness.

And that disgusted him. She had been kindness itself to poor little Jenna, where he had been all fingers and thumbs. Tongue-tied when it came to offering comfort. Much as he had been when he had brought her to her aunt as a child.

His mind hadn't been on Lady Jenna then. The moment he saw Annabelle at that assembly, he'd been lost in a sea of desire.

When she slipped away from the ball to meet him in the courtyard, he'd been enchanted by her bravery. Her spirit of adventure. He remembered her laughter and his clumsy kiss as if it was yesterday. The hesitant brush of their lips. The way she had tasted on his mouth. The warmth and silkiness of her cheek beneath his trembling fingers. And the scent of her soap. He never smelled roses without thinking of Annabelle, he realized. Or the desperate ache of a young man for a first love.

He had never experienced those same heightened feelings again. Not for any woman he'd known. And while the pain of hearing she'd wed had dwindled over time, it was only now he realized an echo of it remained deeply buried. It was time to be rid of it.

"I can't believe it is five years since we met," he said, to break the lengthy silence.

She glanced up at him, shadows filling her expression. "We were so very young, weren't we?"

"Too young, I suspect." He inwardly mocked the recollection of how his body had ached for her for days. "You married soon after I left, I understand." In Boston, when he'd read the announcement in the Edinburgh paper, *The Scotsman,* he'd been angry as well as hurt. "I had no idea you were betrothed when we met." The stars in her eyes when she'd looked at him had led him down a whole other path.

"I wasn't," she said, her gaze fixed on the rutted road. "It was decided very quickly."

The breath left his body as if he had been punched in the gut. "Not because of me?"

Halting in her tracks, she looked up, a frown crinkling her brow. "No. Oh no. Please do not think it." She caught her bottom lip in her teeth as if trying to hold back words. Or trying to decide how much to tell him. "Father made a terrible mistake with some investments. Mr. Jenkins had need of a wife and, well…they came to an agreement." She paused, looking up at Gordon earnestly. "It seemed the perfect answer to our troubles."

As a second son with few prospects, he certainly would not have been the answer to anyone's financial troubles. Nor, despite his very real longing to do so, had he made her any kind of promise. In the optimism of youth, he'd thought they would have more time. Perhaps even that she would wait for him. "You subsequently married Merton?"

"He made a very generous offer."

Something Gordon could not have done then or now. "Jenkins did not leave you well settled?"

"His money went to his heir."

Was he mistaken, or did she sound a little bitter? It really was not his business. He shouldn't be asking such questions. And yet he couldn't stop himself. "What will you do now?"

Again she lowered her glance, looking at the ground as she walked, avoiding the worst of the ruts, giving him a view of the top of her bonnet. Pretty as it was, he preferred seeing her lovely face.

"I have not yet decided," she said finally, her voice low. "But I cannot stay here. Mama finds the gossip distressing."

A surge of protectiveness shot through him. His body tensed, as if preparing for battle. He fought the instinct to stand as her champion. Yet now that she had broached the subject, he could not let it lie there like a social faux pas everyone pretended not to notice. "What happened?"

Her gaze shot to his face. There was a slightly bitter twist to her lips. "Why ask, when you already know?"

"I know only what Mrs. Tracey related yesterday." He gentled his voice. "I prefer my information from the source."

Annabelle lowered her gaze again. "Believe me, you do not want to know the truth." She straightened her shoulders as if picking up a heavy burden, and met his eyes with a calm smile. "And here we are. It is time for me to bid you farewell and thank you for your escort."

The small stone cottage in front of them, with its white picket fence and carefully tended garden, was a far cry from the two-story manse beside the church her family used to occupy. Her mother had indeed come down in the world. But it looked well-maintained, and a profusion of yellow roses adorned a trellis around the front door. "If you will not stay here, where will you go?"

She sighed. "Back to Edinburgh."

A return to the life she knew. "I see."

"Do you?"

He looked down at that damned brim and its jaunty little flowers as once more she avoided his gaze. He had to admit he didn't see anything. "I am not sure what to say," he said stiffly, and she winced.

"Pleased don't be concerned," she said softly. "I won't presume on our acquaintance and trouble Lady Jenna when I am there."

"Annabelle," he said, annoyed with her and surprised by the husky rasp in his voice. "I meant no such thing. And I for one would like to see you again."

Astonishment filled her expression. But slowly, very slowly, a smile dawned on her face. "You are not afraid for your life, then?" This was the old Annabelle, the one who liked to tease.

He squashed the urge to laugh. "Should I be?"

She tilted her head and looked him up and down, amusement in her clear grey eyes. "No. I think a man of your size would have no difficulty fending me off, should I decide to attack you."

He recalled the vague accusation of poison waved

about by Mrs. Tracey, and pushed it aside. "Come for dinner. Tonight. Bring your mother."

The light in her face disappeared. "I must not. I should not have visited Lady Jenna today. I should have known the gossip would have reached the village. I would not have my problems tainting your innocent cousin."

"She will not care. I will tell her there is no truth to—"

"Oh, but you see there is always a foundation of truth to rumors." Annabelle shook her head wearily. "It will not do."

So it was at an end. She was going to walk out of his life again? Unfair. He was the one who'd left, called away on an errand for his father. Not that an offer from Gordon would have been acceptable. Nor was it now, with all his funds tied up in his investment. But he could not let her go. "And if I refuse to take no for an answer?"

"Will you follow me to Edinburgh?"

"If I must."

Her eyes danced with amusement. And a challenge. "Not a wise idea. For either of us, I think."

Reason had nothing to do with it. Passion did. Desire. It shimmered in the air. Sent tingles down his spine. Pumped hot blood through his veins. He clenched his fists to stop himself from hauling her up against his chest and kissing her till she succumbed to his will.

Without warning, she stepped inside the garden gate and pushed it closed between them. Effectively shutting him out.

She looked up at him with a brittle smile. "It was so

nice seeing you again, Gordon. I wish…" She shook her head. "Wishes can't change the past."

It wasn't much, that unspoken wish, but it was all that he needed. He easily vaulted the gate.

Startled, she stepped back. "What are you doing?"

"Seeing you to your front door, as is my duty."

Huffing out a breath, she turned and walked up the path. At the door she turned to face him. "Thank you for walking me home."

The scent of roses filled the air. The scent of Annabelle. He gazed down at her, felt himself falling into those lovely dove-gray eyes all over again. "Annabelle," he breathed.

"Gordon," she said softly. She reached up to touch his cheek with her gloved hand. He caught her fingers and brought them to his lips. Her face tipped up, her eyes watching him, drinking him in, her lips so close, so soft, so sweetly parted. Before he knew it, one arm was around her waist and the other hand cradling her nape. Secluded by roses, he dipped his head and kissed her. The feel of her satiny skin against his mouth only made him want more. Much more. And when she melted against him, he swept her mouth with his tongue, tasting her, wooing her with all the skill at his command.

By the time he let her go, they were both breathing hard. She pressed trembling fingers to her rose-tinted lips for a second. "Are you trying to ruin me further?"

He winced. "No. But I won't just walk away. Not this time. Not unless you insist."

Concern filled her face and he felt guilty, but he

would not let her go. Not yet. Not when he had only just found her again.

"I cannot deny I would like to hear about your adventures in America," she said wistfully. "To know more of your life."

"We owe each other that much," he said, pressing as hard as he dared. "Let me call on you."

She breathed a long sigh, a sound of defeat, as if she had been engaged in some battle with her own inclinations. "No. No calls. Mother would hate it. There is an inn beyond the village. The Bell. It lies some ways east of the village, off the main road. Arrange the private sitting room at the top of the stairs from the side door. The landlord will know. I will meet you there tomorrow after midnight, once Mother retires."

An assignation. The suggestion went straight to Gordon's groin. His mind emptied of rational thought. He could only stare at her.

"I can think of no other way. Is it yes or no, Gordon?"

"Yes," he managed to reply.

"Send word to my coachman if you change your mind," she said softly. "I trust him with my life." With a small dip of a curtsy, she opened the front door and disappeared inside.

And what would he say to her, when he had her alone? Gordon wondered. Would he really be able to reconcile this seductive woman with the girl he had kept frozen in time in his heart?

It seemed he would know soon enough.

# *Chapter Three*

The next evening, Annabelle hunched deeper into her hooded cloak. What on earth had she been about in agreeing to this assignation? Was she trying to recapture her youth, for goodness sake? Her innocence? It wasn't possible.

John Coachman and Betty, her maid, had made no bones about their disapproval when she explained her intention. But she did not doubt their loyalty for a moment. They had helped her under far worse circumstances and would not let her down.

It was the other servants who had gossiped about what had occurred the last night of Merton's life. Although they had never learned the half of it.

And so here Annabelle was, preparing to play the merry widow to the man she had always loved. Tears burned at the back of her throat as she made the admission she'd tried so hard to quell since the first moment she saw him in the village. She couldn't keep him, of course. It wouldn't be right. But didn't she deserve a little happiness after doing her duty to her family and both of her husbands? Some joyful memories to hug to herself?

Letting him go for a second time would be hard. But she had decided that one night in his arms was worth the ensuing pain. Her mother had always said she was stubborn to a fault. And having buckled under his pressure, she would see this evening through. No, not see it through. She would revel in it.

John pulled into the yard and helped her down. "Shall I see you in, my lady?"

"No, John. I can manage."

The frown on his face deepened. "It is not right you should take such risks."

Merton had hired John not only as coachman, but as her protector during his many absences. "There is no danger, John. I swear it." No danger for anyone. A widow did as she pleased, so long as she was discreet. And during her marriage to Merton Annabelle had learned to be the soul of discretion.

So why did her pulse race and her body tremble with doubt? Even her mouth was dry. Cowardice. She was afraid to take something she wanted for herself.

She stepped through the side door and softly climbed the stairs, which were lit by several iron sconces. The door at the top was ajar and she paused outside. Gordon was standing beside the hearth with a glass of wine in his hand. He looked up, saw her, smiled and came to greet her. He took her hands, gazing down into her face as if searching for something important.

"I wasna sure you would come," he murmured finally, drawing her into the room. "I heard the carriage, you understand, but did not look in case it was no you, after all."

She shook her head at him, laughing, feeling as giddy as the girl she had been when they first met. "I am not one to go back on a decision once it is made."

He gave her a considering look, as if wondering if there was something behind her words. Did he feel guilty about leaving all those years before? What had happened was not his fault or hers, it was merely life playing its ugly games.

"May I take your coat?" he asked.

"You may indeed," she said, and began unfastening the buttons.

He brushed her fingers away. "Let me help." He did so with practiced ease, untying her cloak, sliding it off her shoulders and throwing it over a chair. He tugged at her bonnet ribbons, but waited patiently while she removed it from her head. Clearly a man of experience, he knew better than to destroy a lady's coiffure. At least not at the beginning of the evening. The thought made her smile.

He drew in an appreciative breath. "You really are lovely."

Clearly a compliment designed to put her at ease. It seemed they had both learned a great deal in the intervening years.

She chuckled when she saw him frown at the frilly little cap that covered her crown. A nod to her widowhood. Not the kind of thing she had worn when they first met.

He led her to the settle beside the hearth and saw her comfortably seated. "May I offer you burgundy or sherry?"

"Burgundy, if you please." She glanced around the room, the warm glow of the fire and candles on paneled walls making it seem all the more cosy. And of course there was the other door. The door to the bedroom. Discreetly closed. "I hope you find the room to your taste?"

He handed her a glass of wine and sat down beside her, stretching out his long legs. "I do indeed."

She leaned back against the cushions, toasted him with her glass and took a deep swallow, letting the ruby liquid roll down her throat and take the edge off the nerves fluttering in her belly. "Tell me about America."

"It is hard to know where to start. It is a vast country full of opportunity for those willing to work hard."

"A lot of Scots have gone there."

"Not all of their own accord." He sounded a little grim.

"You did not wish to go?"

"I wasna thinking of me. I was thinking of a distant cousin. Drew Gilvry. It was because of his sudden disappearance I was despatched to fill the breech at short notice."

"Oh, I see." She had always wondered why he'd said nothing of his intentions to go abroad the day after they met. Not that it would have made the slightest bit of difference to her life. Once Jenkins made his offer, her path was set. For her family's sake. "But you did go willingly?"

"It was my duty to my family. Recently, I have ventured into business there on my own account."

"I can understand why you would," she said. "It feels good to take control of one's own life." She took another swallow of wine.

His eyes widened a fraction before a frown creased his brow. "Is that what you have done? Taken control?"

Oh, dear. How much had he heard? She gave him a bright smile. "I have indeed."

Silence fell between them. A silence charged with a tension fraught with sensations that tightened her body, and rippled across her skin. Calm as he appeared, there was something running beneath his surface that affected her deeply.

"You have lived in Edinburgh until now?" he asked.

Let him make of her history what he would. Perhaps it would change his mind about wanting to be here with her. "Being half-Scottish, I was soon accepted in Edinburgh society. Mr. Jenkins was a classics scholar at the university and well regarded. My second husband was high in society."

"You have children?"

"No."

His gaze shot to her face. She smiled calmly. Or she thought she had, until he put down his glass and took her hand in his warm grasp and stroked its back with his thumb. "Were they unkind to you?"

Oh, yes, he sensed something was wrong in her marriages. But then she and Gordon had been perfectly attuned from the moment they met. Understanding each other almost before any words were spoken. It had been uncanny then, and magical. Now it made her fear she might break her word. She gave a small shake of her head and smiled. "Not at all, though both were born of convenience."

His grip tightened, then slowly loosened. "It sounds soulless. I can understand why you found your entertainments elsewhere."

Was that a note of jealousy she heard in his deep voice? A traitorous twinge of excitement clenched within her body at the thought he might care deeply enough to feel jealous. Or was it a note of disapproval? A far more likely emotion, she decided. She held his gaze steadily, bravely, daring him to criticise. "Merton gave me free rein to do as I pleased."

Gordon's hand came to her cheek, and as light as a butterfly wing, brushed her jaw with his knuckles. "There is something you are not telling me. But I'll no press you. For what is past is over and done. It is the future I care about."

Shocked, she gasped. They could have no future. "For me, there is only the here and the now."

He frowned, but then bent his head and took her mouth in a scorching kiss.

She felt herself relax in his arms, let the bliss of his wooing lips carry her away, the way it had when she had been young and foolish. When she had thought the world was fair and kind.

And yet she trusted him. Even after all this time she trusted him as she would trust no other. It was an odd realization. Strangely freeing.

As she melted in his arms, Gordon could not have asked for a better response, or been more delighted with the encouraging warmth in her eyes. Even if he was a little disconcerted. He had to keep reminding himself she was just as worldly as he,and not the innocent girl of his youth.

Something for which he ought to be grateful.

Yet the idea was more than a little bittersweet. And he felt a sense of something precious lost.

Then her lips parted to his tongue and he swept her mouth, tasting her deeply, and all regrets faded into the heat of desire and the need to hold her close. He gathered her up, brought her onto his lap the better to plunder the warm sweetness of her mouth and to feel her breasts pressed against his chest.

She made no resistance. Quite the opposite. She tangled her tongue with his, artfully teasing and wooing his tongue with her own until his brain emptied of anything but the most base of urges. The need to get closer. To be skin to skin with a woman he desired over all others.

What a fool she would think him, if she knew.

The small sounds coming from the back of her throat, sounds of pleasure and encouragement, emboldened his hands. One wandered the slight span of her back, explored the bumps of her spine through the delicate fabric of her gown, traced the blade of her shoulder, the ridges of her ribs, while the other shaped the curve of her slender waist and found the swell of the underside of her breast.

Beneath his hands her ribs expanded and contracted, and the flutter of her heart was a live thing against his palm. But there was no fear here. Only longing.

Slowly, his hand drifted upward, cupping the firm flesh of her breast. Learning her shape, weighing the fullness, rubbing the pearled tip at its peak.

He groaned and broke their kiss, looking down into her flushed face, her lips damp and rosy from his mouth and curved in a smile of sensual delight.

"You are more beautiful than I ever remembered," he said softly, and knew it for a truth. She smiled at him so sweetly his heart caught. A painful little twinge.

She ran her fingers down his jaw. "Time has treated you well," she murmured.

It had, Annabelle realized. Maturity sat well on those broad, brawny shoulders. The man was far handsomer than the boy had ever been. As he smiled, looking pleased at her compliment, a dimple appeared in his cheek.

Ah, there he was. The boy she remembered. A little shy and a lot pleased with his daring. The boy she had kept close in her heart all these years. A treasure she had hoarded, never expecting to see him again.

Unbidden, hot moisture prickled at the back of her eyes. A hard lump formed in her throat. Such foolishness. Too feel the heartbreak of it now, after all this time, when she had never allowed it to hurt her before.

"Sweetheart?" he said, concern filling those lovely sapphire eyes.

She fought back the emotion and swallowed the lump with a laugh that sounded a little too husky. "Oh, Gordon. I am so glad to see you again after all this time."

"And I you," he said softly, rising effortlessly to his feet, while holding her in his arms and carrying her to the bedroom door.

A delicious little thrill went down her spine to take residence low in her belly. She reached up and pulled his head down, to press a kiss to his cheek, and whispered softly in his ear, feeling lighthearted. "It must have set you back a pretty penny to order these rooms."

He made a slight scoffing sound in the back of his throat and set her on her feet beside a large four-poster bed with the sheets already pulled back, waiting. For them. "Worth every penny, lass."

The hangings were crimson. The fire in the grate sent shadows dancing across the fabric, making it shimmer and waver. Or was it that surprising welling of emotion once again?

She spun around to face him, to throw her arms around that wall of chest, to make sure he was real and not just a dream.

He tipped her face up, with gentle fingers warm on the skin of her jaw. "Crying?" he asked softly.

"Tears of happiness," she choked out.

He cradled her cheeks in his hands, held her tenderly, his gaze searching her face. "You don't know how many times I wished I had taken you with me the night we met. Whisked you away." He let out a sound that was half groan, half laughter. "I had no money. No way to give you what you deserved, but if there had been anything, any way, I would ha' done it."

She caressed his cheek, his jaw, and smiled. "This is not the time for regrets. We have tonight. Let us make the most of it. I must be home before morning."

A sound like a growl came from his throat. His hungry gaze raked down her body. "Only a fool would let an offer like that go to waste."

A laugh escaped her. "And you are not that."

His hands tore at his cravat. "I am not." He unwound it and tossed it aside, and went to work on his coat.

She untied the bow at the neck of the dress she had chosen so carefully for tonight. Held only by the gathering at the neck and the ribbon tied high beneath her breasts. It opened with the smallest tug at the ties. Smiling, she let the gown slither to the floor and puddle at her feet. Beneath it she wore nothing but her fine lawn shift, her stays and her stockings held above her knees by garters embroidered with roses.

He stared at her in awe. His admiration warmed her from the inside out.

"May I?" he asked in his deep murmur. He reached above her head. She drew back, startled.

"Your hair," he said, looking apologetic. "It was down that night we met. I have never forgotten how glorious it looked around your shoulders."

A small laugh escaped her at the thought he had remembered such a detail. "By all means." She reached up to remove the cap and her pins.

He got there first. "Let me." He freed the little scrap of lace first, tossing it aside, then worked his fingers through her hair, pulling out pins, massaging her scalp as he went. She wanted to purr like a cat as, tress by tress, it tumbled down her back.

He stepped back to admire his handiwork with heavy-lidded eyes. "Just as I remembered," he said with a satisfied nod. He arranged it over her shoulders, patting it in place, stroking it over her breasts. "Perfect."

Laughing, she raised a brow. "You are falling behind," she said, plucking at his waistcoat. With the ease of long practice, she unbuttoned the offending garment and he slipped it off. She then undid the buttons of his shirt and freed it from the waistband of his pantaloons. He pulled it off over his head, exposing all that lovely male flesh to her gaze. Sculpted muscles. A mat of dark hair on his chest, a swirl of it around his beaded nipples and a trail down the ridged hardness of his belly.

Awed, she could only gaze at what she saw. He was a vision of perfection. So very male. So very large. And if the rigid length bulging at the front of his skintight nether garment was anything to go by, so very ready for her.

Moisture dampened the apex of her thighs. She licked her suddenly dry lips. Her insides fluttered, while deep inside her, nerves began to tremble and quake. He was just too beautiful. And she could not keep him.

Perhaps this was going to be the biggest mistake of her life. It wasn't too late to say no. To leave. In disarray to be sure, but not broken. Not quite.

He was a true gentleman, and if she said no, he would let her go.

But she would regret it for the rest of her life.

She forced a bright smile, but could not quite look him in the eye, could not let him see her fear. "Do you think you can manage the rest yourself?"

"Annabelle," he murmured.

The sound of her name on his lips had the ring of an angels' choir.

"Annabelle," he said again, more softly, barely a breath of air passing her cheek. "Sweetheart. Darling. Don't cut me off."

Numbly, she gazed up at him. And every last wall she'd built these past many years crumbled around her. "Gordon. Oh, Gordon."

His name was a cry from her heart.

"Annabelle. Little one." He bent and lifted her onto the bed, laying her gently down on the pristine white sheets as if she were a delicate piece of spun glass. He stripped down to his skin in a few efficient movements and lay beside her on the bed, one hand supporting his head while the other stroked her shoulders, the rise of her breasts beneath the curtain of her hair, and dipped into the valley between. She closed her eyes and drifted on the whisper-soft sensations of his touch.

His lips on her throat, his tongue tracing the veins in

her neck, swirling in the dips formed by her clavicle. Tasting. Learning. His scent invaded her nostrils. Gordon. Wine. The dark notes of a male aroused. Her insides tightened.

Gently, his fingers drew down the fabric of her shift, easing her breast free of her stays, exposing the furled peak to his gaze. His tongue licked, his teeth grazed and tormented the sensitive bud, until she rose up on her elbows, encouraging him to take her into his mouth, to give her the pleasure she longed for.

He came up on his knees, supporting her weight. "Let us have you out of this, shall we?" he murmured softly as his clever fingers worked at the strings of her stays. Finally released, they fell away, and she helped him pull her shift over her head. When she reached to untie her stockings, his hand covered hers. "Leave them. I find them…stirring."

Her insides clenched as his thick, heavy shaft pulsed agreement with his words. A bead of moisture formed at its tip. She smoothed the milky moisture over the surrounding hot, tight dark flesh with her thumb, and then bent to kiss the velvety softness, her palm circling the shaft, feeling the heat and the pound of his blood in time to her own beating heart.

Licking and kissing the salty-tasting silken head, outlining its contours with the tip of her tongue, was more heady than wine. She then took him deep into her mouth.

He groaned, his hand clenching at the sheets beside her head. "You'll be the death of me," he muttered hoarsely. He gently but insistently forced her away. "I'm no ready to meet my end," he whispered against her lips. "Not yet. Not without you."

He kissed her deeply, gently pressing her back onto the pillows, nudging her legs apart with his knee and kneeling between her thighs.

There was a look of deep concentration on his face, a frown between his brows, a grimace on his face. He looked like a man in pain. She smoothed the hair back from his face, rubbed at the crease with her thumb. He caught her hand in his and brought it to his lips, kissing one knuckle at a time, from smallest to largest, until he reached her thumb. He drew it into his mouth and sucked.

Her insides pulsed. Her hips shot up off the bed at the tearing pleasure that rushed to her core. She shivered and shook in the aftermath.

The man was skilled. A maestro. And she his willing instrument.

He encircled each of her wrists with a finger and thumb and brought them down either side of her head. Pinning her to the bed. She undulated her hips, letting him know what she wanted and where.

Clearly delighted, he grinned down at her. "Not yet, my love."

*My love.* If only she could be his love. She could. For one night only. That was all she could allow. One night. Anything more and she would lose her way. Since she saw him last she had come to a decision about how to move forward. At first she'd resisted, but there really was no other way.

She gazed at his dearly beloved face and felt her smile grow and grow. "Soon, though," she said, laughing up at him.

"Aye, soon," he agreed, and lowered his head to worship the nipple he had yet to taste. And the underside of her breasts. And each rib. He delved his tongue into her navel, slowly moving backward between her parted legs, stretching out his arms so that her hands were stilled pinned by his gentle grasp. Like a virgin sacrifice.

She felt a desperately arousing sense of helplessness, being staked out by this amazingly virile man. Because despite the gentleness of his hold, Annabelle had no doubt that she was completely and utterly at his mercy.

A sensual shudder rippled through her body.

He kissed the curls at the apex of her thighs. Inhaled deeply, as if he would carry her scent with him for always.

When they separated.

As they must. He had a future that did not include her. And nor should it.

She lifted her shoulders and glanced down the length of her body, thrilling to the sight of his dark head between her legs, aching in her core as his tongue parted the folds of her feminine secrets and licked delicately. His tongue flicked and delved deep, searching for the tiny budding center. He found it and suckled.

She shattered. Wave after wave of pleasure rolled through her veins.

He released her wrists and raised up over her, his eager shaft dark with blood.

"Yes," she said, smiling through the hot red mist of pleasure. "Now, Gordon. Take me now." She would remember this, for always.

# *Chapter Four*

Gordon gazed down on her beautiful face. This was his Annabelle. Life had torn them apart as little more than children, and chance had brought them back together. Fate had taken a hand. And he was more than glad.

He rose above her, his loins on fire with the need to claim her as his own. And heaven help him, his need was hard to control. Base desires and urges had him by the throat, squeezing all thought, all vestiges of civility from his being. Leaving only one instinct. She was his mate. His woman.

He drove into her slowly, sensing in her little movements beneath him the angles and touches that gave her the most pleasure. Holding himself back, by little more than a soul-deep longing to bring her with him into the abyss.

Again and again he offered himself in the way of a male to a female, giving all of himself. Driving into her body, until he could hold back no longer. Until everything that was in him must break apart. In wonder and thankfulness, he felt her rise to meet him, felt the silken softness of her hot core tighten around him, pulling him deeper, cleaving flesh to flesh until he felt the intertwining of their souls.

She shattered again. Her inner muscles gripping and pulsing around his rock hard shaft, stroking him, as she cried out her pleasure.

Sensual torment threw him into a hot and blissfully overwhelming death. His climax rocked him to the core. Left him splintered in a thousand pieces. It lasted hours and was over far too soon.

Breathing hard, he dropped his forehead to hers, somehow managed to kiss her lips and lift himself clear, before collapsing into warm welcoming sleep, with her head pillowed on his shoulder and his arms holding her close.

Gordon awoke with a jerk at a sound at his side. A soft little sound of contentment. Her. Annabelle. A feral pride filled him.

She stretched. "That was delicious." She turned her face and kissed the rise of his breast above his nipple, where the skin was naked of hair. Nothing overtly sexual, but it warmed him inside. Filled an empty place in his chest with tenderness.

"Aye," he said, and kissed the top of her head while his fingers stroked the tresses that tumbled over her shoulder. "You are amazing."

She lay lax against him. This was what he had been missing all these years. Peace. Companionship.

A sense of coming home. With Annabelle.

He drew her closer, tucking her against his side where she belonged.

She pulled away. “I have to go.”

Her quickness caught him off guard. Unwillingly, he let her slip free of his embrace and sit up.

He rose up beside her, once more mesmerized by the way her hair flowed over her breasts in a toffee-colored tumble of waves. He wound a strand around his fingers just to feel their silk against his skin. “When will I see you again?”

Her head whipped around. “Ouch.”

She clutched at her scalp and he released his grip with a wince of apology. “Sorry.”

“There can be no again,” she said, moving away from him. “Now where is my shift?”

The pain at her rejection was unexpectedly sharp. He caught her upper arm to get her attention as she rummaged through the tumbled sheets. “Cannot, or you do not want to?” Neither was acceptable. Not now.

Eyes wide, she stared at him. “Gordon,” she breathed. “It is not possible.” She swallowed. “Much as I would like it.”

A sop to his dignity? He clung to his calm. “Why is it not possible?” The hurt inside him made his voice harsher than he intended. “Got another noble husband lined up, have you?” The moment he spoke the jealous words, and she flinched, he wished them unspoken.

Her face paled. Her chest rose and fell in an uneven breath. “Another victim, you mean?” A bitter smile twisted her lips. “Of course. Let me go.”

He let his hand drop. "Annabelle, I'm sorry. I didna mean..."

Her eyes misted for a moment. Or did they? Now they were clear and bright and hard. "No need to apologize. You are right. My plans are set. My web woven. If you will excuse me."

For all her brave words, he knew in lashing out in his own pain he'd struck an underhanded blow. "Annabelle. Wait."

Ignoring him, she scooted to the edge of the bed, leaning over to rescue her shift from the floor and presenting him with a lovely view of her delectable bottom.

He bit back a groan and focussed. She was slipping though his fingers like quicksilver. "If this is about Merton, you never told me what happened. Don't I deserve to know?"

Her lips parted in shock. She pulled her shift over her head, veiling her expression, but not hiding her lovely form. "No." She wrapped her stays about her and presented her back. "If you would be so good as to lace me?" She looked over her shoulder. "It is no one's business but my own."

Damn. Damn. He began threading the tapes. Something had happened to change her from the girl she'd been to the woman she had become. But if she didn't trust him enough to confide in him...The idea of her not trusting him hurt, but he'd not exactly shown himself to be a knight in shining armor tonight.

The pain around his heart spread outward. The emptiness inside him returned, deeper, more impenetrable that before. She didn't want him. And he would not attempt to force her to stay. He let go his breath, tied off the bow and leaned back against the headboard. "Then dinna let me keep you." If his tone sounded a little grim, he couldn't help it. It was how he felt.

She'd hurt him. Annabelle felt it in the air. A heaviness. She glanced at him from the corner of her eye. Saw the tightness around his mouth and the hard set of his jaw.

It wasn't her secret to tell. It saddened her to think that if he thought of her at all after tonight, his recollection would not be kind. He'd more than likely assume the gossip he'd heard about her were true. Knowing she had caused him pain hurt her, too. "I'm sorry."

"What have you to be sorry for?" he asked.

She jumped. Had she spoken aloud? "I should not have..." What? Encouraged his attentions? Given in to her wicked desires? She could see from his face that anything she said would only make matters worse. "Tonight was a mistake." She shrugged. It was the best she could do.

She stepped into her gown. It seemed she needed his help once more. She turned her back, saw him in the mirror as he realized her need. Their gazes clashed, his stormy, hers apologetic.

He rose from the bed, gloriously naked and completely unconcerned. She could not help watching the way he moved, the powerful grace, the confidence, the lovely maleness of him, the firming of his shaft under her gaze.

She lowered her lashes. Pretended not to notice.

He set to work on the fastenings.

Her shoulders slumped beneath the weight of her past. She hadn't realized how heavy a burden it would be. But then she'd never expected to see Gordon again. He'd been her dream, her Prince Pharming. The man in the flesh was so much more than her girlish recollections. Hurting him was the last thing she had wanted.

His fingers stilled. She looked up and saw him watching her in the glass. "I don't believe it," he said. "I don't believe the rumors. Why won't you trust me with the truth?" Anger carved stern lines in his face. The anger of a man betrayed.

Something inside her tore. A fountain of emotions bubble up through the gashes. Hope. Sadness. And the love she'd always carried for this man deep in her heart.

Knowing she'd put that look on his face made the ripping in two that much worse. "The truth is not mine to tell," she said, her eyes begging for understanding.

"Then whose is it?"

She closed her eyes briefly. "Please, Gordon."

A soft groan broke from him. He turned her around in his arms, looking down into her face. The effort of holding back her tears made her shake. "I really am sorry," she choked out.

"Hush," he murmured, stroking her back, rocking her gently. "You don't have to tell me if you don't want to."

Not want to? If only she could. To trust anyone with such a dark secret would be beyond foolish. What man would understand? Yet if she could not trust him, what was left to her? Perhaps she could tell him some of it, without breaking her promise. So he would not leave here thinking her completely despicable.

She took a deep breath. "My first marriage solved my father's most pressing debts. I thought there was a settlement for me, too, but it was an either-or situation, I discovered later. I was destitute when Jenkins died."

Gordon made a sound of sympathy. Swept her up off her feet and carried to the large chair by the fire, where he settled her on his lap. "That is better. Now, continue."

She felt safe in his arms. Secure. Protected. She forced herself not to snuggle against him, fearing he might change his mind when he heard the rest of the story.

"Shortly after I came out of mourning, I met Merton. He was handsome. Charming. Witty. And above all, very rich. All one could wish for in a husband."

"It was a love match?"

She tamped down her inclination to laugh. "No. Though at first I did think he was smitten. And I liked him. I thought we would deal well together. Start a family."

"But something went wrong?"

He must have heard the longing, the hope she'd had for children. She brightened her voice. Tried to sound calm, not bitter, though there was some of that in her heart for the way Merton had used her without her consent. "He was not unkind. He just never came to me at night." She shifted away from Gordon, trying to read his expression. It told her nothing. "After many nights of wondering, I could only presume he had a lover. Someone he cared for deeply."

Gordon stroked her back. "Then why marry you?"

Her fingers played with a fold in her skirt as she tried to decide what to say. How to say it. "His lover was not free to wed him."

Gordon cursed softly. "Playing fast and loose with another man's wife, then?"

Annabelle let the question slide. "At first I was angry. I took a lover. I hoped jealousy might bring him back to me. Instead, he seemed pleased. Almost relieved. It was horrible. Demeaning. In my anger, I sought more men. Trying to shock him, I think. Instead, I shocked the world. And still he continued as before, meeting his lover in secret. Creeping from the house late at night. Every night. I finally faced him with it and he admitted it was true."

"He should never have married you."

"Oh no. I needed that marriage. My situation was desperate. Without it Mother and I would have starved. Once Merton and I came to an honest understanding, we rubbed along pretty well. He was always generous and settled a good part of his fortune on me so I would never have to worry about money again." It had all seemed so simple, that night he'd revealed the truth. "Unfortunately, his family are contesting his will." She shuddered. "And accusing me of doing away with him for his money."

Saying it aloud was like a large cold rock landing on her chest. Fear.

"But you didna'."

It was not a question. His faith in her was heartwarming. Strengthening. She shook her head. "No. I didn't. There were circumstances, however…." The injustice of it all caught at her breath. Brought a hard lump high in her throat. Tears of anger and frustration. But she had given Merton her word she would never reveal his secrets, in exchange for the money he had settled on her, and because over the years she had grown to love him. Like a brother.

And he had kept his word. The will had revealed that the settlement he had made on her was vast. It was his heir who was making things difficult. Annabelle took a deep, calming breath. "Still, Merton was not terribly old and his family are suspicious about his death."

And that was as close to the truth she dare go, and still keep to her promise.

"What will you do?" Gordon asked.

She shrugged. "The coroner has declared it was death by natural causes."

"So you have nothing to worry about except gossip?"

She sighed. "Without the settlement, I have nothing. Less. I went into debt to pay the lawyer to plead my case, but it could go on for years, and I have no more credit."

A small hope flickered to life in Gordon's heart. A tiny spark. He kept his voice cool. "How will you manage?"

"I'll have to marry again, I suppose."

She spoke matter-of-factly, almost cheerfully, but

something inside him knew it was all a front. The spark of hope winked out. "You'll marry for money."

"I don't have a choice. Mother's rent is due in a month."

"So once again you will shoulder the responsibility."

She shrugged.

"Do you want to be married again?" It was painfully hard to ask the question calmly. Difficult to hide his longing.

"My wants have nothing to do with it."

The urge to offer himself in marriage was overwhelming. He wanted her and this was the way he could keep her. But he couldn't do it. He could not bear the thought of her marrying him out of necessity. He wanted so much more than that. And if he could not have more, he would prefer nothing but to be of assistance.

"How much money is required?"

She sat up, staring at him. "To fight the settlement? A fortune." She waved a hand. "And I might not win."

He did not have a fortune. "How much do you need to live? You and your mother."

"Not much, if we were careful, I suppose. Two hundred pounds a year would meet our needs. That is what I tried to negotiate with Merton's family, a compromise. They must have seen I was desperate, because that's when they began pressing the authorities to investigate Merton's death."

Two hundred pounds a year. It would take more than half of what Gordon had saved these past five years to produce such a sum annually. It would leave him without sufficient funds to follow through on the purchase of the ship. Leave him working for his father. Something he had come to abhor, as he realized just how far his father was prepared to go to increase the wealth in his coffers.

"I will make the arrangement first thing in the morning." It was the only way he could live with himself after hearing her story.

She pushed away from him to look at his face. "What are you saying?"

"I am saying I will set up an annuity for you."

She leaped from his lap, her face pale, her hands wrapped around her waist. "You want me to become your mistress."

His stomach fell away. But why would she not think that? He had dallied with her this night. He had never once spoken of wanting more. And now it was too late to do so. Because she would see it as her duty. "It is a gift."

Her eyes were wary. "I don't understand. Why would do such a thing? You must want something."

He wanted her to be happy. To be safe. To be able to marry where she willed for once. The thought she might choose someone else was a dagger to his heart. "For old time's sake, Annabelle. A gift. Nothing more."

The shadows in her eyes fled. There was hope in her face. "You really mean it?"

He forced himself to breathe around the pain in his heart. The pain of knowing he would never see her again after tonight. And yet there was a sort of quiet satisfaction in knowing he had done something that meant she did not have to marry if she did not want to. "I mean it." He glanced at the clock on the mantel and forced himself to smile. "What time did you say your coachman would expect you?"

"Oh, heavens. He is probably out there now." Her face softened. "I don't know how to thank you for this."

"Then don't," he said softly. "I don't need any thanks." It was enough to have held her for one night in his arms, and to know he had done something to make her happy.

Something glittered in her eyes. Tears?

"Annabelle," he murmured.

She flung her arms around his neck. "Oh, Gordon." She kissed his lips and they clung together for a moment. He felt her warmth, and her soft curves against him, and in that brief moment he tried to memorise every sensation, every inch of her before he let her go.

She looked up at him. "Will I see you again?"

He didn't know what would be more painful, seeing her again and knowing she did not love him, or not seeing her at all. "Likely not," he said gruffly.

"No," she said, turning away. "No, of course not."

He frowned at the odd tone in her voice. Glimpsed her expression in the mirror before she moved away toward the door. "What do you mean, of course not?"

She looked over her shoulder, surprise in her eyes and a bitter twist to her mouth. "I was wrong to visit your cousin yesterday. I don't blame you for refusing to have any more to do with me, knowing my story."

"Refusing?" He choked on the word. "What the hell are you talking about?"

"My reputation. You must know what the society ladies call me."

Stung by her accusation, he glared at her. "You are wrong, lass. That is not why I said we should no meet again. I want you to be free to marry whom you please, when you please, rich or poor. If you must marry, find a good man this time."

He pulled on his clothes and strode to the door and opened it, gesturing for her to precede him so they could collect her outer raiment from the other chamber.

As she passed in front of him, she looked up. "A good man?"

"Yes," he muttered, trying not to inhale her scent or to look at her mouth as she smiled at him. It was far too tempting a mouth. He wanted to kiss her. To make her melt into him. To tell her…But then she would feel obligated. And he could not bear that.

"There is no better man than you, Gordon."

He stared at her, drowning in her secrets. "I do not want your gratitude."

"It is not gratitude."

"What else would it be?"

She took a deep breath and paused, then shook her head as if changing her mind about what she would say. "Then ignore it, if you wish. But it is there all the same."

His heart stilled, then stumbled into an unsteady rhythm. He closed his eyes briefly, and when he opened them she was still looking up at him. "I do not want to lose you," he said, his voice a low rasp. "I love you. All these years, I regretted not saying so that night. But I didna have the right. I was young. I had no means of supporting a wife. And when I heard you had married…" He swallowed. "Well, I thought perhaps it was nothing but youthful attraction. But somehow I never found another woman who touched my heart the way you did."

"And here was me, marrying one husband after another." Her voice had a sharp edge. She picked up her cloak.

He didn't want her to go. Not when he had the feeling there was something going on. Something she wasn't telling him. "What choice did you have?"

"None." She shook her head. "None at all. But there were other men. Too many to recall. They were my choice. But none of them ever filled the emptiness I felt after you left."

Finally, the heart of the matter. Relief swamped him. Made him reckless. He caught her and swung her around. "Marry me." The words were out before he could think about it.

The way her eyes sparkled for a moment made him think she would say yes. Then she averted her face. "It wouldn't be right."

"Why not?"

She kept her face turned away. "My reputation. I wish I was not so tainted by it all, but I am. I shouldn't even be taking your money. Indeed, I should refuse it. I must.

I don't deserve that you should help me. I…" She broke off with something that sounded like a sob.

Heart in his throat, he lifted one hand to her jaw, gently turned her face so he could look into her eyes, and saw pain. "You what, Annabelle? What? Tell me."

She blinked. A tear clung to her lashes, sparkling in the light from the candles. "I love you too much to let my mistakes spoil your life."

"You love me." He felt as if fireworks had exploded inside his chest. Pain. Joy. Light. "Are you saying you love me?"

"Too well. I should not have come here tonight. Telling you my troubles. It wasn't right." She tried to pull away.

"Sweetheart. Beloved. Stop." With a shaking hand he brushed away the tears from her cheeks. "I gave you the money freely. So you could choose the life you want. Whether it was with me or someone else. But Annabelle, you no longer have a choice." He could not keep the possessive note from his voice. "You say you love me. Therefore, you will marry me, for I, too, have loved you all this time." The words surprised him. A little. But they came from the depths of his being and he knew them for truth. "I loved you the first moment I saw you. I admit I have not lived like a monk, my darling, but I have never for a moment felt for any women what I feel for you."

She collapsed against him as if her limbs had suddenly become too weak to support her weight, and he held her, gladly. Gradually her breathing calmed and she steadied. She gazed up at him and there was wonder in her face. And the love he'd seen that long-ago starlit night. "Are you sure?" she whispered.

"Aye, love. I am sure. Marry me and come to America. We'll start afresh. It has only ever been you, *leannán*. Always. Come away with me, my love."

And she melted against him. Relaxed in his arms, trust a shining, glittering thing between them. Threw her arms around his neck and kissed his lips. Finally, he could bear to break away from her and look into her face. He stroked her glorious mane of hair, gazing down into her lovely eyes. "Let us forget the past and together forge the future."

She hesitated and his gut clenched. "Before you make up your mind, there is one thing I have to tell you. About Merton. The reason the authorities are investigating his death."

Ice ran through Gordon's veins at the fear in her voice. "I don't care what you have done, lass. We will go to America, and hang the authorities."

A small smile curved her lips, but the worry remained in her eyes. "I trust you to tell no one this."

Trust. That he liked. And he wanted to shoulder her troubles. He nodded.

"Merton's lover's name was Albert."

Shocked, Gordon stared at her. "Your husband was…"

"Merton was good to me. I won't hear a word against him. Nor will I expose him to ridicule."

Loyal to a fault. She said she had loved the man like a

brother. Gordon wanted her love and loyalty, too. Badly. "It will be as you wish."

She gave him a grateful smile. "Merton died in Albert's bed. The poor man could have been arrested. Hung. But he didn't care about that. It was the stain to Merton's character that had him in tears when he came to beg my help. I had my servants bring Merton home. I think we were seen. There is no proof of a crime, but Merton's family are furious that I sold the jewels he gave me to fight them. They will do their best to find some way to hurt me."

Gordon had sworn to put the past behind them, and so they would. "Verra well. Then let us make use of that coachman of yours and find a priest to wed us right away. And then, as soon as I have safely delivered Lady Jenna to Carrick, we catch the first ship to America."

A worried look crossed Annabelle's face. "And my mother?"

He thought about it for a moment. So it would take longer to achieve his plans. With Annabelle at his side, he didn't care how long it took. "There is a man I know who might be persuaded to go into partnership wi' me. To make up the shortfall. So she can either come with us or she can stay in her cottage. Whatever she decides, I will support her financially."

"You would do that for me?" Annabelle seemed almost astonished.

"My dear heart, I would do anything for you."

This time the love shone from her eyes, bright and pure and clear. "And I for you."

He grinned at her. "First we marry, then, my own dear heart, I will prove just how much I love you."

He kissed her soundly and knew he had finally found exactly what he had always needed. Annabelle.

* * * * *

# RUNNING INTO TEMPTATION

Amanda McCabe

RUNNING INTO TEMPTATION
is part of Amanda McCabe's mini-series

*Bancrofts of Barton Park*

Look for these novels available from
Mills and Boon® Historical Romance:

THE RUNAWAY COUNTESS
RUNNING FROM SCANDAL

**Other books by Amanda McCabe**

THE TAMING OF THE ROGUE
TARNISHED ROSE OF THE COURT
BETRAYED BY HIS KISS

**And in**
**Mills & Boon® Historical *Undone!* eBooks**

UNLACING THE LADY IN WAITING
ONE WICKED CHRISTMAS
AN IMPROPER DUCHESS
A VERY TUDOR CHRISTMAS

**And in**
**M&B Regency *Castonbury Park* mini-series:**

A STRANGER AT CASTONBURY

# *Prologue*

Melanie Harding struggled to climb up the slope of the hill, holding on to her bonnet as the wind tried to snatch it away. Nature was really terribly horrid, especially to someone like her who had always lived in towns with paved roads and noisy lanes. She never would have thought it, but she even missed pokey, stuffy old Bath! Even *that* was better than living in such a tiny village, with such a dull old uncle.

Melanie sighed as she caught at her skirts, whipped around by the wind. Once she really had thought Bath a narrow, quiet place, especially with those tiny rooms she'd shared with her mother, the evenings at card parties and sipping tea at the assembly rooms. But now she knew what "narrow" really was, when she had no friends at all.

She stopped on the green slope of the hill and closed her eyes, hearing her mother's voice in her mind again as Melanie had tried to stop her from throwing all her clothes into a trunk.

*"Why must I go there?"* she had cried, snatching at

her spencers and shawls, trying to keep her mother from sending her away. Her mother had been all Melanie had since her feckless father died when she was a child, leaving them so poor, so alone.

*"You know very well why,"* her mother had said shortly, as she kept on packing. *"Because no one there will ever have heard of Captain Whitney and your unfortunate behavior. Your uncle the admiral will keep a close eye on you."*

Melanie sighed. The Captain Whitney thing *had* been unfortunate, but surely that was his fault, not hers. She had only believed him when he said his pretty words of love and devotion, read his tender poems, and she'd thought that her dreams were coming true at last. That a handsome officer was rescuing her from their impoverished life.

How could she have known that those poems were copied from a dusty old book by someone called Marlowe—or that Captain Whitney's promises were just as false? That he was like her father, like so many other men. Selfish and careless.

Captain Whitney, in addition to looking handsome in his red coat, had a good income and respectable connections to a viscount's family. If all had gone as he'd promised, her mother would have been ecstatic. But Melanie had been deceived, and now she was being punished for it, being sent to live with her elderly uncle in a tiny village in the middle of nowhere.

Thank goodness for Mrs. Smythe, Melanie thought as she continued her path up the hill. At least she had *one* friend here. Mrs. Smythe knew about fashion and the newest dances, even though she herself was enceinte and couldn't dance for several more months. She would invite Melanie to tea at her cozy village house, where they would sit by the fire to look at fashion papers and share romantic novels.

Everyone else there seemed too serious to be interested in fashion. They never even laughed at all! And at least Mrs. Smythe seemed glad to have a friend, too. Melanie had been feeling all too rejected since her mother sent her away. Mrs. Smythe also had a handsome brother, who was a widower. A brother with a fine estate and a very good income. Sir David Marton.

Melanie reached the top of the hill and turned to look toward Sir David's house at Rose Hill. Its gray stone walls rose against the rolling green fields, its windows sparkling in the sun. It was a pretty enough place, with Palladian columns and rounded towers. It could use a bit of renovation and decoration, of course, but that was what a wife was for. Melanie could certainly settle for being Lady Marton of Rose Hill. Then she would have a home for herself and her mother forever, a home no one could take from them.

The fact that Sir David was reasonably good-looking and smelled nice, not an old, balding man with gout like her uncle's retired old navy cronies, made the idea palatable. But, oh, Sir David was so serious! So quiet and dull, buried in books and work. Not like Captain Whitney had been…

Melanie scowled at the thought. Captain Whitney had

turned out to be a false scoundrel, just as all men surely were. The sparkling, dizzy feelings she'd got when he danced with her were evidently just as false. She had to be sensible now. Sir David was the best chance she'd had in a long time. He was a respectable, established gentleman and she did not care about him too much, so he could not hurt her. She could not let this chance go.

Suddenly tired, and fed up with the wind catching at her skirts, Melanie ran back down the hill toward the road. Her uncle would be waking from his nap soon, and she would have to read to him from the naval reports until dinnertime. She turned back to the village, thinking maybe she could take a bit of tea at Mrs. Smythe's before she had to go back to her uncle's stuffy, overheated house. As she strolled along the deserted lane, all she could hear was the whine of the wind. Until suddenly she heard another sound, the rumble of hooves pounding on gravel behind her and coming on fast!

She peered back over her shoulder, holding on to the straw brim of her bonnet, to see a large, gleaming black horse barreling down on her. It was suddenly so close she could see the sheen of sweat on the beast's flanks and the capes of the rider's greatcoat flying around him like wings.

Terrified, she screamed and dived toward the hedgerows, sure she would be trampled by the hooves. She tripped and fell into a mud puddle, soaking her pelisse. She wanted to sob with fear and frustration. What *else* could go wrong in her life?

"Are you quite all right, miss?" a man shouted. "I am so terribly sorry. I thought no one was around here."

Melanie looked up to see the greatcoated man swooping down on her. He swept off his wide-brimmed hat and for an instant she was dazzled by the halo of sunlight around him. She blinked and saw that he really was quite angelic-looking. Dark, coppery-blond hair tumbled in poetic waves over his brow, and his eyes were a deep, warm chocolate-brown set in a face that looked as if it must have been carved by a master sculptor, all strong jaw and straight, aristocratic nose.

Had she hit her head when she fell? Surely she was caught in some kind of dream. *No one* in the village looked like that.

"Are you injured?" he said, his voice rough with concern.

"N—no," Melanie gasped. "I do not think so." She turned her fascinated gaze away from him to try to check if she was hurt, but she could feel nothing. Nothing but the warm blush in her cheeks at his regard.

"But I did at the very least give you a fright, for which I am profoundly sorry," he said. "Please, allow me to check for any injuries."

Melanie swallowed hard and nodded. He gently drew the muddied hem of her skirt up a mere few inches to reveal her dirty half boots. She watched, her head all a-whirl, as his long, elegant fingers, clad in black leather gloves, carefully touched her ankle and shivered at the sensations his soft touch sent all up her body.

"Does that hurt?" he asked.

"Not at all," she managed to answer. "I think you are right—I was more scared than anything else. I should not have been walking in the middle of the lane."

"Not at all. I am the one who must apologize, I should have had more care. I was in too much of a hurry on my errand. May I help you to stand?" he asked, with a wide, white smile that dazzled her all over again.

"Yes, thank you, sir."

Melanie held out her hand to him. His gloved fingers closed around hers, strong and warm, and he supported her as he raised her up. He held on to her until she could stand on her own, the dazzling dizziness slowly righting the world around her. All the boredom she'd felt only moments before was gone when she looked up at her rescuer.

"I have not seen you here before, sir," she whispered.

"I have just arrived in the neighborhood on a business matter," he said with another dazzling grin. "I would have come much sooner if I had known there were such beauties to be seen. May I beg to know your name?"

After so long spent in the arid loneliness of no society, she was dizzy with his compliments. She laughed. "I am Miss Melanie Harding, sir."

"And I am Mr. Philip Carrington, very pleased indeed to make your acquaintance," he said. He lifted her muddied glove to his lips for a gallant kiss. "Please, let me see you home to begin to make amends for my terrible behavior."

"Thank you, Mr. Carrington," she answered. The name was vaguely familiar to her, but she couldn't quite fathom why amid the delightful feeling of Philip Carrington's touch as he led her by the arm to his horse. She hadn't felt that way for a long time, not since Captain Whitney first appeared in her life.

He lifted her up into his saddle, his hands strong and steady on her waist. Then he swung up behind her, holding her close to him as he urged the steed into a gallop. The wind rustling past her seemed exhilarating now where before she had hated it.

Suddenly the world seemed fun again.

Suddenly Philip Carrington's unpleasant errand seemed a lot more—interesting.

The fear and remorse of nearly running a helpless lady down in the lane faded as the lady in question looked up at him from beneath the dirt-spattered brim of her bonnet. He saw that not only was she unhurt, but she was remarkably pretty. Tousled bright curls tumbled around an elfin, heart-shaped face and her upturned nose was topped with a spray of pale golden freckles.

She gave a tremulous smile as she looked up at him with those large, cornflower-blue eyes.

"Are you injured?" he said, his voice rough with concern.

"N—no," she gasped. "I do not think so."

Her voice was as pretty as her face, delicate as a silver bell. She looked like a fairy princess dropped onto a dull, muddy country lane. He smiled back at her, wondering why he had ever resisted coming to the country in the first place. He had obviously underestimated the charms of rusticating.

Then, in a painful flash, he remembered all too well why he was there in the dismal, muddy countryside. He was there, away from the pleasures of his city life, because he could no longer afford those pleasures. Because he had to find his cousin Henry's widow, Emma Carrington, and get her to pay him what Henry had owed him before he died. Without those funds, he would be forced to desperate measures.

He would even be forced to go to his nasty old uncle, Sir Angus Macintosh, in Scotland to ask for an advance on his inheritance. And that he did *not* want to do, even though Macintosh undoubtedly owed Philip for what he had done so long ago, sending Philip's mother away because she had dared to marry—only to be widowed by—an irresponsible rake. When she had died while Philip was at school, he had vowed to get what she was owed, somehow.

He had also thought to woo Emma while he was here in the country, for she had been a pretty lass and a good friend to him in those heady days on the Continent. Henry had been a great fool not to see what he had in his pretty wife. Emma could give Philip the security he hadn't known for a long time, thanks to his incompetent family.

But surely there was more to life than security. There was excitement, fun. Danger.

All the things he could see now in the sparkling depths of this lady's blue eyes. "Please," he said, "let me see you home to begin to make amends for my terrible behavior."

She nodded, and let him lift her up in his arms to carry her to the waiting horse. She was as light as a thistle in his embrace, and she wrapped her arms around his neck with another laugh. There were no missish airs with her, no simpering. Just laughter and shimmering eyes.

The ride to the village went much too quickly for Philip's taste. It had been many days since he had been so close to such a pretty woman, and Melanie Harding was easy to be with indeed. She asked him a few light, flirtatious questions about his business in the country, and told him she was staying with her uncle, a retired admiral, for a few weeks, and was bored to tears in the village. But there was to be an assembly soon and perhaps Mr. Carrington would come? Perhaps he cared for dancing, as she did?

Philip did care for dancing, now even more so than before.

They arrived at her uncle's house on the narrow village lane much too soon. Philip watched as his pretty damsel in distress dashed up the narrow steps to a house where she paused at the door and turned to give him a flirtatious little wave. Even under the dust of her fall, Philip could see how lovely her pert little face and the bright curls peeking from beneath her bonnet were.

An angel lurking in the dismal depths of the countryside. Who could have imagined such a thing?

*Miss Melanie Harding.* Philip tipped back his head

to peer up at the tall, narrow house. He had a feeling he would be hearing that name again soon. He was determined to see that fair face and slender figure again.

Philip sighed and wheeled his horse around. In the meantime he had to find lodgings and seek out the agent of this dismal journey—Emma Carrington.

At least things looked a little more fun now....

# *Chapter One*

*A few weeks later...*

Melanie took a deep drink from her borrowed whiskey flask. She could hardly believe what she had just done. The strong, smoky liquid made it seem a bit more bearable, but not much.

She stared out the carriage window at the scenery that flew past, a blur of green hedgerows and blue sky that scarcely seemed real. Surely this was a dream? In all the romantic novels she'd read, heroines who had just eloped with handsome heroes did not feel so very… numb.

But then, was Philip Carrington truly hero material? She had been so sorely deceived once before, with Captain Whitney. Whitney had destroyed what little faith she had in men. But she hoped he had not destroyed her spirit.

In the giddy rush of that moment when David Marton burst into Philip's room at the inn and caught her in Philip's arms, Melanie had known all her practical plans of becoming Lady Marton of Rose Hill were gone. Yet somehow she hadn't cared at all. Indeed, she had only felt—relieved. Free. And dizzy with the sheer, bubbling pleasure of Philip Carrington's kiss. He was a most skillful kisser.

Melanie peeked at him from under her lashes. She suddenly felt remarkably shy for a woman who had run away so boldly with a man, but luckily he wasn't watching her at the moment. He sat beside her on the seat of the hired carriage carrying them to Scotland, near but not touching, staring out the other window. She studied his profile against the pale yellow light, as strong and straight and perfect as some classical marble statue, and just as still and unreadable. The tumble of his golden hair fell over his brow and curled on the collar of his greatcoat. Yes—he *did* look like the romantic lover in a story. But how could the tale possibly end? In real life, romantic tales involving such men always ended badly. Look at her parents, at Captain Whitney.

She couldn't see his eyes, so she had no clue what he thought about their impetuous act now. Was he deeply sorry he had asked her to go with him to Scotland to meet his rich uncle? Was he regretting the moment he kissed her and she, giddy with passion, had said yes? He had been remarkably silent on the journey thus far, and last night they had slept in separate rooms.

*"Your romantic nature will get you into terrible trouble one day, Melanie,"* her mother had said sadly as she packed her off from Bath after the catastrophic affair

with Captain Whitney. It seemed Mama was horribly right, and now Melanie was utterly ruined.

Yet she would have done anything to escape from the stultifying tedium of her uncle's house in that horrible little village. Where every day was the same as the one before, long, dull, never changing. She was losing herself there, losing the spark of excitement that made life worth living. Now she felt nothing *but* sparks.

Melanie studied Philip's profile again, so handsome, so strong. Yes, her passion had steered her wrong before. But every day was a new day, at least away from the boring sameness of country life. Anything could happen now.

Especially once they crossed into Scotland. Gretna Green was there, just over the border....

Suddenly Philip turned to face her, as if he realized she was watching him. He studied her, his eyes narrowed, and she had the terrible, cold feeling that he had forgotten she was there. That he wondered why she was sitting next to him.

She pushed those misgivings away. It was too late for doubt now. She took another swallow of the whiskey and passed the flask back to him. He took a long drink of it and tucked it away.

Melanie gave a careless laugh, as if they were merely on a merry little jaunt to a summer picnic. "La, but I can't believe we have come so far like this! It's just like a voyage in a book."

Finally, he laughed, too. It was a golden, wonderful sound, that warmed her even deeper than the whiskey.

His eyes, those beautiful summer-blue eyes, cleared, and she saw the dashing, playful man she had been so irresistibly drawn to.

He reached for her hand and drew her close to his side. His arms were strong and warm when they slipped around her waist, his closeness reassuring. Surely sometimes her instincts steered her right? Surely she was meant to be here with this man? She looped her arms around his neck and smiled up at him.

"It's a grand adventure, Mel," he said, his tone light. But she was afraid she sensed something taut and tense underneath his humor. "The best one I've undertaken in a long time."

Melanie gently touched the fading bruise on his elegant, cut-glass cheekbone. The bruise that was a reminder of the fight with David Marton. Not a fight over her, alas, but over Emma Carrington. Mrs. Emma Carrington—whose own scandalous behavior had only led her to perfect, respectable happiness. It wasn't fair. Yet Melanie wouldn't trade places with her now.

"Are you sure it's an adventure?" she murmured.

Philip caught her hand in his and pressed a soft kiss to her fingertips. "Sometimes adventures go awry, my fair Melanie. I've been on one or two before. Nothing to fear."

He was right; fear was always the enemy. She had decided long ago not to be afraid, not to look back. And she sensed he felt the same way. "Tell me more about your adventures on the Continent, Philip. All the places you've seen, what you did there. My own life has been so dull, and I long to go to all of them! See everything!"

Philip smiled wryly. "Life can be just as dull in Paris or Rome as in a country village. It depends on the people you're with, not where you are."

She wasn't sure she believed him. Her uncle's company could not possibly be as dull if she were with him in Paris! She gave Philip a light, flirtatious smile. "Am *I* an adventure then?"

He laughed again, and reached out to lower the window shade, enclosing them in warm, intimate shadows. "You are assuredly an adventure, Melanie Harding. But I'm not quite sure where you will take me in the end."

Melanie tangled her fingers in the waves of his hair that fell over his coat collar. It was silken and rough all at the same time, wrapping around her skin to hold her with him. "But that's the fun of an adventure, isn't it? The surprise it brings."

He bent his head to kiss the side of her neck, above the embroidered edge of her spencer. "You are assuredly full of surprises."

Melanie laughed at the delicious sensations of his lips on her skin. Her head fell back as he nudged aside the edge of the jacket and pressed the tip of his tongue to the pulsing hollow of her throat.

She moaned.

His mouth met hers, suddenly rough, hungry, as if he had been missing the taste of her as she had missed him. He tasted as she remembered from their last interrupted kiss, of mint and the smoky hint of whiskey, and something that was dark and sweet and only him.

Her lips parted to let him in, his tongue pressing past her teeth to twine with hers. He was rough and fierce, claiming her with his kiss. Her fingers tightened in his hair, holding him to her. She had never felt like that before, completely swept away by a kiss as if seized in a flood wave. She was helpless against it.

Through the hot, blurry haze of his kiss, she felt his hand at the buttons of her spencer. He tugged them free and she helped him push the clothes away from her shoulders. The warm, stuffy air of the carriage swept over her through her thin muslin gown. Then his body was against hers, and she could think of nothing else.

He carried her down to the velvet-cushioned seat, easing her gown out of his way to press a ribbon of hot, open-mouthed kisses to her bare shoulder, then the soft curve of her breast above the ribbon edge of her chemise.

Melanie's heart pounded in her ears, and it was all she could hear with the rough rush of Philip's breath. The carriage walls pressed in close, making it seem as if they were alone in their own secret world of two. There was only him, only the feelings he woke in her, and she forgot everything else.

"Philip!" she gasped, her head falling back. He tugged down the edge of her bodice and her chemise, freeing her white, bare breast to his avid gaze. He traced the tip of his tongue around her pink, puckered nipple and lightly blew on it. Melanie shivered at the delicious, forbidden sensations.

She closed her eyes tightly and bit her lip to keep from crying out in pleasure as Philip drew her aching nipple deep into his mouth, catching it lightly between his teeth. His hand slid over her hip and the curve of her thigh over her gown, and he grasped the hem of her skirt. He crumpled the soft fabric in his fist and dragged it up and up, until her stockings and legs were bare to him.

He moved to kneel over her, nudging her thighs apart as he kissed her other breast. Melanie moaned as she felt the smooth wool of his breeches rub against the soft silk of her stockings, a delightful friction. He was hard beneath the front placket, and though she had never completed the act with a man before, she knew enough to know what *that* meant. He wanted her just as she wanted him.

As their mouths met again in desperate, hungry need, she slid her eager hands down the lean strength of Philip's back, pushing his coat out of her way. Under his linen shirt, she felt the shift of his strong muscles, the warmth of his smooth skin. She caressed his shoulders, the groove of his spine, and shocked herself when she touched his hard, taut backside through his tight breeches.

"Melanie," he groaned as she touched him, and she was glad to hear her name spoken aloud in his rough voice. Glad he knew it was her there with him.

How very handsome he was, she thought through

the haze of her need. How passionate. He made her feel alive again at last. No wonder she had so forgotten herself with him!

But no matter how much she tried to lose herself in Philip Carrington, the jolt of the carriage coming to a halt brought her back to herself. She opened her eyes as she heard voices and laughter outside the window, and remembered they weren't alone after all.

Melanie pushed him away from her, and dizzily sat up against the seat cushions. Her head was spinning from the kisses and the whiskey, the smell of Philip's cologne. He groaned and threw himself onto the opposite seat, his face turned away from her. His face looked so stark. The heat that had surrounded Melanie vanished, leaving her cold and vaguely scared. She quickly sat up straight and smoothed her skirt and hair. She buttoned her spencer with shaking fingers.

"Where do you suppose we are?" she asked, trying to sound light and careless. She would never let him see what she was really feeling.

Without looking at her, Philip eased back the window shade. Melanie caught a glimpse of an inn yard, muddy and rutted around plain plaster walls, where people and chickens and dogs rushed around in a whirling blur.

"It would appear we have reached our destination," he said, his voice quiet and toneless. "Welcome to Gretna Green, Miss Harding."

Philip watched Melanie dash up the stairs of the inn, her slender ankles flashing under the dusty hem of her skirt. He couldn't help but remember the way her leg had felt under his hand, so slim, warm and soft beneath the sheath of the thin silk stocking. So very alive. He heard the catch of her breath in his ear, her quiet moan against his lips as he kissed her, felt again the desire that raged so hot and sharp and urgent, the need to have her, to possess her.

Was he just like his father, then? The old fear that he was just a replica of the careless rake who had married and left his mother rose up in him again.

At the staircase landing, Melanie paused and glanced back at him over her shoulder. For just an instant, a shadow seemed to flicker over her glowing eyes, a cloud. Then she laughed again, that merry, bell-like sound that had first drawn him to her, and the instant of sadness was gone. Had it ever been there? Melanie Harding didn't seem like the sort of woman who lingered in melancholy.

She gave him a little wave, and spun around to follow the landlady out of sight.

"Ach, don't you worry, young sir," the plump, affable innkeeper's wife called to him with a hearty laugh. "You'll have your pretty sweetheart back with you soon enough."

Melanie's footsteps and giggles faded, and Philip ran his hand through his hair. He found it was shaking. His *sweetheart?* Is that what Melanie Harding was? He could scarcely name it, those scattered feelings that flew through his mind. Back in the village, when he had held her, kissed her, just before they were so rudely interrupted by Sir David Marton, it had seemed like a grand idea for her to come with him to Scotland to find his uncle.

There was nothing for either of them in that village, after all. And the passion in her kisses was—surprising. Philip sensed a spontaneous spirit in her that matched his as few other women's ever could. So that spontaneity had taken hold of them and here they were. And he wasn't entirely sure what to do next. He only knew that he had brought Melanie here, and now he had to take care of her. As he had not been able to take care of Emma.

He laughed ruefully as he remembered David Marton bursting into the room as Philip and Melanie kissed, completely wrapped up in each other—and remembered the terrible things he had said, the fight. Sir David hadn't deserved that. He seemed a good enough sort, if rather dull. It wasn't his fault Emma preferred him to Philip's offer. He shouldn't have let matters get so out of control.

His temper had gotten him into trouble far too often. Like his wretched father.

So now here he was in Scotland, come to make a new life with the help of his uncle Macintosh and his fortune. But what could he do with Melanie?

He knew what he *should* do. Send her home before everyone knew she was gone. That was what a true gentleman would do. But Philip had never been a gentleman. And he had the feeling Melanie Harding was not a true lady. Her bright spirit would wither away in a place like that stuffy, airless village.

He found himself most reluctant to part with her. She seemed like a woman who could understand him, maybe even accept him, his wild spirit and all. So they would have to find some way forward together in this strange world they had made.

"You look as if you could use a whiskey, lad," the innkeeper called from the taproom.

Philip laughed. Whiskey had helped get him here in the first place. Maybe just a little more could help him see a way out again.

"Indeed I think I could," he said, and made his way to sit down at the bar.

# *Chapter Two*

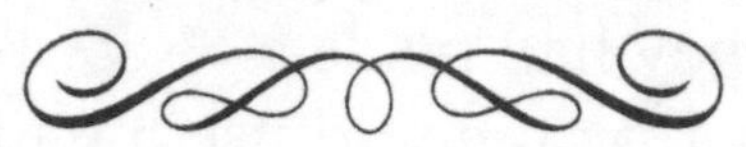

"I am terribly sorry, Captain Whitney, but I fear I do not know where my friend Miss Harding could have gone. Her uncle the admiral has said she returned to Bath, though I did think it most odd that she would leave without talking to me." Mrs. Smythe held up her gilded teapot with a simpering smile. "More tea?"

"Thank you, Mrs. Smythe. You are very kind." Captain Bartholomew Whitney smiled affably at the silly Mrs. Smythe, even though inside he could feel his temper kindling. He had come so far to find Melanie Harding, all the way to this dismal little village, only to find she had already flown away.

How could she have escaped him already? And just when he discovered she had an uncle who might be a wealthy admiral?

"I must say I am most disappointed to hear I cannot see dear Miss Harding," he said. "We were such friends in Bath. Yet it seems even her uncle does not know what has really become of her."

He took an obligatory sip of the insipid tea as Mrs.

Smythe fluttered her handkerchief at him. *Friends*—yes, that was one way to put it. When he had kissed Melanie behind a screen at the assembly rooms, he'd only been looking for a diversion during a dull time in the watering place before his regiment was posted elsewhere. She was pretty enough, and her smile flirtatious as they danced.

But that kiss—ah, it had been most surprising. The young Miss Harding had depths of passion and need in her that were most attractive indeed. Addictive, even. Captain Whitney was a man who liked to control his women, and a woman of spirit was the greatest challenge of all. Surely she was made for him, made to be tamed by him in bed. She seemed quite sure to soon be his mistress, to be *his,* as she was meant to be. But then the silly girl, or rather her mother, had discovered his betrothal to Miss Banbury, and Melanie had pushed him away, sobbing and shouting. The next thing he knew she was gone from Bath.

What did she expect? That he would marry *her?* Miss Banbury had twenty thousand pounds, and Miss Harding not a farthing. At least so he had thought until he discovered her connection to Admiral Harding. But that didn't mean she could not be Captain Whitney's mistress, in the bedchamber where she belonged.

He did not like to be thwarted. At all. Especially not by a chit like Melanie Harding. He was going to find her, and make her his. Make her sorry she'd left him. Then she would know her place.

He took another sip of tea and smiled at Mrs. Smythe.

"I understand you are great friends with Miss Harding. Or so the lady working at the bookshop tells me."

"We are such dear friends. It has been a long time since I had someone to talk to like that." Mrs. Smythe sighed and laid her hand over the swell of her belly. Above their heads there was a crash as her two energetic sons dashed around the upstairs floor. She didn't seem to notice. "I do hope she will come back one day soon."

"She was not here very long."

"No. Her uncle the admiral, while certainly a respectable man, was no fit home for a lively young lady, I fear. I knew she would not stay long." Mrs. Smythe giggled. "I do wonder she didn't go back to Bath, with such friends as you waiting for her there!"

Captain Whitney gave a regretful smile. "Alas, I fear I did not fully appreciate such a treasure as her friendship until it was gone. But I hope to remedy that now, if I can only find her. Are you quite certain, Mrs. Smythe, you have no idea at all of her whereabouts?"

Her smile faded. She put down her teacup and gave him an uncertain glance. He tried to encourage her with a smile tinged with just the right amount of romantic sadness.

"Well," Mrs. Smythe said nervously. "She did have a new friend, Mr. Philip Carrington, who is also now gone from the village. He was very charming, a relative of my own sister-in-law. And quite well-off, I believe. He mostly lives on the Continent. He seemed to like Miss Harding a great deal indeed…."

Captain Whitney felt fury catch at his heart, white-hot, flaming beyond his control. Melanie had already found another admirer? How could she? The little whore.

But he had much experience hiding his true feelings. He pushed down his anger and smiled at Mrs. Smythe, carefully putting down his cup before it could snap in his hand. "And this Mr. Carrington disappeared at the same time as Miss Harding?"

Mrs. Smythe's brow creased. "It was certainly most odd. She had said little to me about him, except that she found him handsome."

"Perhaps you could tell me more about Miss Harding's stay here, Mrs. Smythe. Everything you know."

# *Chapter Three*

"Oh, ye'll tak' the high road, and I'll tak' the low road, and I'll get to Scotland afore ye! But me and my true love will never meet again, on the bonnie, bonnie banks o' Loch Lomond..."

Melanie laughed and took another drink of ale as she listened to the song. It was a rough, strong brew, much like the crowd at the inn's taproom. As evening gathered over the village, darkness closed in at the windows. The only light now was from smoking, guttering candles set on the rickety tables and the long, sticky stone bar.

It seemed like the whole neighborhood was gathered there after their work was done for the day, and when Melanie ventured down in search of Philip and some dinner, they'd welcomed her as if she were their long-lost sister.

At first she felt strangely shy, but the music and fun of the evening quickly overcame that, and she became engrossed in learning their Scottish songs, joining in their laughter.

The sound grew louder and louder, wrapping around

her, rising to the smoke-encrusted beams of the low, whitewashed ceiling. The musicians in the corner, a small collection of drums, fiddles and pipes, played wherever the crowd led. A few couples even danced, twirling between the tables.

Melanie couldn't remember when she had last had such fun. Not in her uncle's house, certainly. Not even in Bath, where there were assemblies and card parties. There was much dancing in Bath, of course, but of the carefully chaperoned, precisely regimented sort.

This made her want to laugh and twirl, to revel in the feeling of being free at last! When she danced she had no worries that she wasn't good enough, that she didn't deserve fine things in life. When she danced, nothing else mattered.

She only wished Philip would join in the fun with her. Then it would all be perfect.

She studied him over the edge of her tankard. He stood by the bar, where he had gone to order her some supper and watched the crowded room with lazy, unreadable eyes, lightly tapping his fingertips on the stone.

He'd been polite when she appeared; he found her a seat, made sure she had ale. Yet he was so…distant. She started to think she had only imagined that fiery kiss in the carriage.

Then he turned and caught her staring. He smiled, a knowing, sensual grin that told her he *knew* what she was thinking. That he remembered, too. It made her face turn hot, made her want to grab him and pull him close to her so he could kiss her again.

She quickly turned away and took a deep gulp of ale. It was not at all like the watered wine she was used to; it made her head swim.

"Having a good time, Mel?" Philip said, sliding onto the bench next to her. She could feel the warmth of his body reaching out as if to caress her, and she had to force herself not to move away.

"I like it here very much. It's so—so full of life," she said, trying to get back the feeling of being swept away on the tide of music and laughter. But now all she could see, all she knew, was him. "It's been too long since I heard such music."

Philip reached over and took her hand. He turned it over on his palm, studying the curve of her wrist, her fingers. She stared, fascinated and speechless, as he raised it to his lips for a warm, soft kiss. It was a swift, fleeting caress, but it suddenly made the evening even lighter. Even more exciting.

"An adventure, eh?" he said. He gave her another lazy smile, and she wished she knew what he was thinking. What he saw when he looked at her.

"Perhaps not much of one to you, but I have been trapped in respectable quiet for much too long," she said. She ran her fingertips lightly over his wrist, feeling the heat of his skin under her touch. "I do like it here. I'm glad you brought me on this adventure, Philip."

She only hoped *he* was not sorry.

"Will you think that later, pretty Melanie?" he said, a stark hint of bitterness in his voice.

Before Melanie could answer, he suddenly wrapped

his fingers around the nape of her neck, dislodging some of the pins in her hair. He drew her closer to him and kissed her. Despite the quickness of his movement, the sudden hunger of it, his lips were gentle on hers, as if he gave her time to push him away.

But she couldn't leave. She only wanted him to be closer, to forget everything in the delight that overcame her with his touch.

She leaned toward him, opening her mouth under his.

He groaned. His fingers tightened in her hair, and his kiss turned hotter, hungrier. He tipped her head back, and she reached up to hold his face between her hands, half-afraid he would slip away from her and she would lose the way he made her feel.

Suddenly, there was the clattering noise of a plate landing on the table, and Melanie sprang back from Philip. Her face flamed even hotter as she remembered where they were, the crowded room, the music. Philip Carrington truly did make her forget everything else.

She peeked up to find the innkeeper's wife smiling at her.

"Ah, young love," she said, reaching out to give Melanie's cheek an understanding pat. "We see it all the time here, don't we lads?"

Philip sat back on the bench, but he didn't leave her entirely. His arm lay lightly around her shoulders. "Forgive us for forgetting ourselves."

"Never you mind that," the landlady said. "We know why you're here, to be sure."

Melanie's thoughts raced. Why *was* she there? She

could hardly remember. Maybe she had never known, but now that kiss had driven all other thoughts out of her head. "Why is that?"

The woman laughed, her plump cheeks glowing pink. "Why else does anyone come over the border so quick-like? To marry, of course! Maybe you have a disapproving guardian chasing you?"

"The blacksmith's shop is open all night," the innkeeper called from behind the bar. "Why don't we take you there after you have your supper? 'tis been too long since I got to give away a bride!"

A bride? *Her?* Melanie's heart pounded like a drumbeat in her ears. But wasn't that what she wanted? What she had secretly wished for, deep down inside, when they came to Scotland together?

She was so confused. Yes, she did want Philip. But only if he wanted her, too. She had made so many mistakes in the past, and this was surely her greatest one. But would marrying make it better—or worse?

She glanced toward Philip, hoping to see some magical answer in his eyes. Some clue as to what she should do next. But his glorious blue eyes were just as unreadable as ever. He gave her one of his lazy smiles, his chin propped on his palm as he studied her.

"Why not?" he said. "We've come this far, after all. What do you think, Mel? Care to get married over the anvil?"

It was hardly the most romantic proposal a girl could ever dream of, with moonlight and flowers and jeweled rings. But to her, those words sounded so sweet. Especially after Captain Whitney's contemptuous laughter, his derisive words about how she wasn't a worthy wife…

Melanie pushed away the old hurt of disillusionment, and drank down the last of her ale. Captain Whitney was in the past. Philip Carrington, a better man in every way, was here now. Perhaps he was not the ideal husband, but he was handsome, fun and willing to wed her right now. She knew she had to take what she could get. Philip was right—they had come too far to turn back.

"I say I am assuredly in the mood for a wedding," she said, and the room around her erupted in cheers.

Philip's smile widened, and he leaned over to kiss her again. The touch of his warm lips reassured her. Surely this was fate, this whole strange scene. Surely this was meant to be….

"…and do you take this man as your wedded husband? Will you…"

Philip studied the woman who stood beside him at the makeshift altar. Melanie's golden head was bent, and he had only a glimpse of her expression. Usually, he only saw her laughing, her passionate curiosity for life lighting up her delicate features, making her eyes glow. Now she looked most solemn as she listened to the Gretna officiant. Solemn, and—startled?

Surely she was just as amazed as he was to find themselves there. Her hand shook in his. Would she flee and break this strange dream-trance?

Philip closed his eyes for a second to see a vision of

Melanie doing just that. Melanie running out the door into the night, the pale skirts of her gown vanishing into the darkness.

Surely he should feel relieved if she *did* flee. He'd always been so sure he would never find himself in the parson's mousetrap. Instead, he found his hand tightening on hers, as if he would hold her with him.

Very strange indeed.

Melanie glanced up at him, and at last she smiled. "I will," she said, softly but firmly.

Philip remembered why he had brought her here, so impulsively. Why he had decided to marry her.

When they kissed over the supper table at the inn, their need for each other so strong they didn't care where they were or who might see, he'd realized that here at last was someone who could understand him.

After his father's death, his mother's sending him away and then his cousin Henry's false friendship, after all the glittering falseness he'd found on his travels, Melanie seemed *real.* She shared his impulsive nature, his wanderlust, his carelessness. Perhaps they could explore life together.

Perhaps, just perhaps, neither of them had to be alone now. Philip dared to do something he had never done before. Hope.

"Ach, lad, do ye or do ye not?" someone cried.

Melanie's smile dimmed a bit, and Philip realized he had just been asked a very important question.

He smiled at her and squeezed her hand. "I will."

Melanie laughed, making him laugh, too. He only

ever wanted her to laugh from now on. The crowd around them cheered.

Philip slipped a newly purchased gold band on Melanie's finger, and it was done. She was his wife—for better or worse.

# *Chapter Four*

"Welcome back, Mrs. Carrington," Philip said, laughing as he swung her up into his arms and carried her into the small room at the inn. "It may not be much, but for now it's home."

Melanie laughed, too, feeling giddy as he spun her around and around. As he slowly lowered her to her feet, she slid her palms down his chest until she reached the buttons of his waistcoat. She slid one free as she kissed his throat.

*Melanie Carrington.* How very unreal that sounded. The whole night seemed most unreal, from the noisy procession through the streets to Philip taking her hand and repeating their vows. Had it all truly happened? Melanie wasn't sure at all. But if it were a dream, it seemed very fun and she didn't want it to end.

The candlelight glinted on the new ring on her finger as she slipped another button free. Philip smiled down at her lazily, letting her play.

Another button was free, the fine silk of the waistcoat falling away to reveal his linen shirt, and Melanie suddenly felt rather shy. Did he feel as she did, excited and scared, thrilled? Did he still want her at all, now that she was his?

She pressed her palm flat against him, feeling the beat of his heart. "Kiss me, Philip. Please," she whispered.

And then she had her answer. His cool distance melted away, and he groaned as his arms came around her, dragging her up against him to cover her lips with his. His tongue slid deep, twining with hers, and she greeted him eagerly.

Her shyness fled. They were married now, for better or worse; she was his. She unfastened the last button of his waistcoat and slid her fingers over his shirt, feeling the heat of his skin through the thin linen.

His kiss deepened, grew hungrier, and she wanted to know what he felt like. She tugged the shirt free of his breeches and finally touched his bare skin. Her fingers skimmed up under the hem of his shirt and teased over his hard abdomen, his ribs, his shoulders. She scraped her nails over his smooth chest, and he groaned again.

"Melanie," he whispered against her lips. "What you do to me…"

What she did to *him?* But she was the one driven mad! All the time she had been so restless, always searching, always seeking something that inevitably eluded her. Surely this was exactly what she had sought.

He kissed her again, roughly, holding nothing back, and she could think of nothing at all but the way she felt with him. He forced her head back as his tongue plunged deep into her mouth, and she met him with equal fire.

She felt his arms lift her higher, and they moved across the small room until they tumbled back onto the bed. She pushed his coat and waistcoat away, and he tore his shirt off over his head. His clothes landed in a careless heap on the floor, and he pressed her back to the tumbled blankets, his body coming over hers.

His kissed her arched throat, her shoulder, licking a soft, delicate ribbon of fire over her skin.

"I can't—bear it," Melanie gasped, wrapping her arms around him.

He laughed roughly against her shoulder. "I'm sure you can bear it just a little longer...."

She felt him reach between their bodies to unfasten his breeches. His manhood sprang free from the fabric confines, hard and hot as iron under velvet. Curious, Melanie ran her fingertips over him. She gasped at the feeling of it.

"Melanie..." he moaned, and jerked against her touch. Emboldened, she caressed him again, but he pushed her hand away. "If you don't stop now, I fear our wedding night will be over before it begins."

Melanie laughed, and laid back to watch as he quickly stripped away his boots and breeches. She had never seen a naked man before, only drawings of ancient statues. Philip was more beautiful than any of them, powerful, gilded gold in the candlelight.

"I fear I feel rather overdressed now," she said, tugging at the skirt of her best pink muslin gown. Her wedding dress.

"I can help you with that," he said.

Melanie laughed again as he seized her in his arms. He quickly unfastened her gown and slid it away from her body to reveal her bare shoulders, her thin chemise. She shivered as he eased away even that meager cover and pressed his lips to her bare back. He touched her skin with the tip of his tongue, as if to taste her.

He tossed her gown to the nearest chair, and as she waited, breathless, to see what would happen next, he slid the pins from her hair and ran his fingers through the tumble of curls. He raised one lock to his nose and inhaled deeply, and that one tiny, tender gesture made her want him even more.

She lay back down on the bed, staring up at him in fascination. He was so very beautiful. She could hardly believe he was her husband now, that he was about to make love to her.

He watched her, too, and his blue eyes narrowed, darkened. She could only hope he liked what he saw in her, that he wanted her as she wanted him. She held her arms up to him in silent entreaty.

He knelt back over her, sliding his hands slowly up her stockinged legs as he parted them and drew her to the edge of the bed. As she stared at him, her breath catching, he knelt between her trembling thighs and softly, softly kissed the bare skin just above her ribbon garter.

"Philip!" she cried, as he traced her most intimate

spot with the tip of his tongue before plunging shockingly deep to taste her very essence.

She let him kiss her there until she could bear it no more. She tugged at his rumpled hair, drawing him up until he braced himself over her. She could tell he held himself carefully so he wouldn't crush her, but she wanted him so much closer.

She wasn't afraid at all now.

She wrapped her legs around his lean hips and arched up into him. His skin was so warm, damp and smooth over his strong muscles. She traced a caress over his back, his taut buttocks, reveling in the way he felt against her.

She kissed his shoulder, tasting the salt-sweetness of him. How she craved him, needed him! It was like coming alive again at last after a long, dark night.

"Melanie," he said hoarsely. He buried his face in the curve of her neck, and she felt him breathe her in deeply. "I can't fight this any longer..."

"I know," she whispered. "Neither can I."

He kissed her neck, his mouth open and hot as it slid over her shoulder, the soft curve of her breast. "Melanie, you aren't like anyone else I've ever met."

"Neither are you." So surely, she thought, that must mean they were meant for each other.

She slid her hand over his chest, the sharp angle of his hip. She felt his back stiffen and his breath catch as she dared to touch him again. She was fascinated as he grew even harder under her caress.

"You'll kill me yet," he said, half laughing, half pained by his restraint.

"I—I want you, Philip. Now," she whispered.

She felt his hand between her legs, his thumb sliding into the wet core of her. "I want you, too, Melanie. But I don't want to hurt you."

"You won't. I trust you," Melanie said, surprised to find that those words were true. Despite everything, she did trust in him. Trust in what they had together. She closed her eyes and eased her legs wider to welcome him. "Please."

She heard him draw in a ragged breath as he reached between their bodies again and gently parted her damp folds as he sought entry. Then she felt a stretching, a burning, as he slowly slid inside of her.

Melanie gasped at the warm, unfamiliar friction, the sensation of sudden fullness and pressure. Of being joined with him.

"I'm sorry," he whispered. His whole body went still, his arms rigid as he held himself balanced above her.

Melanie was afraid he meant to leave her. "No!" she cried in protest, holding him with her. "It feels better now."

And it did. The shocking ache was fading as her body grew accustomed to him, leaving only that delicious new fullness, and a glimmer of something wonderful she couldn't quite grasp.

Philip nodded. He drew back from her one slow, enticing inch at a time, then plunged deep again.

"Oh..." Melanie sighed, closing her eyes tighter to

feel him moving within her, faster, deeper. That tiny seed of pleasure grew deep inside of her, flowering, expanding. Every nerve ending in her body seemed to come to fiery life, awakened only by him.

She learned his rhythm and moved with him, a strange, exotic dance where they were perfectly partnered.

The night outside the window, the small, warm room—the whole world narrowed to just the two of them. Behind her closed eyes, Melanie saw gold and silver sparks, shimmering, sparkling. It seemed this was what she had been waiting for forever.

Then all her thoughts flew apart in an explosion of fiery stars and she felt as if she was soaring into the sky, the past burning away, leaving her free.

Above her, Philip called out her name, his back arching. He pulled out of her, and she felt the damp heat of his seed on her skin. He collapsed beside her on the bed, their arms and legs entangled.

Melanie slowly sank back down to earth, as light as if she drifted on a feather. She had never felt so tired, so light, so—confused. Yet somehow she knew that, whatever happened tomorrow, right now she was where she should be.

Beside her, she heard the soft rush of Philip's breath. She opened her eyes and rolled onto her side, gazing at him in the hazy moonlight. His eyes were hooded, and he gave her his lazy smile, the one that always made her heart pound.

"Are you all right?" he murmured.

"Oh, yes." Far better than all right. She kissed his cheek softly, and he smiled. His arms came around her and drew her down against his shoulder. Wrapped up in each other, they fell into sleep.

"Tell me more about your travels, what you did before," Melanie said lazily, as they drowsed in the shadows of deepest night. She felt his fingers trail through her hair, and she curled closer to his side. She wished the night would never end, that they would never have to leave the warm little cocoon they had created in their little inn room. "It must have been so exciting."

Philip gave a rueful laugh. "It was exciting sometimes—but also most uncertain. Sometimes I would never know where I would be the next day, who I would meet, if there would be any friends. If I would have to drag my cousin Henry out of trouble yet again. If the turn of the cards would favor me. Perhaps that was what made it exciting. But I am growing too old for it all."

"Ah, yes. You are so old. Just look at all this gray hair!" Melanie teased. She tousled his tumbled, shimmering golden hair until he laughed. It was a beautiful sound, one she wanted to hear more. "I think it sounds wonderful, to go wherever you like, wherever the whim takes you."

"Is that not what you did with me? Go where your whim took you?"

Melanie thought about that. Yes, it was a whim that made her run away with him. A whim that could easily lead to disaster. Yet she was beginning to think it was the best thing she'd ever done. "I suppose I did, and it feels wondrous! Though I know I will have to answer for it soon enough, to my mother and my uncle, but it was wonderful to feel free for a while. Is that how you felt, when you left for the Continent? Did your family chase after you?"

His fingers, which had been softly tracing her skin, went still. "My family was what urged me to go. My father died when I was a boy, and my mother didn't have the energy to deal with a boisterous son. I was a terrible troublemaker, I fear, even when I was young. I spent most of my boyhood at school. It was her brother, my uncle Macintosh, who urged my mother to send me away with my cousin Henry. Said it would be the making of me."

"And was it?"

"I suppose it was. Though not in the way he hoped. I found out what my own strength was, far away and on my own."

Melanie had also been on her own ever since she could remember. On her own, and never managing it all quite well enough. "I wish I could do that. My mother sent me away just so she wouldn't have to think about me any longer. I fancied I was in love with the wrong man, you see, and I was sorely deceived." She swallowed hard, remembering how heartbroken she was to find out the truth about Captain Whitney, and how her mother could not help her. "I don't think she cared whether I found my strength or not."

"Have you?" Philip said. "I think you are very strong,

Melanie. One of the strongest people I know. You aren't afraid of being yourself."

He thought she was *strong?* No one had ever said that to her before. Mostly she had just been a nuisance. She sat up to study his face in the silvery moonlight. He was so handsome in the night, so solemn and austere. "Do you really think so? I never felt strong at all. Only weak and easily tempted. I never can seem to help myself from following my feelings, even when I know they are wrong and improper."

"Surely that only proves your strength. You are true to yourself, to your own heart. You should be admired for that, not condemned."

"As you have been condemned for being true to yourself?"

Philip was silent for a long, tense moment. His face was smooth and expressionless in the moonlight. "I suppose so," he said slowly. "But I have led myself into great trouble, as well."

Did that trouble include marrying her? Melanie lay back down next to him, curling herself into his side to make herself feel safe again. "Well, now we can keep each other from trouble. Starting with this visit to your uncle. Surely he won't turn away a repentant and reformed nephew with a new wife? I am very good at charming irascible old people, like my own uncle."

Philip laughed. His arms came around her, and he spun her to the bed beneath him, kissing her bare shoulder until she could remember little else. "The respectable Mr. and Mrs. Carrington, eh?"

"Most suitable to be your uncle's heirs. But being suitable doesn't mean being dull, does it? It doesn't mean no more adventures."

"My dear Mrs. Carrington," he whispered, his lips tracing her neck, "I think dull is the last thing you could ever be."

## *Chapter Five*

Melanie let herself out of the silent, sleeping inn and into the fresh, pale morning. It was cooler there, north of the border, than it had been at the village with her uncle. She drew her shawl closer around her shoulders and headed off down the lane, barely restraining herself from skipping.

It seemed like such a glorious day. A whole new, exciting beginning, just as she had been longing for. When she awoke in the predawn grayness, she couldn't go back to sleep as her mind raced over all the new possibilities ahead of her. She couldn't be still, but neither could she wake Philip who looked so gloriously handsome, so peaceful, as he slept beside her in their rumpled sheets.

She was also half-afraid that he might not share her wild joy if she told him how she was feeling. He had confided in her last night, and his confidences showed her a way they could happily move forward together. Have adventures together.

But what if that was not at all what he wanted, in the cold light of day?

She wanted to hold on to every bit of happiness she could, for as long as she could.

Melanie hurried down the deserted lane, peering into shop windows, imagining the lives that went on in those gray stone buildings. Lives different from any she had known before. She and Philip would see many such places together. There was so much to explore in the world!

The only person she saw on her walk was an errand boy, hurrying past her on his task. He tipped his cap to her and then was gone. She came to the end of a row of cottages, where the road twisted away into the low, rolling hills. It was the same road she had arrived on, but this morning it was shrouded in mist, like torn bits of tulle caught on the gray-green landscape.

For a moment, it seemed she was all alone, poised between civilization and wilderness—just as she had felt all her life. But then she heard the faint rumble of hooves on gravel, coming closer and closer. It seemed she wasn't the only one up so early after all.

Melanie quickly climbed over a rail fence at the border of a field, out of the way of any hurrying, careless traveler. A horseman emerged from the mist, moving fast, intent on some urgent errand. She had a glimpse of dark, sweat-dampened hair, a familiar profile....

"Melanie! Is it really you?" the rider shouted. He drew in his horse in a shower of dust and swung down to hurry toward her. “What a piece of luck. It’s as if you sensed I was near, and came to meet me!”

Melanie watched him with growing horror. Was this some sort of dream, or a nightmare? Perhaps this was her punishment for being too happy? For it was Captain Whitney hurrying toward her now. Captain Whitney, who had betrayed her. Why was he here, now, when she had finally forgotten him?

She wrapped her hand around the fence post, and felt the wood dig into her palm. She wanted to yank it out of the ground and throw it at him, the foul deceiver.

“What are you doing here?” she said, as cold and calm as she could make herself be.

“My dearest! When we last met, you called me Bartholomew.” His steps slowed as he moved toward her. He still smiled, that ever so charming smile that had once drawn her in. Now she saw a grim strain behind the lightness.

His smile was not nearly so beguiling as Philip’s.

“And the last time we met, you told me you were engaged to another woman,” she said. “Has the nuptial event taken place? Should I wish you happy?”

“My dearest Melanie, no. I came to my senses and realized *you* were the only lady for me. I rushed to tell you that, to beg you to stay with me, but you had gone. I’ve been searching for you for weeks.”

He had been searching for her? Melanie shook her head. She remembered too well the pain she’d felt at his treatment of her, the hurt of his rejection. The way it had sent her to something better in the end. Melanie gave a humorless laugh, and held out her hand to keep him from coming closer. The morning light caught on her new gold ring.

"Now *you* are too late, captain," she said. "Today I am Mrs. Carrington. The wife of a much better man than you could ever hope to be."

Suddenly, like a summer storm slashing through bright sunlight, an expression she'd never seen before on Captain Whitney's handsome face transformed him right before her eyes. A scowl twisted his mouth, and his eyes went dark.

"You little harlot," he said, as calm and easy as if he'd said *shall we have tea?* Somehow that very coolness made the words seem even worse. More threatening. "You went right from my arms to his? When you knew you belonged to me?"

Belonged to him? Melanie suddenly felt very cold. She instinctively took a step back, trying to resist the urge to run. Something told her that if she fled, he would just chase her. That he would like to see her fear, as all bullies did.

And she refused to show her fear.

She tilted up her chin and stared at him in challenge. "You are betrothed to another woman, as I should not have to remind you. How could I possibly belong to you?"

Captain Whitney took another step toward her. "I was engaged to her only for convenience, Melanie. Surely you knew that. You and I could have been together in other ways."

"As your mistress, you mean? Tucked away in cozy little side-street rooms?" Melanie said, cold with the knowledge of just how close she had come to such a fate. If not for Philip…

"But that was before I knew you were an admiral's niece! An admiral who took some fine prizes in the war," Captain Whitney said, his voice growing rougher. Louder. Melanie took another step back into the field beyond her fence. "Surely we could have made sure you were his heir. Then we could marry. But your whorish ways…"

Suddenly, before she could run, he lunged forward and grabbed her arm in an iron-hard grasp. Melanie gasped, and twisted hard against him, but she couldn't free herself. She couldn't breathe for the fear squeezing at her throat.

"Let me go!" she cried, her voice faint.

"You are just like all the others," he growled. His face came closer to hers, and she could feel his hot breath on her skin. "So pretty and sweet on the outside, but greedy and unfaithful at heart."

She stared up at him in a daze of fear. How very different he looked, all dark and twisted. How had she ever thought him handsome?

"I am greedy and unfaithful?" she cried. "You are the one with a fiancée, who you have abandoned now as you did to me, just because you think I am an heiress. Well, I am no heiress, but my new husband does not care. He is twice the man you could ever be…"

"Shut up!" he shouted. His hand shot out and cracked across her cheek, leaving fiery pain behind.

Melanie's head spun, and she was so shocked she couldn't even cry out as Captain Whitney dragged her closer. His lips touched her skin.

"Let her go," a voice rang out, ice-cold. "Right now."

Melanie almost collapsed on a sob. *Philip.* Philip had come to her. Captain Whitney dropped her to the ground, and for a moment all she could feel was the pain when she landed.

Her hair tumbled into her face, and she reached up to push it out of her eyes, trembling with the mixture of fear and relief. Then she saw Philip's face, and his expression was distant and as cold as ice.

Philip awoke slowly, like swimming to the surface of a wonderfully warm sea. He stretched and chuckled, feeling lighter, freer than he had in a very long time. The problems that had weighed down on him like loops of steel chains for too long seemed to have fallen completely away.

Who would ever have guessed that a woman could change the way he felt so completely? That suddenly he would realize something he had never known before—that he didn't have to make his way alone in life. That someone could understand him, and not wish that he was different, better, than he truly was. *Now we can keep each other from trouble,* she had said. She had understood as no one else ever had.

Philip laughed, and sat up to tell her the extraordinary way he felt. He wanted to look into her eyes, to kiss her….

But she wasn't in bed beside him. The sheets were drawn smooth, the pillows neatly piled up, her side of the bed cold to the touch, as if she hadn't been there for a while. He quickly scanned the small room. Her shawl was gone from where she had draped it over a chair. The dress and chemise she had worn last night were also gone. There was no trace of her in the room, except for the faint lingering scent of her perfume in the air.

The hard, cold knot in his very core grew and solidified into the certainty that no one could bear to stay with him. Not his parents, not his cousin. Now not even his wife.

Philip threw back the bedclothes, and quickly pulled on his own clothes. He splashed cold water from the basin over his face and ran his hands through his hair. The chilly water helped him think a bit clearer. Surely Melanie had just gone downstairs to find some breakfast. She wouldn't have run off so suddenly.

And even if she had—why would he care? His whole adult life had been spent assiduously avoiding the snares of matrimony. He should be glad of the chance to escape them again, to be free and on his own.

But, somehow, he was not glad at all. He was angry, and something else he couldn't even recognize. Something that threatened to make his heart turn to stone and crack wide open.

He hurried down the stairs, swirling on his coat and hastily tying his cravat. There was no one in the taproom, which had been so crowded and noisy last night, but the scent of stale ale and old smoke hung in the air. Only the landlady was there, sweeping at the stained floorboards, her face weary.

"There's tea by the fire if you want it," she said.

"Have you seen Miss Har—that is, Mrs. Carrington this morning?" he asked.

She gave a snort of a laugh. "Lost her already, have you? I haven't seen her, but the errand boy said he saw her leaving early this morning. Sneaking out, I suppose."

Lost her already? It seemed he had.

"Can you arrange for a carriage for me?" he said tightly. "As soon as possible. I must leave for my uncle's house immediately."

The landlady's eyes widened in surprise. "Without waiting for Mrs. . . ."

"Now, please." Philip knew it was no use waiting for Melanie. She had left him, as assuredly as everyone else had.

The carriage came quickly, barely giving him time to throw his things into a valise. As it rolled toward the edge of town, he felt the old coldness descending on him again, the numbness that had carried him through so many days. It had left for a few moments, when he held his new wife in his arms, but now it was back. Perhaps forever.

It was only beyond the crowds of the streets that he caught a glimpse of Melanie. She stood in the middle of a deserted field beyond a rail fence, her pale pink skirt a banner against the dark green. But she wasn't alone. A tall, dark-haired man in a red coat stood with her—and reached out to pull her into his arms.

A freezing anger swept over Philip as he watched the pair, seemingly entwined in a passionate embrace. He gave a bitter laugh, and started to turn away, to leave his wife of one day to her lover. To be proven right was a terrible vindication indeed. He was right to leave.

But then he heard Melanie scream. Not a cry of delight, but a piercing shriek of raw fear. He spun back around to see her struggle in the man's arms, trying to push him away. And then the man slapped her across the face.

In one flash, burning fury replaced the ice of disappointed betrayal. Philip ran toward them without thinking. He leaped over the fence, barely realizing what he was doing. He could only see Melanie, only know that she had been hurt and he had to save her.

Melanie saw him before the man did, for he had his back to Philip. Her eyes widened, and he could see the swirling fear in the blue depths. She gave a choked sob just as Philip seized a handful of the man's woolen coat and swung him around.

"I will thank you not to accost my wife," Philip said coldly. Time seemed to have slowed down, the air around him chilly. He was overcome with rage that anyone would dare hurt Melanie.

The man's face twisted in such a contorted way that even if Philip had known him he wouldn't have recognized him. He was sure he had never met the villain, but he wondered if this was the man Melanie had mentioned, the man who broke her heart.

"Your *wife?*" the man sneered. "So you are the man who was fool enough to marry such a whore. She was mine first…."

At the vile word *whore,* it was as if a red mist lowered over Philip's vision, blocking out everything but his anger. How dare anyone treat a spirited lady like his Melanie this way? His fist drove into the man's face, shoving him backward. The man shouted as blood spurted from his nose, staining his fine coat. Melanie screamed.

Philip only heard her as from a distance. He could think of nothing but the fact that this man had hurt her—and he had to protect her. His mind seemed to clear, as he frostily assessed his opponent. Gazing into the hate-brightened eyes above the broken nose to read that intent before the man launched a counter-attack. Every sense was heightened; his blood seemed to flow fast and hot in his veins.

Once, when he was young and foolish, wandering the Continent with his cousin Henry and their wild friends, Philip had lived for such moments. He'd loved the danger and thrill of a good fight. It was one of the few times he felt truly alive.

But now—now Melanie made him feel alive. Made him *want* to live, to see what adventure awaited them next. He just had to vanquish this one last enemy, for her.

When he looked at the furious man across from him,

he saw himself as he had once been. Empty. Seeking escape in wilder and wilder sensations. He knew with a sudden flash of deep knowledge—that was over for him.

Philip finally saw the shift in his opponent's eyes. He lunged toward Philip, his fists flying toward Philip's face. Philip ducked and parried, landing a swift, hard right to the man's vulnerable midsection.

The two of them went down in a clash of blows. The man's fury seemed to grow as Philip became cooler and more calculating. It forced his opponent to make foolish mistakes, become clumsy and blinded, which Philip took full advantage of. At least his misspent youth had been for something.

Finally, he pinned the man to the ground. Sweat stung at his eyes and in his cuts, but a wave of victory washed over him. The man gave a stifled sob as he stared up at Philip.

"Do it," he sniffled, all his bravado gone.

Philip laughed, and raised his fist to deliver the coup de grâce. Suddenly, a soft hand caught his, holding him still.

"No, Philip, please," Melanie said gently. "No more of this."

Philip's anger faded as suddenly as it had come over him, and he felt weary. He looked up at his wife, shocked to see tears in her beautiful eyes. Tears—for the man who had hurt her? The coward Philip now held with his fists?

"Melanie…"

She shook her head. "I can't bear to see you hurt anymore, Philip. Please—he is beaten now. He won't bother us any longer. Let's go home. Let me take care of you. That's all I want now."

Philip couldn't quite believe what he was hearing, what he saw in her eyes. She cared about *him?* No one had done such a thing before. No one had ever cared if he was beaten to a pulp or not.

Certainly no one had ever wanted to take him home.

"Yes," he said, hauling himself to his feet. Melanie slid her arm around his waist, not even looking at the man who now sobbed on the ground. "Let's go home."

# Chapter Six

"Sit here now, Philip," Melanie said soothingly. She slid her husband's arm from around her shoulders and helped him sit down on the rickety wooden chair by the fire in their room at the inn. "Whatever possessed you to do such a thing? Brawling in a field with Captain Whitney! What if your uncle heard of it? He already thinks you are a great scoundrel."

"And so I am. This just proves it."

Melanie shook her head, and turned away to pour out water into the basin and find some clean rags. Once her back was to him, she allowed her stern expression to slip into the tiniest of smiles. When she had seen Philip coming toward her, she'd felt such happiness and relief as she had never known before. She was no longer alone.

"He tried to hurt you, Mel," Philip said, his voice hard, touched with ice. "He deserved far worse than the thrashing he got."

"Perhaps so. But I don't think he'll be bothering us again." Melanie turned back to him, the damp cloth in her hand. She leaned over him to carefully dab at the cut over his eye. It all seemed too good to be true for a girl like her, to have a knight in shining armor come to her rescue. "But did you not think perhaps I was there of my own accord? After all, I told you I once fancied myself in love with that villain."

Something flickered in Philip's eyes, and he glanced away from her. Melanie felt her heart sink, leaving her cold. She went on cleaning his cuts and bruises, but all she wanted to do was turn away and cry. Suddenly she felt even more alone than she had before. It was like being shown a beautiful jewel, told it could be hers, then having it snatched away.

Philip grabbed her hand and held on to it tightly, not letting her pull away. "Mel, look at me."

She reluctantly dragged her gaze up to meet his. He looked right at her now, his expression fierce. "Melanie, I did think for a moment, when I first saw you in his arms, that you had gone to him. That you had left me. After all, I have never done anything good enough to deserve you. To deserve what we have found here together."

Melanie felt the tiniest touch of the most reluctant hope, deep down inside of her. "Wh-what have we found here?"

He looked up at her steadily, never wavering, so serious. "Do we not understand each other? In a way no one else has ever understood either of us? I've never had a home, Mel, not really. But last night, here in this shabby little room, I felt I could never be anywhere else. And I thought—hoped—you felt the same."

"Oh, Philip, I did! I do," Melanie cried, her hope bursting free. "I never knew anyone like you. So full of adventure and fun, so complicated and fascinating."

He grinned up at her, wincing through his bruises. It was the loveliest smile she had ever seen. "And handsome, too?"

"Gloriously handsome." Melanie gently kissed his cheek. "I never thought there could be anyone like you in the world, either. I felt ill when Captain Whitney grabbed me, so scared. But not as scared as I was thinking you would imagine I went to him."

"My darling." Philip drew her down onto his lap, and she buried her face in his shoulder. He smelled of sunlight and starch, sweet, faint traces of cologne—and of his own delicious self. She had never felt safer. He pressed a gentle kiss to her hair. "Melanie," he said, "after last night, I never should have had a second's doubt. When I heard you cry out—I was so furious, I couldn't think at all. I only knew I had to get you away from him. It was the first time I had ever thought of someone above myself."

"And it was the first time I had not felt alone," she whispered. She curled her hand into his shirt and held on as if she would never let go.

"I know I am a terrible wager as a husband," he said. "We will have to beg my uncle for a home, and I have no great riches to give you. But I promise, Melanie, you will never be alone again."

*Never be alone again.* She had never heard sweeter words, never been so wonderfully happy. "And I promise *you* will never be alone, either. We have each other now. Even if we have to make our home in this room, it won't matter. We can finally be happy."

"Yes," he answered, turning her face up to his. She glimpsed his tender smile just before he kissed her. His lips touched hers as if she was the most delicate, precious thing in all the world, and she knew that at last she truly could belong somewhere. "We can finally be happy…"

# *Epilogue*

*Macintosh House, six years later*

"Mama! Hurry up! The carriage will leave without us."

Melanie looked up from the piles of luggage in the foyer of their home, an ancient stone pile high in the Scottish hills. Her son, Peter, stood in the doorway, waving at her. She laughed at the eagerness on his handsome little face.

"It can't leave without us, my darling," she said. "It's *our* carriage. And Italy will certainly be waiting for us no matter how long it takes us to get there."

"But I want to get there *soon,*" he answered, his bright blue eyes glowing just like his father's did at the prospect of an adventure. "I don't even remember the last time we were there."

"That's because you were barely out of leading strings. You nearly did yourself an injury running about the ruins at Pompeii!" Melanie said, still smiling. Peter was completely bold and unstoppable, just like his father.

"And Louisa wasn't even born yet. It will be her very first chance to see Rome."

She picked up her little cherub from where she crawled on the marble floor. Melanie's little blond-curled angel. She kissed Louisa's plump, pink cheek. The baby laughed and patted Melanie's neck.

"Take your sister to nanny, darling, and tell her we will be ready to leave very soon," Melanie said, giving Louisa's hand to Peter. "There just might be some new books about pirates in the carriage…."

"Pirates!" Peter cried. Next to travel, high-sea skull-duggery was his favorite thing. He took his sister's hand and gently helped her toddle out the door. "Just wait until I tell you about Blackbeard, Lou…"

Melanie smiled as she finished checking over the trunks. Sometimes she could not quite believe this was *her* life. The wild leap she had taken into the unknown when she ran away with Philip Carrington had led her to so much more than she could ever have imagined.

Uncle Macintosh, beneath his Scots bluster, had proved to be quite a darling. An old man just as roguish as his nephew in his youth, and full of grand tales. Melanie had become quite fond of him, and missed him when he'd passed away two years before and Macintosh House became their home.

Not that they were always there. In the cold, windy winters, they went to Italy and Greece and Switzerland, exploring new places, meeting new people. Building their little family. Melanie had to smile when she thought of it all. It was riches beyond what she ever thought she could deserve.

"And what are you smiling about, my pretty wife?" Philip said, sneaking up behind her. He drew her close to him and pressed a soft kiss to her neck.

Melanie laughed, and leaned into him. "Peter and his pirates, Louisa walking now. And envisioning Italy. The sun, the blue sky..."

"The long, warm nights?" he whispered.

"Definitely those. Most of all." She turned in his arms and looped her arms around his neck as she looked up into his eyes. How she loved him! How she treasured what they had built together, against all odds. "Oh, yes. The nights above all else."

* * * * *

# HOW TO SEDUCE A SHEIKH

Marguerite Kaye

If you enjoy this sheikh story, then be sure to check out further sultry desert settings in Marguerite Kaye's

INNOCENT IN THE SHEIKH'S HAREM
THE GOVERNESS AND THE SHEIKH

**Other novels by Marguerite Kaye:**

RAKE WITH A FROZEN HEART
OUTRAGEOUS CONFESSIONS
OF LADY DEBORAH
DUCHESS BY CHRISTMAS
(part of *Gift-Wrapped Governesses* anthology)
THE BEAUTY WITHIN
RUMOURS THAT RUINED A LADY

**And in**
**Mills & Boon® Historical *Undone!* eBooks:**

BEHIND THE COURTESAN'S MASK
FLIRTING WITH RUIN
AN INVITATION TO PLEASURE
LOST IN PLEASURE

**And in the**
**M&B Regency *Castonbury Park* mini-series:**

THE LADY WHO BROKE THE RULES

Don't miss
Marguerite Kaye's
STRANGERS AT THE ALTAR
Coming soon

# *Chapter One*

*Arabia, September 1801*

'Who will bid five hundred? Yes! Six hundred. Now seven.'

It was the suppressed excitement in the man's voice as much as the sums of money involved that roused Prince Zafar al-Zuhr's curiosity and distracted him from his careful inspection of a magnificent snowy-white camel. His interest in the animal had been half-hearted, founded in a desire to be seen to spend generously and thus spread goodwill in his neighbour's kingdom rather than a desire to purchase yet another beast to add to his already impressive herd. Having no wish to risk causing offence, however, Prince Zafar al-Zuhr summoned Firas, his man of business, to commence the bartering process without which the camel seller would be insulted, and headed off in the direction of the excited bidding that had floated over the marketplace and piqued his curiosity.

The market was a busy one, situated as it was on the

Red Sea. Merchants from as far away as India traded here, selling silks and exotic spices. There were carpets and camels for sale, expensive oils and rich unguents, even some ancient artefacts from the tombs of pharaohs, though the trade in such things had largely migrated north as first the French and then the British had moved into Egypt. If such trade existed in Prince Zafar's kingdom of Kharidja, it was kept very much under cover, for his people knew how much he frowned upon the loss of their cultural heritage to foreigners.

Zafar came to a halt at the edge of the crowd that filled the palm-tree-shaded square. The air was redolent with the smell of unwashed bodies, acrid with the palpable stench of fear emanating from the small group of African men who were huddled together for protection. Manacled and half-naked, their ebony skin glistening with perspiration, they awaited their turn on the rostrum, terrified and bewildered. Zafar's fists clenched automatically. Common as these markets were all the way along the Red Sea coast, accepted practice as it was, he could not help his natural repugnance at the sight of human bondage. He had banned such slave markets from Kharidja. Zafar turned, anxious to be gone.

'One thousand!'

The exorbitant sum stopped him in his tracks. The throng melted before him as he pushed his way roughly to the front, intimidated by the fury on his face as much as the trappings of power that were apparent in the pristine white of his robes, the glinting gold of his sabre and dagger hilts. In the centre of the dusty space stood the slave trader, a Turk, and long-travelled if the condition of his clothes was an indication. Beside him, striving to keep herself upright, her arms crossed over her bared breasts, her eyes glistening with a mixture of terror and defiance, was a woman. A foreign woman. European by the look of her, her pale skin raw with sunburn, her hair, the colour of chocolate, streaming down her back.

The urge to yank his sabre from its sheath and to set about clearing the crowd was almost irresistible. Zafar's hand was already on the hilt, his other on the dagger he wore strapped across his chest.

'One thousand and fifty. And one hundred. One thousand two hundred.'

There were three competing bidders. He knew without a doubt the horrors that awaited this woman whose eyes darted between each of the men who held her fate in their hands. In their purses.

She was trembling. He could see, from the way she clenched her jaw, from the tightening of the muscles on her neck, the effort it took her to stay upright. The dress she wore had been ripped from her upper body, the bodice with its empty sleeves hanging in tatters at her waist. Though she seemed to have escaped the whip or any obvious molestation, her bare feet were filthy and bloody. French or English, most likely, left behind when their respective armies left Egypt. He could not imagine what travails she had already suffered. He had witnessed the indignities she would have been put through as potential buyers examined her.

Zafar's hand tightened on his sabre, but it had been

a long road, this bloody battle towards a lasting peace, too long and too hard-fought for him to risk such a provocative action now, despite the still-raw horrors the situation invoked. Yet there was something about the woman that drew him. She was perhaps twenty-four or-five, slim in the way some Western women were, her waist narrow, her breasts small. Her face had a remote beauty about it in the sculpted cheekbones and finely drawn brows. In contrast, her lips were full. Despite her terror, it was her determined aloofness, the way she refused to cower or to shrink, that earned his admiration. There was defiance in those surprisingly blue eyes of hers, and courage, too.

'Three thousand.'

A ripple of excitement greeted Zafar's bid.

Two of the three contenders shook their heads, but the third remained in the game. 'Four thousand,' he growled.

Zafar did not recognise the man, but he recognised his intentions. 'Five.'

'Six thousand.'

'Highness, this is madness. What use can you possibly have for such a scrawny specimen?'

Zafar, now grimly determined, ignored Firas, who had appeared at his shoulder. 'Ten thousand for the girl and the men,' he said.

An audible gasp greeted this bid. Behind him, his man of business groaned. His opponent hesitated for a painful moment, then he muttered something vicious under his breath and turned away. The slave trader nodded jubilantly. No doubt he would now retire on his profits, but Zafar did not care. He allowed himself a small, triumphant smile. A victory, and bloodless to boot. It was worth every gold coin in his considerable purse to spare this woman. He turned to Firas. 'Have the men freed from their manacles. Give them food and water, and get the caravan ready.'

'Highness, why?' Firas expostulated. 'You could have purchased a herd of prize camels for such a sum.'

Zafar, who was just beginning to ask himself the same question, eyed his man haughtily. 'You dare question my judgement?'

Firas did not flinch. 'No, Highness. I have no need, for I understand very well why you acted as you did,' he said quietly.

'Then you should also understand that I will *not* have that matter discussed.'

The menace in his voice was unmistakable. Though he allowed Firas much latitude, this was one topic upon which he would not be questioned. His man bowed low and scuttled off to do his master's bidding.

Colette Beaumarchais pulled the ruins of her bodice around her to cover her nakedness and struggled desperately to hold her shattered nerves together. Nearly two weeks in captivity, snatching sleep in short bursts, acutely aware that at any moment her captors might turn on her, had taken a severe toll. When she realised the brigands had decided not to molest her for fear of reducing her value, her relief had been extremely short-lived. No one who had lived as she had, travelling with the French army across Egypt and Syria, could be ignorant of the fate that awaited a female sold into slavery.

Leon had been forever warning her of the dangers of straying far from the camp, as had her dear papa. Both her husband and her father were dead now, and for the first time she discovered she was glad of that. They would never know the fate that befell her. Which was not, at least, going to be determined by the evil-looking man who had been defeated at the last minute.

It made no difference, she told herself. The outcome would still be the same. But surreptitiously eyeing the man who had bought her, she could not suppress the tiniest little surge of relief. That he was rich, she had no doubt, for her basic grasp of Arabic had allowed her to follow the bidding. That he was powerful was also indisputable, for there was an indefinable air of authority about him—not arrogance but confidence. A man used to complete and unquestioning obedience.

His tunic and the cloak he wore over it, which she had learned to call a *bisht,* were an immaculate white. His headdress, too, white and what looked like silk. The *igal,* the band that held it in place, was threaded with gold, and the curved sheath of the sabre he wore at his waist was studded with what looked to be emeralds and rubies. Rich and noble, if the way the people were bowing and scraping around him was anything to go by. Yes, there was something extremely attractive about him, in the fluid way he moved, like a prowling predator, both graceful and lethal. A warrior? There was that, too, in his face, which had not Leon's classical good looks but had that hewn, hard-planed look of the battle-hardened soldier. His skin was tawny, the colour of the sands at dusk, and his eyes were dark, hooded. A man who gave nothing away. He wore no beard. His mouth was strikingly sensual. Her captor. Her owner. The man who now held her life in his hands.

He turned away from the slave trader just then and met her gaze for the first time. Colette inhaled sharply. Under other circumstances, it was true she would find him most attractive, intriguing even, but these were not other circumstances. *Sacré bleu,* what was she thinking! This man had just purchased her like some chattel. He could—and without doubt would—do with her what he wished. *Bien,* she was not a general's daughter for nothing. Garnering all her courage, Colette straightened her shoulders and stood proud, meeting the man's gaze defiantly, knowing full well how offensive such a gesture could be perceived from a mere woman. *'Monsieur,'* she said unwaveringly, 'you may have purchased my body, but I must warn you, you will never break my spirit.'

She spoke in her native language, not expecting him to understand, the words uttered as a boost to her flagging courage rather than from any desire to antagonise. Her purchaser's eyes, however, a curious colour, amber or gold, flashed fire. His brows were drawn together in a fierce frown.

'You should be very glad, *mademoiselle,*' he replied in perfect, softly accented French, 'that it is I and not one of the other bidders who prevailed today. Be assured that having paid such an exorbitant amount, they would take great pleasure in breaking both your body and your spirit.'

He was clearly furious, yet his fists remained unclenched, and he made no effort to close the short distance between them. Did he mean that he would not try to break her, or that the breaking of her would give him no pleasure? 'Why?' Confused, Colette asked the question uppermost in her mind. 'Why did you pay so much for me? I am sure a man such as yourself could have purchased any number of slaves more beautiful than I for such a sum.'

He surveyed her, not lasciviously but as her father was wont to survey the strategy board when planning a battle. 'Why do you think, *mademoiselle?*' he asked.

Confused, she could only stare. On one level she *was* afraid, but another part of her was inclined to doubt his intentions. A warrior he may be, but he was no violator. Her instincts told her she could trust him, but she knew better than to trust instincts when her mind was affected by the intense heat, her fierce thirst and, above all, the trauma of the past few weeks. 'I think you paid such an *exorbitant* sum merely for the pleasure of winning, *monsieur,*' she said. 'I cannot imagine that you wish such a—a meagre example of womanhood as I in your harem.'

'Meagre?'

'Skinny,' Colette replied warily. Horribly conscious that her meagreness was barely covered, she tightened her grip on the tattered remnants of her gown before recalling how pointless it was, for he had already seen for himself during the bidding the smallness of her breasts, the narrowness of her waist. Leon used to tease her about her slimness on the occasions when they shared a bed. 'I had as well married a schoolboy,' he had said once as she lay beneath him, eyeing her breasts in a disappointed way. It had hurt, though she had tried not to show it, for he had never pretended that he married her for love of her person.

*En fait,* she should be glad that her person was so unwomanly, for it may yet be her saving. Colette let go of her bodice, deliberately baring herself. 'As you see, *monsieur,* I have none of the attributes that would make me fit for your harem.'

Cursing low under his breath in Arabic, he unfastened his cloak and threw it over her shoulders, pulling it close to cover her nakedness. 'The first law of the harem, *mademoiselle,'* he said, 'is that a concubine should be seen only by her master.'

His fury took her aback as much as his protectiveness confounded her. The silken folds of the *bisht* caressed her bare skin as it swathed her. She had never worn anything so luxurious. Colette pulled it closer around her, as if it could form a barrier between her and the crashing reality of the situation. She had little fight left in her, but there was still some. 'You will be disappointed,' she said. 'I warn you, I am no virgin.'

Now his fists did clench. 'The men who captured you?'

Hastily, Colette shook her head as she saw the direction of his gaze, towards the slave-driver. *'Non!* My husband.'

'Your husband! He cannot be much of a man to have allowed his wife to be captured.'

'He is dead, *monsieur.* But if he were alive, he would assure you that I am not—that I know nothing of the arts of love,' she said desperately. 'You will be disappointed in me. I am not fit for your harem, but I have other skills. If you will allow me to work, I can—'

'You think I will set you to work?'

'I am much stronger than I look,' Colette said, defensive in the light of the stark disbelief in his tone. 'I can clean and cook and sew, and I am an excellent organiser. Papa always said so. Also, I can nurse. In the field hospital, I was—'

'Enough!' He held his hand up as if to fend off her words. 'I have no need of slaves, and my kingdom is not at war, *mademoiselle—madame.* I wonder what kind of man were you married to, that he made you so certain of your lack of womanly charms?'

The distance between them had not changed, but Colette shivered under his heated gaze as if he had touched her. Fear warred with a flicker of excitement low in her belly. It was wrong to feel this way. She licked her cracked lips. 'My husband was a soldier,' she said.

'Your husband was a fool.' He reached out to touch her, smoothing his hand over the fall of her hair. The flicker of excitement tightened into a knot. 'What is your name?' he asked.

'Beaumarchais. Colette Beaumarchais.'

'Madame Beaumarchais, you should not be so quick to leap to conclusions.'

*Cat's eyes, like a tiger,* she thought, mesmerised, trying to ignore the way her skin was heating as he brushed her hair away from her face, his fingers feathering over her cheek, down the column of her neck.

'I don't understand. If you do not want me for a slave or a concubine, then why did you buy me?' Colette demanded, shrugging away his hand, which was resting on her shoulder.

He moved swiftly as she made to walk away, pulling her hard up against him, breast to chest, thigh to thigh. Heat flooded her at the shocking nearness, at the overwhelming maleness of him, his solid muscle and sinewy strength. A warrior. And a very potent man. *'Laissez-moi!'*

He laughed. 'Release you? Into the desert and no doubt into the hands of another set of slave traders? You do not wish that.'

'No. I mean yes. I am perfectly capable of looking after myself.'

'As you have shown by your appearance today.'

Silenced, she ceased struggling. 'Who are you? Why won't you let me go if you don't want me?'

'I am Prince Zafar al-Zuhr of the Kharidja.'

Her heart began to hammer in her breast. He held her so closely that she could feel the slow, steady beat of his. One hand slid down her spine to her waist. The other slid up her arm. There could be no doubting the heat in his gaze. There could be no doubting his intent as he bent his head towards her. He was going to kiss her. She braced herself and at the same time she tilted her face, parting her lips invitingly, only to find herself released as suddenly as she had been caught up against him. Mortified by her contrary behaviour, Colette staggered. 'You have not answered my question, Prince Zafar,' she said.

His eyes flashed. Drawing himself up to his full height, he eyed her disdainfully. 'I am Prince Zafar al-Zuhr of Kharidja. I answer to no one. You would do well to remember that.'

## *Chapter Two*

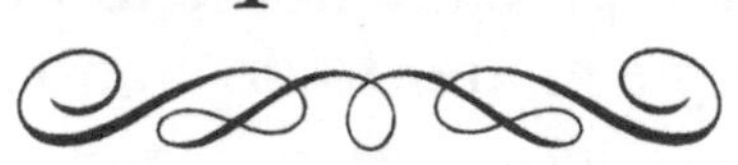

Zafar strode off towards his caravan, forcing the Frenchwoman to break into a trot to keep up with him. He was appalled at how close he had come to surrendering to the desire to kiss her. No matter that she seemed to think him a savage, Colette Beaumarchais was under his protection, and he would never violate that trust.

Rattling out a stream of orders to Firas in the vain hope that the man would be too taken up with obeying him to comment further on his prince's aberrant behaviour, Zafar was all the time conscious of the woman at his side wrapped in his *bisht* who was now, legally if not morally, his property. His responsibility. His, under the ancient custom of the land, to do with as he liked. It was a custom he wished he could outlaw, but so far progress in Kharidja had been slow, and resistance by his people—or the men, at any rate—strong.

He cursed himself inwardly. What in the name of the gods was he going to do with the woman! He had bid on impulse, intent only on saving her, without actually considering how he would do so. He had not expected gratitude, yet her attack on his honour, though completely natural under the circumstances, had hurt. It angered him that she had so misjudged him, that she had had the nerve to question his intentions. It pleased him to think how abject her apologies would be when he obtained a safe passage home to France for her. It would be no simple matter to do so, for there were few he could trust to escort her to Egypt, and he had no idea what the diplomatic situation was in Cairo. No, the best thing would be to take her to Kharidja and to make proper arrangements from there. This too would allow Madame Beaumarchais plenty of time to reassess her opinion of him, something that he was strangely set upon her doing. Later, when they set up camp, he would inform her of his plans and she would thank him. For now, though, he would allow her the time to repent of her attitude. Satisfied, Zafar nodded to himself and turned his attention to Colette. 'Have you ever ridden a camel?'

She stared at him blankly. Her eyes were smoky blue, the colour of the midnight sky over the endless desert. Dark shadows spoke eloquently of long, sleepless nights. The full, sensual lips he had been so intent on kissing were dry. He remembered the angry sunburn on the delicate skin of her body and cursed himself for being a thoughtless fool. How long had she been captive? Such a tender specimen as this with such pale European skin must find the heat of his beloved desert almost unbearable. 'Come,' he said gently, holding out his hand to her. 'There is shade and water aplenty where my caravan is being readied for the journey home to Kharidja. My kingdom is three days' ride away, over the desert.'

'Kharidja. I have never heard of that place. Why are you taking me there?'

She was clasping her hands tightly together, holding the folds of his cloak closed. Despite the burnish of the sun, her face had an ashen pallor. Even as he noticed this, Zafar saw her legs buckle and leapt forward to catch her, but she struggled to right herself. As her legs buckled again, he swept her into his arms, ignoring her flailing arms and protests. 'Stop struggling. You must save your strength.'

'For your bed, you mean.'

She was as stubborn as a mule! Zafar tightened his grip. 'For the camel,' he said curtly.

Colette clung to the high sides of the strange saddle, which swayed alarmingly. The ground was a lot farther away than it was from horseback. The animal smelled so different, too, and the constant bleating noises it made, as if in protest at being forced to carry an extra load, were most disconcerting. She fixed her eyes firmly on the horizon for fear of being sick. The dusty, stony track was giving way to sand. The sun was past its peak, and the headdress, one of Prince Zafar's own, was really most effective in keeping her cool, though she had protested at first, thinking it would make her much hotter.

A strong arm snaked around her waist and held her firmly. 'Do not resist it,' Prince Zafar said. 'If you let yourself be taken by the movement, you will find it easier.'

Nervously she eyed the reins, which were threaded with gold and decorated with little tinkling bells. 'I am perfectly well.'

'Forgive me, but you look far from well. Now, let go of the saddle. Feel the movement of the camel as you would the movement of the sea on the deck of a ship.'

Tentatively, she did as she was bid, letting her body move with the motion of the saddle. 'You are right,' she said in surprise some moments later.

'You will find that I almost always am.'

'I doubt that,' Colette replied. 'More likely it is that no one dares tell you that you are wrong.'

She knew as soon as the words were out that she had been not only rude but disrespectful, but he surprised her. 'That is very true, Madame Beaumarchais, none dare. I wonder why you do?'

It was beyond foolish of her, but there was something about this man that made her want to challenge him. His unconscious assumption of power that was no doubt well deserved, that was part of it, but there was, too, his determination not to explain himself, an aloofness that she wanted to break down. And then there was her own challenge to him. She would not allow him to break her spirit. Attack was the best form of defence. Papa's favourite maxim; it would serve her as well as any other. 'When one has nothing to lose,' she replied, 'one dares anything.'

'I wonder, would you have been more conciliatory

were I one of the other bidders?' Prince Zafar asked, his voice suddenly cold.

Colette bit her lip, reminding herself of the many tales she had heard, of the fact that this man, no matter how civilised he may appear, was a desert sheikh who had bought her. Had she misjudged him? 'You must understand, my experience of your countrymen has not exactly been pleasant,' she said warily.

'The men who captured you were Turks.'

Another faux pas, obviously. 'I would find it easier to trust you if you would tell me what you intend to do with me.'

'That very much depends on whether you trust me or not.'

'My papa would call that a non sequitur. It means—'

'I know perfectly well what it means.'

'I beg your pardon. Your command of my native language is most impressive.'

'For a barbarian, you mean.'

'For anyone, I mean!' Colette snapped. 'You are determined to put the worst interpretation on everything I say.'

'And you are determined to put the worst interpretation on everything I do,' Prince Zafar snapped back.

'It is surely understandable, given the circumstances.'

'You think so, Madame Beaumarchais? Have you actually considered the circumstances? We make camp in an hour. I would advise you to spend the time contemplating your situation most carefully.'

* * *

The night sky was inky blue, littered with stars which seemed to hang much lower than they did at home. There was a vastness about the desert sky that made Colette feel insignificant and utterly alone. Roused from a light doze as the camel came to a halt, she looked around her in astonishment. Enormous sand dunes spread out into the distance in soft folds and sharp ridges. A half-full moon cast its eerie light over the oasis, where the caravan had drawn to a halt. A cluster of goatskin tents stood on one side of the glittering water, while a much larger tent was pitched under the shelter of a group of palms.

She staggered as she dismounted from the camel. Her legs stiff, her eyes gritty with sand, she looked about her in wonder at the beauty of the desert night, at the hive of activity near the tents, the mules and camels hobbled for the night, the slaves, freed of their manacles, helping to light fires and prepare food. Beside her, Prince Zafar was silent, surveying the camp with a frown. 'What will you do with them?' she asked, pointing to the Africans.

He shrugged. 'My kingdom is small but growing fast. There are many opportunities for those who wish to take them. Those who wish to return to their native land will be assisted to do so.'

'They will be free?'

'I have outlawed slavery in Kharidja.'

Which begged the question of her own status, Colette thought but did not say. Through the long journey across the desert she had tried, as he had bid her, to consider the circumstances but had managed to do so only fitfully. Relaxing into the swaying motion of the camel meant relaxing into Prince Zafar's body. His arm had circled her waist protectively, his hand resting lightly on her hip. Her rear was tucked into him, the outside of her thighs brushing the inside of his. It was shockingly intimate and even more shockingly pleasant. Her body tingled with wholly inappropriate awareness, little flickers of pleasure darting along her skin, heating and tightening her belly.

Leon had never affected her like this. When he made love to her, there were moments, the glimmer of something in the distance she never quite reached. Was it the fact that this man was so fantastically exotic, so blatantly masculine and clearly powerful, that appealed to her? Casting a sidelong look at the powerful figure outlined against the desert night, she reminded herself to be on her guard, but the gnawing feeling that she had misjudged Prince Zafar refused to go away.

She had always been an excellent judge of character. Papa said so, and Leon, too. *Vraiment,* she had been through a dreadful experience, but it was very wrong of her to allow it to shape her views of every man she met. Besides, though she had unintentionally angered him, what she had said to Prince Zafar was true—she really had nothing to lose.

Colette took a deep breath. 'Highness?' He turned towards her, frowning. 'Prince Zafar,' she said tentatively, 'I fear I owe you an apology. I believe I have misjudged you.'

His eyes narrowed, though he said nothing. 'I can see you are a good man,' she continued doggedly, 'from the esteem in which your servants hold you. And freeing the slaves, too, your kindness in offering to send them home if they wished it.'

Still no reply, but his very stillness reassured her that he was listening. 'I have no idea why you paid such a very large amount to save me from those other bidders,' Colette said, 'but I do know that you have saved me as surely as you have saved those Africans, and for that I thank you from the heart. I am in your debt.'

Impulsively, she dropped to her knees and took his hand, pressing a kiss to his fingers, but seeing his startled look she realised she had probably broken all sorts of unwritten rules and hastily let him go.

He grabbed her hands, pulling her to her feet. 'Never abase yourself before me like that.'

'I am sorry, I only meant—'

'You owe me no debt. I do not want your gratitude and I certainly have no need of a woman on such terms.'

Colette stared at him in confusion. 'I was not offering myself to you on any terms. I was merely saying thank you.' Despite herself, her temper flickered. 'I know perfectly well that I am not—not to your taste, Highness. You told me so yourself.'

'I told you I didn't want you as my concubine. I did not say that I didn't find you attractive. Which does not mean I have any desire at all to take you in gratitude any more than I would take you by force.'

Relief and exhilaration made Colette giddy. Despite

the crowd of freed slaves, servants and animals just a short distance away, it felt as if they were alone at the oasis. The desert air was warm and sweet, enveloping them in its soft caress. Awareness of the scent of him, the heat of him, the sheer power and overwhelming maleness of him, shot through her blood, making her heart pound. His hands, which had been resting in hers, now slid up her arms. Though he did not urge her, she stepped towards him. Beneath the soft folds of his tunic, she could see his chest rise and fall. The thin line of a scar ran from his ear to his throat, she noticed, stopping frighteningly close to the fragile pulse, which would have meant certain death had the wound been a fraction longer. She could not resist reaching out to touch it. 'You had a narrow escape,' she said softly.

His face hardened as he pushed her brusquely away. Something that looked like pain darkened his eyes. 'No,' he said. 'Quite the contrary.' He turned away from her and nodded down at the oasis. 'You will wish to bathe.'

Nonplussed, Colette stared at the glinting water longingly. 'How can I?' she asked, indicating the throng of the camp.

He held out an imperious hand. 'Come with me.'

# *Chapter Three*

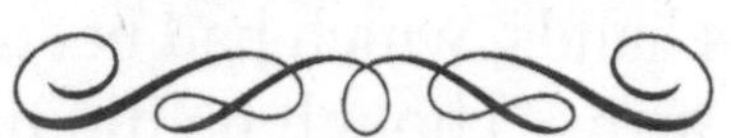

The oasis was shaped like a figure eight, with the caravan set out by the larger of the two pools. Prince Zafar led her to the smaller one, which was bordered by large tussocks of spiky grass and small shrubs. Though she could still hear the chatter of the servants, the snuffling and bleating of the camels and mules, Colette could see none of them from the pool's edge.

'Your privacy is guaranteed,' Prince Zafar said. 'I have given orders that no one is to disturb us.'

Orders that would be obeyed unquestioningly, Colette thought with a small smile.

'Here, there are drying cloths, soap, a fresh tunic for you to change into. I shall wait on you while you bathe. With my back turned, you may rest assured, *madame.'*

He had obviously gone to some trouble to make the arrangements for her. Touched by his consideration Colette dropped a small curtsy. *'Merci,* Highness, you are most thoughtful.'

A brief nod greeted this remark before Prince Zafar turned his back. Had she offended him again? She had no idea. The man was unfathomable; there was no point in trying to understand him. Shrugging to herself, Colette made her way to the edge of the water and undressed.

He could hear the rustle of her clothes as she slipped out of them, the gentle ripple of the water as she entered the pool. He could picture her, tall and slim, pale in the light of the moon, the warm waters lapping at her toes, her calves, her thighs, her derrière, her waist, her breasts, as she made her way into the centre of the pool. He could picture her all too clearly. The urge to turn around, to see for himself how closely his imagination matched reality, was almost irresistible.

Zafar tried to focus his mind on more important matters—the business of running his kingdom, of achieving lasting peace, of promoting prosperity, matters that never failed to occupy him—but the little splashes that told him she was washing, lathering her body with his own lemon-scented soap, distracted him. Desire had not deserted him in the past two years. Since there was no shortage of willing and beautiful women eager to share his bed, it was easily sated, but this was different. He didn't want *a* woman but this particular disrespectful, brave, opinionated woman.

The stillness of the desert night carried every sound. Colette Beaumarchais's sighs of pleasure floated across the water to taunt him. He imagined her lying on her back, floating under the stars, the small mounds of those perfect breasts exposed to the sky. So different from— so different. And perhaps that was why she was so desirable?

An exclamation, quickly muffled, made him whirl around, his hand going instinctively to his scimitar, drawing it swiftly from his belt, slicing the vicious blade through the air above his shoulder in readiness as he covered the short distance to the water's edge. 'What is it? What did you see?' Zafar scanned the surroundings for sign of an intruder.

'What are you talking about? I dropped the soap.'

'You dropped the soap!' The fingers of his left hand were tight around the dagger that was strapped across his shoulder. He waded out towards her. She shrank away from him. Realising that he was still holding his scimitar at the ready, he dropped his arm. 'I thought you were in danger.'

She shook her head. Zafar realised that she was shaking at the same time as he remembered she was naked. 'I frightened you,' he said remorsefully, determinedly keeping his eyes on her face.

'I— It was just—seeing you with that sword—I just remembered…'

Her eyes were bright with tears, though she was valiantly trying to suppress them. She was hugging herself tight, obviously much more shaken than she cared to admit. Zafar threw his scimitar onto the shore and pulled her against him, wrapping his arms tight around her. 'I am deeply sorry.'

'I am perfectly fine now,' Madame Beaumarchais said, and burst into tears.

Her head was on his chest, her hair soaking into his tunic, her naked body pressed against the length of his own, but he desired only to comfort her. He held her, telling her again and again that she was safe.

The storm was over as quickly as it began. Her sobs quieted. She stopped shaking. 'I don't usually cry. Papa always said that tears are for those who can do nothing else,' she mumbled into his chest.

'Women cry, men act,' Zafar said.

'But a general's daughter must lead from the front.' She pushed herself free of him. 'I am sorry I alarmed you. And I'm sorry you have endured an unnecessary soaking.'

The water was waist height. She had wrapped her arms around her breasts again, but she did not cower or shrink. She was blushing, but her eyes met his bravely. His own tunic clung to him like a second skin. 'I intended bathing after you,' Zafar said.

'I'm sorry I lost the soap.'

His laughter surprised him as much as it did her, echoing over the water. The strangeness of the day, the strangeness of the situation, all suddenly seemed absurd. 'Please, *madame,* allow me,' Zafar said, casting off his headdress, his belt and his dagger, throwing them all onto the shore and diving into the water.

Colette watched in amazement. He looked so much younger when he laughed, though she got the impression he didn't laugh very often. He surfaced, water streaming down his face, took a breath and dived again, giving her a glimpse of firmly muscled buttocks, long legs, narrow feet. She knew she should not be looking, but she couldn't drag her eyes away. His hair was short-cropped. Without his headdress he looked less intimidating and much younger.

'Voila!'

Prince Zafar surfaced triumphant, holding the block of soap in one hand, smiling widely. His tunic clung to him, completely transparent, revealing the broad expanse of his chest, a smattering of dark hairs, the dip of his belly. Somewhere low in her own belly, the muscles tightened as she stared at him, his skin the colour of caramelised sugar at the open throat of his tunic, the strength and power of his warrior's body, the smooth cap of his hair. His smile faded under her gaze, his eyes seeming to gleam in the moonlight as they focused on hers. Heat sizzled under her skin as he looked at her and she saw her own burgeoning need reflected on his face, though he made no move towards her.

She knew now why he hesitated, why he would not move. Honour rather than a lack of desire. He would not make the first move. Colette had never been bold, but nor had she ever felt the headiness, the power of being wanted so blatantly. If she did not move, nor would he. But if she did… Though she had only the haziest idea of what she would be missing, she did not want to miss it. She had come so close to death she wanted, needed, to feel alive.

She reached out her hand and touched his cheek, running her fingers down the long column of his throat to the opening of his tunic. His eyes widened. His breathing quickened with hers. She stepped closer, dropping the arm that covered her breasts, and pressed herself against him, pressed her naked flesh to the damp fabric of his tunic.

He shuddered. The waters of the pool caressed them. She was dimly aware of the talking, the muted laughter, the sounds of the animals coming from the encampment. The night sounds of the desert—the cry of a hawk, the rustling of animals in the shrubs—added to the mystery, the strangeness, the exoticness of the scene. Practical Colette Beaumarchais, war widow, general's daughter, captive, with Zafar al-Zuhr, warrior, prince, rescuer, in an oasis in the desert.

One of his hands was twined in the long strands of her hair. The other was clenched tight at his side. She could feel the rapid rise and fall of his chest against her breasts. *'Madame,'* he said, his voice husky, 'I told you, I do not want your gratitude.'

'This is not gratitude.' That he could resist, even while she offered herself so blatantly, was no longer an insult but the best, most flattering of compliments. She closed the final gap between them, moving her hips against the thick length of his erection under the water, knowing that he wanted her, knowing that despite his wanting her he would not take what she did not offer. Leon would be appalled by her utter lack of modesty, by the very idea that she might just be surrendering to desires of her own, wishes of her own. This thought gave her confidence. The look of raw passion that Prince Zafar gave her made her bones melt.

She pulled him towards her so suddenly that he staggered as her mouth found his. For an appalling moment she thought he would shrug himself free, that she had misread the whole situation . Then he put his arms around her, lifting her feet from the sandy bottom of the pool, and kissed her hard on the mouth.

Her lips were cool and soft. Her body was wet, hot, surprisingly supple, delightfully curved. Her kiss sent him spinning almost out of control as she clung to him, wrapping her arms around his neck, pressing her breasts against his chest. In an instant he was aflame with desire, lost in the smell of her, the taste of her, the exoticness of her, this conundrum of a woman, this astonishingly generous woman, this woman of so many contrasts and contradictions.

She tasted of soap and clean water and something most definitely female, spicy and sweet. He pulled her closer, kissing her more deeply, groaning as his tongue met hers, touching, tasting, tangling with his. He wrapped her legs around his waist, holding her high against him in the water, shuddering as the throbbing hardness of his erection was enveloped in the soft, damp heat of her thighs.

She was panting, moaning, kissing him, astonishingly just as wild as he, clinging, tugging at his flesh to bring him closer, closer. He staggered to the water's edge, setting her down in the sand, breaking contact for the briefest of aching seconds to yank his sodden tunic over his head.

Casting it onto the sands, he caught her watching him, her eyes wide, unblinking. No woman had ever dared to look at him so. No woman had ever expressed such raw desire before. He found he liked it. He stood there as her eyes travelled over his body, relishing the way she looked, taking her hands, urging her to touch where her eyes fell, his shoulders, his chest, his belly, his flanks. As her fingers curled around his shaft, he groaned aloud. Blood pulsed through him, stretching the skin taut. That smile of hers, did she know what it did to a man?

Gently, reluctantly removing her hands from him, he cupped her derrière and kissed her swiftly, encouraging her to arch into him, feeling the heat, the wetness of her, against his shaft. He kissed his way down her throat to her breasts, taking one pink, hard nipple into his mouth and sucking, still supporting her, holding her tight against his erection. She gave a rousing little gasp.

Her other breast now, sucking, licking, sucking. Another little gasp. He was throbbing, concerned that he would lose control, he whose life was all about control, succumbing to his urgent need to be inside her too swiftly, too soon.

Easing her down onto the sand, he kissed her mouth again, her breasts again. She writhed delightfully, bucking up under him. Parting her legs, he moved between them to kiss her belly. A startled gasp greeted this move, and he remembered what she had said, that she knew nothing of the arts of love. The arts that it was a husband's job to teach his wife. Obviously the man she had married had been a very poor husband. No wonder she thought herself unattractive. Zafar smiled with satisfaction as he kissed his way down her belly to the apex of her thighs. A cluster of dark curls, damp with her arousal, smelling of vanilla. Placing his hands under her bottom, he tilted her towards his mouth, parted the soft folds of skin with his lips and set about showing her just one of the many things she had been missing.

# *Chapter Four*

Colette felt taut, every muscle, every sinew focused on riding the wave of spiralling heat that was building inside her. Shocked then excited, exhilarated, her body thrumming and pulsing in response to the way he licked, sucked, kissed, a part of her that she had never considered any man could do such outrageous, delicious things to.

She dug her hands into the sand, feeling the warm grains trickle through her fingers, and dug her heels in, too, bracing herself for the inevitable surrender to the aching, tingling, tightening within. Brief glimpses she had had of this feeling, but always they had dissipated before completion. Once, she had touched herself in the hope of reaching this place but had been too ashamed to continue. She was not ashamed now. She cared for nothing but the way he slid his fingers inside her and thrust high, the way his tongue swept over the hard, hot centre of her, his other hand reaching up to cup her breast, and the whirl of her climax sent her spinning headlong, pulsing with heat, left breathless, panting, shuddering, clinging, crying shamelessly for more.

He held her tight against his mouth, licking more slowly, bringing her gently down to earth. She opened her eyes and saw stars. Real stars, low in the desert sky. A deep chuckle made her skin prickle and her muscles tighten in some primal response. He was hovering over her, his eyes gleaming with something that looked like triumph. She did not grudge him it but reached for him, pulling him towards her to kiss him deeply, tasting her arousal on his lips. 'I have never…'

'I know,' he replied with another throaty chuckle.

'I didn't,' she said, laughing too.

'And did you like it, *ma petite* Colette?'

'I fear the entire camp must be aware that I did.'

He laughed aloud at that, and she wondered why she felt only this wild excitement and absolutely no shame. Then his erection pulsed against her belly, and the ebb of her climax began to turn, demanding a different kind of satisfaction. She ran her fingers down his spine to rest on the taut muscles of his buttocks and arched up against him.

'Colette.' He shuddered. His smile fading, he kissed her again, and then again. She dug her heels farther into the sand, embracing his thighs with hers. The tip of his shaft was nudging between her legs, tantalisingly close. She ached to have him inside her, but she sensed him hesitating. 'What is wrong?'

He closed his eyes as if in anguish. Then abruptly he rolled away from her and got to his feet. *'Non.'* He cursed quietly in Arabic. Quickly pulling on the clean tunic that had been left out for him, he handed her another. 'There is food in my tent, the large one under the palm trees. I will escort you there. Eat and then sleep. I have many things to attend to. We leave at dawn,' he said, and led her to the tent, where he left her alone with her thoughts and a burning sense of shame.

For the first two days and nights of the journey he kept his distance, trying to make sense of the emotions the Frenchwoman had awoken in him. Guilt predominated, for he had come alarmingly close to betraying his own code of honour by taking advantage of her. For all that she had been married, she was a relative innocent. Not only was she under his protection, but she had been through a terrifying ordeal, had come horrifically close at that slave market to enduring worse. Under such near-death circumstances, it was not surprising that she behaved so out of character. In the aftermath of a battle, lust was one of the most natural emotions for a soldier, after all.

He had not taken advantage of her fragile mental state, but it had been far more difficult than it ought to have been. Finally, today, watching her tend to the festering sores on the ankles and wrists of several of the freed slaves, admiring the gentle but firm way she dealt with the most horrible of the infections, her calm, authoritative manner earning her patients' trust, Zafar admitted to himself that it was the simple fact that he had not found it easy to refuse what she offered that was most disturbing. He wanted her with a passion, an intensity he had thought beyond him.

He had assumed, from the fact that she made no effort to close the distance he placed between them, that she regretted what had happened at the oasis. As the third day drew to a close and night fell, Zafar began to see how his abandoning her by the water's edge left her no option but to do so. She must think herself callously rejected. *That* he must put right immediately.

Though the caravan had settled down for the night, Colette was sitting on the divan wide awake when he arrived in the doorway of the tent. 'May I?' Zafar asked.

She scrambled to her feet, covering herself with one of the tasselled silk covers. 'Of course. It is your tent, Highness.'

'Zafar,' he said, waving her back down onto the divan, taking a seat beside her. 'I wish to talk to you as a man, not a prince.' She eyed him uncertainly but sat beside him as he bid her, primly holding the emerald silk cover around her. 'I owe you an apology,' he said. 'When I left you at the oasis two nights ago, I thought only of myself. I did not consider how my behaviour must have appeared to you. It was not that I did not desire you or that I was shocked by your reactions to me.'

'It wasn't?'

She was blushing, playing with one of the tassels on the cover, refusing to meet his eyes. He took her hand between his. 'I thought my desire for you was obvious. Your reaction delighted me, Colette. I had not expected and I could see you had not either. I wanted more than anything to complete our lovemaking, but you have been through so much these last days and weeks and you told me yourself that you were behaving quite out of character.'

She blushed. 'I can certainly say hand on heart that I have never thrown myself in such a brazen manner at any man before, never mind a desert prince in the middle of a desert oasis.'

'And I can say hand on heart that it was only a supreme effort of will that made me stop. You did nothing to be ashamed of, Colette, but I very nearly did.'

'I don't understand.'

'It is one of the first laws of the desert, to keep safe those who are under your protection. It is a rule I intend *never* to break.' He did not say *again.* He had no need to remind himself—the guilt was there always, like a rogue cloud in a clear desert sky.

'I thought you were just too polite to refuse an overwrought foreigner.' Colette shook her head, half smiling. 'I thought I had broken all sorts of protocols and probably offended you in every way possible by making advances, and I've been worried that I'd offend you even more by apologising.'

Zafar laughed. 'And I thought you kept your distance because you regretted what had happened. One thing I have come to realise in our brief acquaintance is how very isolated protocol has made me. I am not infallible, though it is customary that I appear so to my people, and I would prefer that you keep that information to yourself.'

'Then I didn't embarrass you?'

She blushed charmingly. Her smile was generous, like the woman herself. He closed his eyes as the memory of her stretched out on the sands beneath him, crying out with pleasure, sent the blood hurtling to his groin. 'Colette, I deeply regret that you should have thought so.'

'I thought perhaps it might be that you're married? I would understand if you were.'

He flinched. 'No.' Conscious of her scrutiny, Zafar jumped to his feet and made a show of adjusting the wick of the lamp. 'I have no— I am not married, and I don't have a harem—at least, I do have a harem, but it lies empty,' he said, which was the truth and calmed him enough to allow him to sit back down again. 'My duty is to protect those in my care. I failed in that duty once before. I vowed never to repeat that error.'

Colette frowned, distractedly pleating the tassels on the cover together, then shook her head emphatically. 'My actions were nothing to do with being taken prisoner and sold, though I suppose there was an element of being simply glad to be alive. But that was only a small part of it.'

'Why, then?' he asked, intrigued.

She did not answer him directly. 'Zafar, what do you intend to do with me?'

'Send you back to France, of course. Did you doubt it?'

'No. Yes. I can't understand why you are taking me to Kharidja.'

'It will take time to make the appropriate arrangements. I don't know what the political situation in Cairo is, and I will not allow you to travel without being assured of your safety.'

'The first law of the desert again.'

He nodded. 'You have not answered my question.'

'I will, but it's a bit of a long story.'

Zafar pulled off his headdress, throwing it onto the floor and running his hands through his hair. 'We have all night, and you have my undivided attention.'

Colette settled back on the divan, curling her feet underneath her, trying to decide where to start. It was an immense relief to discover that she had not misread Zafar's attraction to her, a more than pleasant surprise to hear that it was every bit as unexpected to him as it had been to her. It had cost him to speak to her as he had done tonight, when he had no need at all to justify himself to her, was indeed quite obviously unaccustomed to justifying himself to anyone. She owed him the truth in return.

'I told you I was a general's daughter,' Colette said. 'I've followed the drum all my life. First with Papa and then with Leon, my husband. I met him when he was one of my father's junior officers and when Papa died, Leon asked me to marry him. He never pretended that he was in love with me, though I know he cared for me as I did him. Ours was a marriage of convenience. When an army is on a campaign, there are advantages in having a wife to take care of the practical arrangements. I had a lifetime's experience of doing so, and as I told you, I am also an excellent nurse.'

'I saw that for myself today. You did not flinch at even the most horrible of those wounds.'

Colette shrugged. 'What is the point in a fit of squeamishness when there is work to be done? Besides, I have seen much worse. Sometimes a man can lie for days in the sun in the aftermath of a battle before he is brought back to camp.'

'So you were in Egypt with your husband. Were you happy?'

She pursed her lips. 'I wasn't unhappy. I didn't know any different, you see. Papa instilled in me the need to be useful and Leon was very like Papa.' She found herself colouring again, this time with mortification, but forced herself to continue. 'To be very blunt, my husband found carrying out his marital duty something of a chore. I felt guilty for wishing it could be more pleasurable and assumed it was my fault that it was not. I thought I was simply not that kind of woman.'

Zafar cursed in his own language. 'In my culture, we are taught that such a failure is always the man's.'

'In my culture, we are not taught anything, which is part of the problem, I suspect,' Colette said tartly. 'I had no idea—but then, you sensed that.' She broke off, blushing.

'Your husband sounds like a fool.'

Colette shook her head. 'He was a good man and a good soldier. Leon died of typhoid in the last throes of the campaign. I stayed behind to nurse the wounded when the other wives were sent home. Then there was a delay in sending more ships, and while we were waiting, I heard of a group of deserters who had been attacked in the desert and I foolishly agreed to be part of a group that went to their aid. We were attacked, I was the only woman, the men were all killed and—*bien,* you know the rest.'

'You were fortunate indeed not to have been molested.'

'And even more fortunate in my rescuer,' Colette said warmly. 'I haven't thanked you properly, but…'

'I don't want your gratitude, I told you that. I don't think you realise what a lucky escape you had.'

'Trust me, I do. I simply don't see the point in dwelling on it. To snatch victory from the jaws of defeat was one of Papa's maxims. Even when he lost a battle, he could find something positive.'

'Admirable, though wrong-minded in my view.'

'You do like to view every situation in the worst possible light, I've noticed. You sit guard in the doorway of this tent every night with your dagger at the ready. I am a very light sleeper,' Colette said in answer to his questioning look. 'It is very noble of you, though what danger you think I can possibly be in with an entire caravan of armed men besides yourself to protect me…'

'You know nothing about the desert,' Zafar exclaimed. 'You nothing of its dangers, the ruthlessness of some, the cunning that can make use of the smallest lapse. You know nothing of it.'

His hand had gone to the dagger at his chest, his

knuckles white as he tightened his hand around the hilt. Taken aback at the sudden change in his mood, Colette tried to reassure him. 'I only meant that I feel safe here with you. I cannot imagine that anyone would dare attack—'

'Then you are beyond naive.' Zafar took a deep breath. 'I did not mean to alarm you, but there are things you do not know, things you are better not knowing….' He broke off, moving to the doorway of the tent to stare out at the desert.

What didn't she know? It was something far more complicated than a mere underestimating of the power of desert marauders, that was for sure. Colette hesitated, but she knew him well enough by now not to pursue the matter. 'Zafar, please don't go back to being a prince, not just yet. I don't know why you are so upset, but I promise you, I have no intention of allowing myself to be kidnapped again.'

She meant it as a joke. She could see him trying to see it as such and wondered why it was such a struggle. 'You are a very brave woman.' He reached out to touch her face, curling a long strand of her hair around his finger. 'I am glad we talked.' He unwound her hair. 'We leave at first light. You should get some sleep.'

'Wait. I haven't finished yet. You wanted to know what it was that made me behave so wantonly, especially when I told you that I know nothing of the arts of love.'

'You need no artifice to arouse me, I assure you. You did that simply by being yourself.'

'Really?'

Zafar took her hand and kissed her palm. It was the most fleeting of touches, his lips on her skin, but it sent her pulses fluttering. 'Really,' he said.

'That is most—interesting.' Her voice sounded breathless. Her mind was racing, thinking outrageous thoughts. The tone of this conversation was becoming more shocking by the second. Even more shocking, Colette was finding it exciting rather than shameful. 'That is most interesting,' Colette said again, 'because that is the main reason I behaved as I did. You being you, I mean. Just kissing you, just being near you, to be honest, I find that I cannot— That I— I've never felt like that before and I liked it. A lot, actually, I liked it a lot.'

She paused, trying to order her thoughts, and when Zafar made to speak, she held up her hand to silence him, momentarily distracted at the way he tried to hide his shock at being told to be quiet. 'I thought that I was never likely to meet anyone like you again,' she continued. 'I thought that I would regret it if I allowed modesty, propriety, whatever you wish to call it, to get in the way. After what I'd been through, such things seemed so trivial. In that sense, I suppose you could say I was affected by my ordeal.'

'Do I have your permission to speak?' Zafar asked, putting his hands together and lowering his eyes the way she had seen Firas do.

'Yes, I'm quite finished,' Colette replied, laughing.

'Thank you. I am honoured that you feel able to be

so frank with me. And in that spirit of frankness I want to assure you that the attraction between us is entirely mutual.'

Relief—not only at having finally been able to confess such intimate truths, but at realising that she was not the woman she thought she was, that the secret pleasures of the flesh were not beyond her reach—gave way to a recklessness in Colette. Having come this far, once again she felt she had nothing to lose. It was a liberating feeling. 'Have I reassured you that you would not be taking advantage?'

'You are still under my protection.'

'But you cannot harm me if you take only what I want to give,' she persisted. 'Knowing that I give myself freely to you, that would satisfy your sense of honour?'

'I…'

'How long do you think it will take to make the arrangements for my return to France?' Colette interrupted impetuously.

'A month, perhaps less. I will try to expedite things—I have contacts—but I will not compromise your safety. Colette, what are you proposing?'

'What I am proposing, for once in my life, is to do something purely and simply for the pleasure of it,' she said, and the truth of this gave her confidence. 'I am proposing that for the next month I occupy your empty harem and you—you induct me into the arts of love.'

He stared at her for so long she began to wonder if he had understood her. 'What I mean is, Zafar—'

'You are propositioning me!'

'I suppose you're going to tell me that's against protocol, but you did say that you wished to talk to me as a man and not a prince.'

'You are not asking me to believe it is any more common in your culture, surely, for a woman to proposition a man? No, don't answer that. I know it is not. You are quite outrageous, Madame Beaumarchais.' He was laughing, though he was trying not to let it show, but his eyes were sparkling and his mouth was trying desperately to curl up at the corners.

'I am sure I could learn to be much more outrageous, under your tutelage,' she said, allowing the silk cover to slide enough to reveal her shoulders, the faintest glimpse of her breasts.

Zafar, she was pleased to note, was momentarily distracted but did not, she was also pleased to note, allow his eyes to linger. 'Are you serious?' he asked.

'Very serious. When I return to France, it will be to a rather more mundane life.' Which was putting it mildly, Colette thought, recalling just how pitiful Leon's pension was. 'I will never again have such an opportunity to indulge my senses. In a royal palace. With a prince. In his harem.'

'With this prince. In my harem.' Zafar's smile, like his eyes, had a tigerish quality. 'I only hope I can live up to your expectations.'

'From what I saw at the oasis, I think there can be no doubt of that,' Colette said, risking a meaningful glance.

'Something, *chérie,* for which you must take all the credit.' Catching her unawares, he leaned across the divan and kissed her swiftly. 'I think you have a natural talent for this,' he whispered, nipping the lobe of her ear. 'It is a talent I would very much like to explore, but not tonight.'

Zafar got to his feet and picked up his headdress. 'If you are still as certain when we arrive in Kharidja, then it will be my pleasure to accept the challenge you offer. And, I very much hope, to our mutual satisfaction. *Bon nuit.*'

He pulled the curtain of the tent closed behind him. She could see his shadow as he sat guard, as he would sit guard all night. Colette blew out the lamp and settled down on the divan. Tomorrow she would be inducted into her brief career as a concubine. She could think of nothing that would have scandalised Leon more, save the fact that she knew without a doubt that she would enjoy every single second of it.

# *Chapter Five*

Kharidja was built around an enormous oasis. Irrigation allowed orange and lemon groves, vineyards and olive groves, and palm trees heavy with dates to flourish, creating a vibrant green contrast to the golden desert sands. The palace stood perched on a hill overlooking the city. Four large battlemented towers connected by high walls protected the inner buildings, which glittered white under the fierce heat of the sun above. At the gatehouse the caravan split, with the majority heading through the outer courtyard to the stables and servants' quarters. Firas jumped down from his camel, handing the reins to one of the house servants, and immediately hurried off, presumably to his office.

Alone with Zafar, Colette stared about her at the tinkling fountains, the refreshing leafiness of the plants, the gold, green and blue mosaic of the floor. Above the walls of the courtyard the palace loomed, more beautiful and much larger than she had imagined. At the highest point stood a minaret, the brilliant blue, gold and green tiles that decorated it sparklinglike jewels. 'It is truly lovely,' she exclaimed.

Noticing the shocked look on the guards' faces, she realised she ought not to have spoken to Zafar in public thus. Managing just in time to bite back an apology, she instead dropped her head and tried to look suitably respectful. Now she thought about it, no one had looked Zafar in the eye. In fact, several people had thrown themselves in front of his camel in obeisance, despite his impatiently signalling that he wanted them to do no such thing. She began to realise the extent of the liberties she had taken with his person and wondered, not for the first time, what it was he saw in her that made him tolerate, even encourage, such impertinent behaviour.

'Come,' Zafar said, 'I will show you to your quarters.'

She walked in his wake, through the door at the far end of the courtyard into another, much more elaborate courtyard containing a huge pool with a fountain at the centre. Following him around the pillared terrace at what Colette thought was a respectful distance, she began to feel quite intimidated by the majesty, the power and the wealth that this enormous palace represented.

'There is no need to walk like a servant.' He stopped, waiting for her in the next doorway.

'The guards were all staring at me when I spoke to you.'

'Because you are a foreigner. And a woman. You are my guest, Colette, not an inferior.'

'I feel very inferior.' She clutched the cloak she wore over her borrowed tunic more closely around her. 'I hadn't expected this to be so grand. It is as big as Versailles.'

'Don't you like it?'

'It's beautiful. Truly beautiful,' she said as the courtyard opened out into a high room adorned with so much gold leaf she blinked, 'but I can't help but feel under observation. There are so many guards.'

Zafar laughed. 'These are the public rooms. In the private rooms, one can be quite alone. Let me show you.'

She felt as if she had been walking for miles when they came to the huge oak door of the harem. 'No eunuchs,' she said half-jokingly.

'Another custom I have outlawed. No key either.' Zafar pulled the door open and ushered her in. 'Your harem, Madame Beaumarchais, which has not been used since my father's day. I trust that the rooms have been adequately prepared. I am afraid I must leave you to explore them, but I will return to take dinner with you in a couple of hours. If there is anything you require, just ask Barika.'

She had not noticed the maid hovering at the far end of the courtyard, which was smaller than any she had so far passed through and much more domestic, with cushions strewn around the little fountain and a table with chairs set in the shade, upon which was a tall silver pitcher of iced tea.

Her basic Arabic and the gentle maid's intuitiveness made the next two hours very pleasant indeed. After the reviving mint tea, Colette luxuriated in a sunken bath sprinkled with rose petals. In the adjoining bedchamber, she found to her delight a selection of clothes, gauze-like pantaloons and tunics in silk, chiffon and satin all in dazzling jewel colours, kidskin slippers decorated with seeded pearls, scarves and cloaks and headdresses. 'How?' she asked the maid in wonderment.

'Highness's orders,' Barika replied with a smile. 'The seamstresses worked all night. You like?'

'I love.' Wriggling into a pair of pantaloons made of coffee-coloured chiffon threaded with gold, pleated and tied at the waist with a gold sash, pulling the matching tunic over her head and staring at her reflection in the tall looking glass, Colette barely recognised herself. Her hair was glossy from the special treatment Barika had given her. She looked exotic, sultry. 'Like a concubine,' she said, laughing.

The maid, however, shook her head. 'Like a princess. A beautiful princess.'

The courtyard door opened and Zafar entered, followed by a procession of servants bearing large silver-and-gold salvers. Once the feast was laid out to their master's satisfaction, the servants emptied out of the harem. The nerves that had been banished by the novelty of her situation flooded back, making Colette feel slightly queasy. Since Zafar had accepted her audacious proposal, they had not been alone together. Now they were quite alone, and in a harem.

'Our native dress suits you very well,' Zafar said, seemingly quite at his ease as he sat down on the cushions beside the low table where the food had been set out.

'I should thank you for being so thoughtful.'

'It's nothing. Won't you join me?'

She perched awkwardly on a cushion, wishing she had his easy grace. 'The food looks delicious.' She doubted she'd be able to eat a thing.

'Are you hungry?'

'Honestly?' She forced herself to put aside the cushion she had been hugging to herself. 'I'm too nervous to eat.'

'We don't have to do anything other than eat. If you are having second thoughts…'

'No.'

'I would understand. It is one thing to discuss such an idea, another to face the reality of it in cold blood.'

Her blood didn't feel at all cold now that she looked at him, but she wondered if he was referring to himself. 'If you have changed your mind…'

'No.' Zafar reached over to touch her knee. 'The clothes are a gift. You do not owe me any obligation.'

'I know. I didn't think that for a moment. I'm just— It is simply that I don't know what to do.'

She only realised she had been clutching the cushion to her again when he reached over and removed it before holding out his hand and drawing her to her feet. 'The only thing you have to do is relax and enjoy,' he said softly. 'Let me show you.'

He caught her up, holding her high against his chest, and carried her to the bedchamber, but instead of laying her down on the divan, Zafar set her down in front of the looking glass. 'What do you see?'

'What do you mean?'

'Tell me, who is this person in the mirror?'

'Colette Beaumarchais.'

Standing behind her, he shook his head impatiently. Her body was framed by his in their joint reflection. He wore a flowing robe in royal blue, the high neck and cuffs braided and embroidered in darker shades. The simplicity of the tunic drew attention to the muscled form of the man beneath it, the stern, handsome face above it. 'In our culture, the body is a temple of delights. In order for you to enjoy them, to share your body with a man, you must first learn to love it yourself.'

He bent over to brush a kiss on the top of her head. 'When I look at you in the mirror, I see a beautiful woman who has not yet learned to appreciate her beauty.'

'I'm not beautiful. Please, Zafar, there is no need to pay me compliments. I would far rather you were honest with me.'

'I am not complimenting you, I am telling you what I see.' He brushed his hand down the length of her hair and wound a long tress around his hand. 'When I see your hair like this, I think of how it would be spread across my pillow. I think of how it would be wrapped around my wrists, manacling me to you. I imagine how you would be naked, with your hair caressing your breasts, your back, the curve of your spine.' As he spoke he stroked her, trailing a path over her breasts, down her back.

'You think your breasts are too small,' he said, cupping them in his hands, 'but they are incredibly sensitive. When I touch you like this, I can see from the way your eyes change colour, from the flush on your cheeks, what effect it has.'

He stroked her nipples with his thumbs, back and forward, back and forward, through the silk of her tunic. Beneath the filmy fabric she could see them puckering in the mirror, saw too the flush of her arousal on her cheeks, the way her eyes darkened, just as he said.

'Now, I see a woman who is ready to be pleasured,' Zafar said, pushing her hair back to nibble on the lobe of her ear, pressing tiny kisses onto the tender skin at her nape, returning his attention to the front of her tunic, slowly undoing the row of tiny buttons that fastened it. The tunic parted, and Colette gasped, closing her eyes on her nakedness.

'Look, *ma chère,* do not hide from your beauty,' Zafar urged. 'See how lovely is this curve.' He ran his hand from her cheek down her neck across to her shoulder. 'And this one.' His palms flattened on each of her sides down to the indentation of her waist. 'And this one.' Spread out over the curve of her hips. 'There is nothing more beautiful than curves. Your slenderness makes them all the more alluring. Do you see?'

She was beginning to. The creature in the mirror didn't look a bit like her, but then, Colette could not remember ever examining herself naked in such a way. Zafar was untying the sash that held her pleated pantaloons together. She wore nothing under them. Even now, she could see the outline of her legs, the shadow of her sex, beneath the chiffon. The pantaloons slid to the floor, leaving her naked, and this time she did not close her eyes. Behind her, Zafar was staring at her reflection as if mesmerised. His eyes too had darkened, his cheeks too were flushed with desire. She could feel the length of his arousal pressing into her back.

He spread his hands over her thighs and pulled her back against him in a rocking movement. 'I dream of you wrapped around me. When I see you like this, your skin so pale against my own, your shape so soft and pliant against mine, I can think only of what it would be like to be inside you, my hardness melded, enfolded by your softness. I think of your flesh, so cool yet capable of heating mine to boiling. I look at you and I see fire and ice, hidden pleasures waiting to be explored. Do you see it, Colette? Do you see yourself as I do?'

Holding her firmly against him, his shaft a solid weight in her back, Zafar covered her sex with his palm, sliding one finger inside her. She moaned, saw her refection moaning and moaned again.

He withdrew his finger and put it in his mouth. 'You taste as delightful as you look.' He cupped her sex again, sliding his finger inside her, over the heat of her, slowly circling, then took her hand and placed it under his. 'My pleasure is your pleasure,' he said.

She was shocked. He made no move to force her, merely covering her hand. 'It is your body, *chérie.* You should learn to love it. Explore it.'

Tentatively, she touched herself, doing as he had done, sliding in, over, circling. She was so wet. Again, she touched herself. Zafar's breathing quickened as she did so. Their reflection showed his eyes fixed on her hand, his face dark with desire, his hands gripping her hips, rocking her back against him. She touched herself more boldly, roused by her own touch, by his watching her, by her watching him.

'My pleasure is your pleasure.' His words in her voice, husky and sensual, made her smile, and her smile too was sensual. Who would have thought? Confident now, and too taut, too close to the edge to stop, she slid her fingers deeper inside herself and began to stroke harder, feeling her muscles tighten. Zafar's grip on her tightened, the gentle rocking of their bodies echoing each stroke, until she was so tense she could hold on no longer and came, crying out, panting, held firmly against him, as the waves of her climax shook her to her core.

When it had passed, she was astounded to find herself still upright, still gazing in the mirror, the woman reflected there wild-eyed and sated, the man behind her…

Definitely not sated, judging from the hardness she could still feel jutting against her back. 'Did I do something wrong?'

Zafar shook his head. 'You have done everything perfectly.'

'But you…'

'We are not finished yet. The second lesson in the art of love, *ma petite.* Our mutual pleasure.' Leading her gently over to the divan, he divested himself of his robe, lay down on the bed and pulled her on top of him.

# *Chapter Six*

'We have had word from our contact in Cairo, Highness. The French consul is most grateful to hear that Madame Beaumarchais is alive and well. I have taken the liberty of making preparatory arrangements for her journey in line with his proposals.'

Zafar scanned the papers Firas handed him. 'But this suggests she will leave in less than a week's time,' he said, frowning.

'It is already five weeks since she arrived, Highness. If you remember, your orders were to make the arrangements as speedily as possible. I thought you would be pleased to finally have the matter resolved.'

Zafar got up from behind his desk and stared out of the window at the courtyard, where a bird was singing in the ancient cypress tree. 'Has it really been five weeks?'

'Indeed, Highness. Long enough for your people to speculate as to the…er…exact nature of Madame Beaumarchais's position here. It has been a rare day when she has not been by your side, talking to you like a male courtier.'

'Madame Beaumarchais is helping me with my plans for the establishment of a hospital, as you well know.'

'Forgive me, Highness, but your people are wondering if you also have other plans for her? It has been two years since— It has been two years. It is not good for a man to be without the comfort a woman can provide, not good for Kharidja to be without the comfort of an heir. Every sovereign needs a consort. '

'You would do well to remember that topic is taboo, Firas.'

His man of business blanched but pressed on resolutely. 'Forgive me, Highness, but I must speak up, for the good of our kingdom. You need a wife. I have seen how you are when you are together. There is clearly something between you. It would be unconventional to say the least, but taking the Frenchwoman as your wife would meet with your people's approval, I'm sure of it.'

'Enough, Firas!' Zafar interrupted tersely. 'You go too far. I strongly suggest you restrict yourself to carrying out my wishes.' Zafar handed the man the document outlining the proposals for Colette's repatriation. 'Make the necessary arrangements,' he said, dismissing him with a curt nod.

As the door closed, Zafar returned to the window, staring out sightlessly at the courtyard. Never had five weeks passed so swiftly. It was not just the pleasures of the flesh he and Colette shared, though each night it seemed that they reached new, unimagined heights of ecstasy. Just thinking about it made him hard. That first night together, the exquisite pleasure of their joining, it had been almost overwhelming. Almost. He had been so close to spilling himself inside her, to losing himself in her. He had taken care not to do so again, even though the primal urge to possess her completely was almost impossible to resist. He could not risk the consequences. He did it for Colette's sake, he told himself, though he knew it was as much for his own. To surrender in such a way would be folly when he knew she must leave. They were from different worlds, he reminded himself, and soon they must each return to their own.

Though he kept up the pretence of teaching her, he was learning far more from Colette than he cared to admit. Never before had he been with a woman so liberated by her sensuality, so unreserved in her expression of it. *My pleasure is your pleasure,* he told her, and never before had the words held such truth. Knowing that he had been her first true lover made him feel ridiculously pleased with himself. Thinking that she would take another…No, he could not think of that.

But they had shared more than just passionate nights. As Firas pointed out, she was more often than not by his side during the day, a friend and a confidante. He had never had either. He had not realised how lonely and isolated he had become. Colette had blurred the boundaries between night and day, prince and man.

He would miss her terribly. There, it was said. He would miss her, but there was nothing to be done about it. She did not belong here, and he could not, in any event, keep her with him. That, he had known from the beginning. Two years ago he had sworn never to take such a risk again. He would honour that vow.

Colette pushed the hospital plans to one side. She would never see it completed. It was unlikely that she'd even be here to see the foundations laid. A month, Zafar had said it would take to make arrangements for her return, and it had already been five weeks. How much longer did she have? She hadn't asked, because she didn't want to know the answer.

How was it possible to fall in love in five short weeks? Sighing, she made her way out of her quarters to take her favourite walk along the battlements. It was impossible not to fall in love with a man like Zafar, she thought, leaning over the parapet to watch the date harvest. She had loved Leon in a gentle way, but she had never been in love before. With Zafar it was different. What was surprising was that it had taken as long as five weeks for her to lose her heart to him. Not that it made any difference at all, for he did not love her, and even if he did, he deserved much better than a penniless foreign widow. A prince deserved a princess.

But he did not love her. Every time he made love to her, he gave a little less of himself, held himself back more. She no longer believed he did it for her sake only. It was a mental as well as a physical act, a retreat. It hurt, but she had only herself to blame for that fact. For her the passion between them had been a revelation, opening up the world of sensuality to her and in doing so giving her a new confidence in herself. She no longer felt incomplete, or that she was missing out on a secret. For her their lovemaking was just that, making love, mentally as well as physically. For Zafar it was merely physical.

Last night, when she had been floating blissfully in the aftermath of her climax, she had reached for him, wanting to prolong the intimacy. He rolled away from her on the pretext of fetching her mint tea, but she knew she had overstepped a mark. He never spent the whole night in the harem, never slept there. She had given up hoping that he would.

Yet in daylight, it seemed to her, they were truly intimate. He shared his thoughts, his ideas, his ambitions without reservation. She had never been with a man who was interested in her mind before. She had never had an intimate friend. With Zafar she had found both, and here was the root of the love that had blossomed in her for him. They were both by nature solitary. Together they had discovered the pleasure of not being alone, of sharing.

With another heavy sigh, Colette pushed herself away from the parapet and completed her tour of the battlements. The sun was at its highest, so she returned to the cool terraces around one of the many courtyards in the palace, wandering aimlessly from one to another before heading back to the harem. Still restless, she climbed the stairs to the second terrace. Her footprints left a trail in the dust as she went from room to room stacked with furniture and boxes.

Bending to examine a pretty inlaid chest, she caught

her tunic on one of the handles. As she pulled open the drawer to free herself, something in the bottom glittered up at her. An ornate bracelet, made of gold and decorated with jewels. Blue, red and green, the royal colours. It was a beautiful piece, and undoubtedlyextremely valuable. She clasped it around her wrist and was admiring the intricate filigree work when the door to the courtyard creaked open.

'Zafar, I'm up here.' Colette ran lightly down the stairs to greet him. 'You look very serious.'

'Firas has had word from Cairo. You can leave within the week.'

Her heart plummeted. 'Within the week.'

'Yes, it is good news. I know how eager you must be to finally return to your homeland. It has been a long time.'

'Yes.' She nodded and summoned a bright smile because it was what he wanted of her, though she felt like bursting into tears. 'And anyway, our agreement was only for a month. We are already on borrowed time.'

'Indeed, I— Where did you get that?'

He was staring at her arm. At the bracelet. 'Oh, I forgot I had put it on. I found it in a chest upstairs.'

'Take it off. Immediately!'

His face was set rigid. Obviously it was very valuable. 'I wasn't going to steal it, if that is what you are thinking,' Colette said, struggling with the clasp.

'I said, take it off.' Zafar cursed.

When she finally managed to undo the catch and hand it to him, Zafar stared at the bracelet as if it were cursed or possessed or both. Tentatively, she put her hand on his arm. 'Zafar, what is it?'

'It belonged to my wife. I gave it to her on our wedding day.'

'But—you said you are not married.'

'I'm not. Afifah is dead.'

'Afifah,' she repeated foolishly.

'It means chaste and modest one. It suited her well.'

'Afifah was your wife.' Colette rubbed her eyes. 'Why did you not tell me? Why has no one so much as mentioned her name? Why is there no trace of her here in the harem? I don't understand, Zafar.'

'I told you, this harem has not been used since my father's time. My wife had her own quarters.'

'Did you love her?' The question was out before she could stop it.

'Of course. She was my wife.'

*Of course.* Colette clasped her hands together tightly under the folds of her tunic. 'What happened?'

*What happened?* Zafar stared down at the bracelet. Never since that fateful day had he talked about it. He could not think about Afifah without being overwhelmed with guilt.

'Zafar?'

Colette was pale, her eyes dark with concern. Colette, who had been through so much but who was so fiercely determined not to allow herself to be broken. He twisted the bracelet around and around, remembering the care with which he had chosen each of the jewels, emerald, ruby and sapphire, remembering Afifah's delight when he presented it to her. She was a hothouse flower, his wife, charming but fragile. Colette was made of sterner stuff. Colette was determinedly independent, infinitely practical, and yet in some ways she was more of a woman than Afifah had ever been. She challenged him. She gave as much as she took, in the dark of the harem and in the light of day. Would she understand? She would not lie to him, of that he was certain.

Zafar set the bracelet down on the edge of the fountain and sank down onto the cushions, holding his hand out in invitation. 'I have never talked of this,' he said.

She took his hand and held it to her cheek, pressing a kiss on his palm. 'Tell me.'

He gazed into her eyes, the colour of the night sky. *Tell me.* It was like the rush of a wave formed from a swell, breaking suddenly and unstoppably to shore, the need to do just that, to unburden himself, to share the guilt in the hope that she might just be able to help him dissipate it. Clasping her hand tightly in his, he began.

'We had been married for just a year. We were in the desert, making camp at an oasis in the next kingdom. It was a routine visit. We had been allies for some time. I would not usually have taken Afifah with me, but she had just discovered she was expecting our child and had developed a morbid fear of being alone. I thought it was safe.'

He closed his eyes on the memory of that morning, Afifah teasing him, pleading to travel with him, torn between tears and laughter as she had been since first telling him about the baby. 'Our tent was set apart from the others. There was no guard—I didn't think we needed one. Afifah was having trouble sleeping. I had not thought she would be so foolish as to stray from the tent alone, but she was young. She had been raised in the old-fashioned way in a harem. She knew nothing of the dangers of the desert. And I—I thought there was no danger.'

His brow was clammy with sweat. He felt sick. So many times he had replayed the chain of events in his mind, castigating himself at every point when he had missed an opportunity to change the outcome. Beside him, Colette sat silent. He could sense the tension in her. He raced on. 'I heard Afifah call out. She was only a few feet from the tent, but it was far enough. There were five of them. She was thrown onto the camel as I reached her. I fought like a dervish. I killed two and mortally wounded a third, but the others spirited her away. By the time I had my own guards roused, we were miles behind them. But I followed them, Colette. I thought they were random marauders, but I was wrong. An old enemy with a long memory had commissioned some mercenaries to abduct her, knowing that I valued my wife's life more than my own. They left her body where they knew we would find her. She was— She had been defiled. I cannot describe— When I saw her— When I saw her…'

He dropped his head into his hands, grinding the heels of his hands into his eyes. Colette put her arms around him, trying to pull his head onto her breast. He was tempted to surrender to the comfort she offered, but he did not deserve it and would not give way to such weakness.

Pushing her away, he sat up, taking jagged breaths. 'What I saw will remain with me forever. I failed to save Afifah and must forever carry the burden of that failure. I vowed that day never to fail in my duty again.'

# *Chapter Seven*

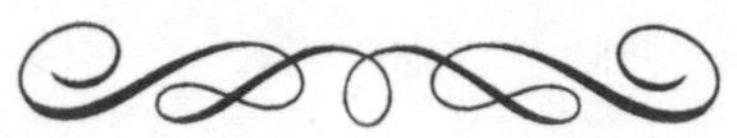

'That was what prompted you to come to my rescue,' Colette exclaimed. 'That is where you got the scar on your face. And that is what you meant when you warned me of the dangers of the desert.'

Zafar nodded silently.

She was horrified by what he had told her. When he had seemed about to break down, she had assumed it was grief. But his grief had been replaced with anger and guilt, she saw now.

'I am so sorry,' Colette said tenderly, 'but you must see it was not your fault, Zafar.'

'Afifah was in my care and I failed her. I dispensed with the guard. I did not accompany her when she left the tent.'

'You didn't know she had gone.'

'They took her because of me, Colette. She died because they wanted to hurt me. All I want is to bring peace and prosperity to these lands, but Afifah paid the price for my ambition.'

'Zafar, it is the noblest of ambitions. I wish the same

could be said for the wars my father and husband fought for France. I have seen many innocents die for the sake of Napoleon's hunger for power.'

His smile was twisted. 'Always you look at things from the best possible viewpoint.'

'And always you look at things from the worst. Why not try my outlook for once? It was a terrible thing, a tragedy, but you must not let it dictate your life, Zafar.'

'What do you mean?'

He was frowning heavily, warning her not to step over the mark, but she loved him too much not to speak out. 'You told me once that although you must appear infallible to your people, you know in your heart that you are not. You did everything within your power to save Afifah, but there are some things that are beyond even your powers. It was not your fault.'

'If I had ordered a guard to stand outside the tent. If I had not fallen asleep…'

'If Afifah had not chosen to go outside without waking you. You cannot take responsibility for the actions of others, Zafar.'

'She was under my protection.'

'She was a grown woman with a mind of her own.' He had a stubborn set to his mouth. Obviously she would not succeed on that front. Thinking like a general's daughter, Colette marshalled her thoughts and tried another line of attack. 'You are afraid it might happen again, aren't you? You must be, else you would have married again. You have dedicated yourself to Kharidja in every way, yet you have not provided the one thing that is essential for the future, an heir.'

'You don't know what you are talking about.'

'I do, Zafar. I know you very well. I think you are afraid it would happen again, and it is that fear that keeps you solitary, isolated and lonely.'

'How dare you! I fear nothing!'

She flinched in the face of his icy rage but would not back down, for she was now certain she was right. Face the enemy without fear. Good old Papa! 'Since Afifah died, you have let your enemies win, Zafar,' Colette said, meeting his angry gaze fearlessly.

'That enemy no longer lives. My vengeance was swift and merciless.'

'But he still lives in your memory. He is victorious in death because he rules your life.'

'I am ruled by no one!' Zafar exclaimed.

'You are angry because I am right.'

'I am angry because you have no understanding of the matter at all. It is a matter of honour. I may as well have killed Afifah with my own scimitar, but I should not have expected a mere woman to understand that. At least I will be spared your homespun philosophy when you are gone.'

He turned on his heel and would have stormed out of the harem had she not caught his hand. 'We have precious little time left, Zafar. Let us not fritter it away in pointless acrimony.'

For a long moment he simply stared at her; then suddenly she was in his arms and he was kissing her hungrily, greedily, devouring her with the kind of kisses that were completely lacking in any restraint. Passion flared like a shooting star. She threw her arms around him and kissed him back just as avidly, knowing that it meant nothing to him, knowing it was merely a result of the emotional turmoil his confession had generated, knowing it may be her one and only chance to make love to him, to really make love to him, without reservation.

His kisses were dark and deep. His hands moved feverishly over her body, tearing at her clothes in his hunger for her flesh. Colette was equally fevered, tugging so frantically at the buttons that held his tunic in place that they scattered across the tessellated floor of the courtyard. His belt dropped to the floor with a clatter. Her shoes, her sash, her pantaloons went the same way. He yanked his tunic over his head to stand before her naked, breathing harshly, his erection jutting. She pulled her own tunic away, casting it over her shoulder, wanting only to kiss, to stroke, to touch, skin on skin. His mouth brought her nipples to hard, aching peaks. She wrapped her hand around the silken hardness of his shaft, making him moan. His fingers slid inside her. She was hot, wet, tight. He was so hard he was pulsing in her hand. Their kisses grew wilder. She wanted no finesse this time, no slow climb.

'Now,' she muttered. 'I want you inside me now, Zafar.'

He perched on the edge of the fountain, pulling her onto his lap, his hands cupped around her bottom as she sank slowly, deliciously, onto him. Her feet trailed in the fountain, the water cool, a delightful contrast to the inferno raging inside her. She clenched around him, holding him, forcing him to still as she kissed him slowly, deeply, and then she began to move, bracing herself on his shoulders, sliding away from him, then taking him inside her again, slow and hard. His eyes were glazed. His skin was taut, stretched tight across his cheekbones. Her nipples grazed the rough hair on his chest, sending little frissons of pleasure through her. She slid up and thrust down again, holding him so tightly that she could feel him throb. Her climax was not far away, but she held on, waiting for him, wanting him. Harder. Faster. Again and again. She felt his shaft thicken, causing her blood to thicken, her own muscles to tighten. One final thrust and he cried out, pulsing into her as she pulsed around him, spilling himself, abandoning himself to the power of his climax, surrendering to her for the first and only time.

'I love you,' she whispered, knowing he could not hear her. 'I love you, Zafar.'

Firas proved as efficient as ever. Over the next few days the preparations for Colette's departure were completed. Smarting at the accusations she had flung at him, confused by the intensity of their lovemaking, Zafar distanced himself from her, telling himself that the sooner she was gone from Kharidja, the sooner he could return to the relative calm of his old life.

In a few short hours she was due to leave Kharidja

under escort. Zafar prowled the battlements gazing up at the night sky. He didn't want her to go. He did not want to return to the solitude of his old life, but he had no alternative. The vow he had made when Afifah died haunted him. Colette's accusation, that he lived his life in fear, taunted him. He feared no one and nothing. He lived as he wished and by no one else's rules. He was Prince Zafar al-Zuhr.

He was also a man. And he was not, as Colette had pointed out so fearlessly, infallible. Afifah was dead and there was nothing he could do to change that. If he had placed a guard at the tent. If she had not gone out alone. If he had not defeated the man who arranged for her abduction in battle. If he had not spent his rule fighting for peace…

No, there were some things he would not, could not, change. For the first time, he could see that day's events in the context of the preceding months, even years. It was not guilt he should feel but regret. Colette had taught him that. He could begin to imagine a future where he was not weighted down with remorse, driven by the need to atone. And he could see now that Colette was right. These past two years of his life had been a victory for his enemies. He was frozen in time by the vow he had made, yet to break it…

The only possible justification there could be to break it dawned on him suddenly. A feisty, fearless Frenchwoman. He was in love with her. Zafar shook his head in wonderment. How could he have been so blind? He was in love. Not the gentle, protective love he had felt for Afifah but a love every bit as feisty and fearless as the woman who had captured his heart. The woman who would leave tomorrow for her native land if he did not try to stop her.

Taking the battlement stairs in several bounding leaps, Zafar made for the harem. He did not know what her answer would be but he knew if he didn't ask her, he would regret it always, and thanks to her, he was finally done with regrets. Throwing open the door of the harem, he called for Colette.

The courtyard was empty. Her name echoed around the terrace as he called, running frantically from room to vacant room. Panic clutched at his heart as he strode along the corridor, calling loudly for his man of business.

'Where is she?'

Firas bowed. 'You wished me to expedite matters, Highness.'

Zafar stared at him uncomprehendingly. 'What are you telling me?'

'She is gone, Highness, just as you commanded.'

'But she was not due to leave until the morning.'

'She insisted, Highness. I think she wished to spare you the pain of a farewell. And herself, if I'm any judge.'

Colette sat straight in the saddle of the camel, trying desperately not to cry. Above her, the silver carpet of stars winked in the vast desert sky, oblivious to the forlorn woman beneath. For two days she had waited, telling herself that Zafar needed time to come to terms with the truths she had hurled at him. For two days she had nurtured a dwindling hope that he would seek her out, that they would somehow be reconciled before she left. On the third day, she knew he would not come, and she could not endure the pain of waiting, nor could she risk giving way to the more desperate urge to throw herself at him and tell him how she felt. Zafar had suffered enough guilt to last a lifetime; she would not add unrequited love to his burden.

She could not bear to say goodbye, and so she had left, quietly and unobtrusively. She would survive, because it was in her nature to do so. She would make the best of things because that was what a general's daughter did. But she would never forget, and she would always love him.

They reached the tiny oasis where they would camp in the dead of night. Colette had been eager to continue, desperate to put as many irrecoverable miles between herself and Kharidja as possible, but the guide was adamant. The camels needed rest, and so too did she. Sitting at the mouth of her little tent, she was watching the small caravan of trusted guards take their meal when a cry of alarm went up.

'Get in the tent, *madame,'* the guard urged. 'Take this. Use it if necessary—it is loaded. Be assured I will die before I allow any harm come to you, for if it did, my own life would be not worth living,' he said with a twisted smile. A gun was thrust into her hand.

She did as she was bid, crouching in the far reaches of the goatskin tent, her heart pounding. She could use a gun, of course; it was one of the accomplishments her father had insisted upon. Outside, a shot was fired. A shout, curses and then a stream of furious Arabic, followed by a dark shadow looming in the doorway. 'Do not move, or I will shoot,' she said, her voice tremulous.

Zafar strode in, wild-eyed and dishevelled. She almost dropped the gun but remembered just in time that it was primed and set it carefully down on the floor. 'What on earth are you doing here?'

'Colette.' He stopped short in front of her. 'Colette. No. Do not speak.'

She wasn't sure she could. She waited, her heart fluttering, trying to quell the vain hope that she could not prevent from rising in her breast.

'You were right,' Zafar said. 'I did all I could to save Afifah but it was not enough. I have not yet ceased blaming myself, but I know that in time I will. And you were right about the consequences, too. I have allowed the fear that it would happen again to rule me. You were right, and I thank you for having the courage to show me.'

'Oh. Well, that is most— I am very pleased to hear it Zafar, but—'

'I am not finished yet! By the gods, woman, I am trying to ask you to marry me. You might at least have the decency not to interrupt.'

She opened her mouth, but no words came out.

Zafar pulled his headdress off and cast it to the ground. 'I love you,' he said baldly. 'I am in love with you. I want you beside me, with me, in my life. Always.'

'But you said you would never take another wife. You said—'

'I know what I said! Must you throw my words back at me? I was wrong! I am not infallible, as you know only too well. I was wrong. I want you to be my wife. I don't know whether it is possible that you return my feelings, but—'

Finally, she found her voice. 'I do,' Colette said hurriedly. 'Zafar, I do. I love you so much, and I'm sorry for interrupting you, but I have waited so long to tell you—'

'You love me?'

'I am in love with you. I have been for…I don't know, days, weeks, it feels like forever.'

'Then you will stay?'

'If you want me.'

'If I want you!' He burst into hearty laughter, then pulled her tight against him, holding her so close she could scarcely breathe. *'Mignonne,* I have never wanted any woman the way I want you. I want you in my bed and in my life and I never, ever want to let you go. I know there is danger—I will always have enemies, but—'

'Zafar, I would far rather be happy with you no matter what the dangers than unhappy without you.'

He laughed again, though softly. 'You stole my very words. Will you marry me, *chérie?*'

'Yes, yes and yes, my desert prince,' Colette replied.

'Yes!' Zafar exclaimed in a most unprincely manner, taking her into his arms amid the awesome vastness of the desert landscape and kissing her.

* * * * *